HELLBOY

THE LOST ARMY

HELLBOY

THE LOST ARMY

by

Christopher Golden

Illustrated by

Mike Mignola

POCKET BOOKS
New York   London   Toronto   Sydney

POCKET BOOKS, a division of Simon & Schuster, Inc.
1230 Avenue of the Americas, New York, NY 10020

Copyright © 1997 by Mike Mignola

Published by arrangement with Dark Horse Comics, Inc.

ISBN: 0-7434-6282-3

First Pocket Books printing February 2004

10   9   8   7   6   5   4   3   2   1

POCKET and colophon are registered trademarks of
Simon & Schuster, Inc.

Cover art by Mike Mignola

Manufactured in the United States of America

For information regarding special discounts for bulk purchases,
please contact Simon & Schuster Special Sales at 1-800-456-6798
or business@simonandschuster.com

Original Book Design by Cary Grazzini

FOREWORD

In 1993, with some help from the Legendary John Byrne, I introduced the comic-book character Hellboy, the World's Greatest Paranormal Investigator, and his world of secret-agent fish men, fire girls, and Nazi supermonsters. This thing you're holding in your hands is a bold experiment and (I hope) a smooth transition from Comic Book to Novel. How did it come about? Here's the way I remember it . . .

Big-shot horror writer Chris Golden, who had written some nice things about Hellboy in one of those rock 'n' roll, video game, comics magazines, asked if I would consider having him write a prose Hellboy story to appear as a backup feature in the *Hellboy* comic. I must have been intrigued, because I went out and read Chris's two vampire novels (*Of Saints and Shadows* and its sequel, *Angel Souls and Devil Hearts*). I was impressed by the weird atmosphere and giant-sized monster action, and we upgraded the project from backup feature to novel. Chris told me a rough idea of what he wanted to do, and I said, Great. The powers that be at Dark Horse said yes to the whole thing, and there you go. Pretty easy.

Storywise, my only contribution to this thing was the opening sequence. When Chris mentioned that he wanted to open the book with the final moments of some unrelated case, I came up with the burning car and its passenger. Everything else is Chris, including giving Hellboy a sex life—something I'm sure Hellboy appreciates.

My thanks to Chris, and to Scott Allie, who agonized over every line of this bad boy from beginning to end, and who had to figure out where to put all my pictures.

To you, whoever you are—enjoy.

Mike Mignola
Portland, Oregon

DEDICATION

This novel is respectfully dedicated to Mike Mignola: artist, writer, and friend. It was a tremendous honor to be allowed to work with Hellboy & co., particularly since Mike is so protective of the children of his imagination.

I would like to gratefully acknowledge the invaluable input of Scott Allie, who suffered every word with me. Told ya I'd meet my deadline.

Thanks, guys.

Now, as Sniegoski would say, "For my next trick . . ."

Christopher Golden
Bradford, Massachusetts

HELLBOY

THE LOST ARMY

PROLOGUE

T he Bentley was in flames as it crested the hill. The jagged edges of the broken windshield were blackened by fire. The paint on the hood bubbled, heat blisters popped. The tiny two-lane strip of Vermont highway was deserted at just past three in the morning. There were no streetlights, just the moon and the burning Bentley to illuminate the night. The car drifted from one side of the road to the other, then was jerked suddenly back on course. It repeated that pattern several times.

There was no one behind the wheel.

Which did not mean the Bentley was unoccupied. Not at all. Merely that nothing human rode in that infernal vehicle.

A massive tentacle shot through the demolished windshield. Purple and pustulent, it whipped from side to side, probing the other windows of the car, then trying to beat down the flames that rose from the Bentley's engine.

Other tentacles sprouted from windows all around the car, dripping vile fluid. The interior of the Bentley did not have room for those tentacles. Never had. And certainly, it did not have space for the creature which had spawned them. Something that might have been a tail—thick and green with vicious-looking razor spines along its length— burst through the rear window. It was burning with a cold, blue flame quite unlike the fire in the Bentley's engine.

A ropy, muscular proboscis spiked through the roof of the car, then sniffed the air like the snout of an aardvark. A bulbous, fleshy boil seemed to balloon up through the hole the proboscis had made. It quickly inflated and, after a few moments, eyes began to open all across its surface.

Within the Bentley, something bellowed. Something almost human. Most certainly not the repulsive terror which now seemed to be pouring from the burning vehicle. The tentacled thing issued a keening whistle which may have been a cry of pain, or of triumph.

As the car approached a darkened roadside diner, two quick shots rang out, resounding in the silence of the night, and echoed back to the car from the dense forest on either side of the street. Then a third shot. That was all.

The proboscis abandoned its search; the bulbous sack of eyes exploded in a shower of viscous liquid which set the fire blazing even higher, as if it had been sprinkled with gasoline.

With a screech of metal, the passenger door blew off the side of the car, trailing flames and whipping tentacles.

A body tumbled out, a huge figure which appeared to be covered with blood. The body hit the ground, rolled, stopped. The long, brown duster coat the figure wore was on fire.

The Bentley rolled on toward the diner.

Its former passenger rolled around on the pavement, then leaped to his feet. He batted at the flames already eating holes through his coat.

"Damn," he hissed, putting out the last of them, cursing the ruined duster and the way his ribs hurt from hitting the ground.

There was a tumultuous crash, followed by the tinkling of shattered glass hitting pavement. He turned to see that

the Bentley had come to a stop, half in, half out of the diner. The flames began to catch. The loathsome thing inside the automobile shrieked its pain and anger, tentacles burning, lashing side to side, slowing down.

Limping slightly, the surviving passenger began to walk across the diner's parking lot toward a phone booth.

He was huge. Tall and broad.

And red.

His skin was like a scarlet callus, worn down and healed over time and again for millennia. But it wasn't callous at all. It was, merely, his skin. His hooves clicked on the tarmac, and his long tail curled out from under the bottom of his duster, never touching ground. On his forehead were two round protrusions, flat, amputated stumps of what had once been thick, proud horns. The perfect redness of his flesh was marred only by a goatee and sideburns of coarse black hair and a bristly stubble on his scalp, chest, and legs.

A terrifying face. Made all the more disturbing when he smiled.

But he wasn't smiling now. Not even the hint of a smile.

He slid back the door of the phone booth, and was forced to stand sideways and bend his knees slightly to move inside. His right hand was huge, oversized even for his body. It wasn't made of flesh, but, rather, some kind of stone. Or, perhaps, some other substance which human beings had not named as yet. He held the phone with that hand and dialed with his left. Such delicate operations were always done with his left hand.

"It's a collect call," he said, and though the tone was pleasant enough, there was something unsettling, something cold about his voice.

"Just say a collect call from Vermont," he insisted, a bit testily.

After several moments of listening, he said, "Thank you," and waited some more.

"Tom," he said finally, "it's Hellboy."

As he listened to his superior's questions, Hellboy scratched idly at the stubble on his head.

"Yeah," he said. "Yeah, it's all set. Mrs. Crittendon didn't care about the house or the car, she just wanted the thing out of there. Too bad, though. It was a nice car."

Hellboy cocked his head to one side, then raised an eyebrow at the next question.

"Tom, I'm telling you it's all set," he said. "The damn thing's on fire, after all . . . What do you mean it can't be killed by fire?

"Well it isn't moving, anyway.

"Of course I'm sure."

As he said this last, Hellboy turned to glance at the diner.

"Tom, hold on a minute, okay?" he said, then dropped the phone.

In the calliope flash of the firelight, Hellboy could see that the thing within the Bentley had begun to move. It was flowing, tentacle after tentacle, through the crater it had ripped in the car's roof, and had begun to pull itself out onto the top of the vehicle.

Hellboy reached for his gun. It wasn't there. A quick glance told him he had dropped it when he'd rolled around trying to put out his blazing coat. Not that it mattered, though. He was pretty sure he'd used all his ammunition.

The infernal beast dragged the bulk of its body out onto the roof and began to slide down the Bentley's rear windshield, leaving a trail of putrid mucus in its wake. It looked smaller, and he wondered if the thing had somehow detached itself from the rest of its body to escape the fire. Or, since the fire didn't seem to be killing it, maybe it was just pissed off and was coming after him.

That seemed more likely.

Hellboy rifled through the pouches of his belt and then the seemingly endless pockets of his duster. Charms, talismans, and a rosary blessed by Pope Pius XII fell to the pavement in a clatter. A ward against evil made for Hellboy by a Santeria priest pricked his left index finger.

"Jeez!" he hissed, and sucked on the finger for a moment before resuming his search.

Out of his pockets, he produced dozens of objects invested with the power to protect him from evil. They didn't always help. In this case, he knew they wouldn't be enough.

His left hand wrapped around something metal, hard. He pulled it out. It was a flashlight. Seconds later, something else substantial . . . some kind of weapon! Hellboy aimed the weapon and was about to fire when he realized what he was holding.

A flare gun.

Lot of good that would do.

He could hear Tom—Dr. Manning—yelling over the phone. He couldn't make out the words, but he assumed the man wanted to know if he was all right. Or at least if he'd succeeded in his mission.

The vulgar obscenity that had been within the Bentley began to slide from the trunk to the parking lot just behind the burning car. Its tentacles stretched out, blindly attempting to sense his location. When they stopped swaying, Hellboy knew the thing had somehow pinpointed him. In a moment, it would start after him.

"Come on!" he shouted, not at the shrilly screaming creature, but in frustration with his search.

His fingers touched something hard, and square. If not for the smooth metal surface, it might have been a child's block, innocently lettered "A, B, C." Not so innocent, though. A smile contorted Hellboy's features into a menacing grimace. He withdrew the square from his pocket. On one of its six sides, there was a circular impression, a slight indentation.

It was a thermite charge, leftover from the Finland debacle two years before. He knew it would come in handy now. Fire might not kill the thing, but the explosive power of the tiny bomb would do the trick. All he had to do was . . .

The Bentley blew up. The flames had finally reached the gas tank, and the car exploded in a rain of shrapnel and charred demon flesh. The glass of the phone booth blew out, and Hellboy lifted his stone hand to shield his eyes.

He stared into the conflagration left behind, the diner starting to burn now as well. Where pieces of the beast had fallen, they were now melting into the pavement, leaving oddly designed scars behind on the parking lot.

After a moment, he remembered his interrupted call. He limped back to the ruined booth, and was surprised to hear Dr. Manning's shouts still coming from the dangling phone.

"Tom," he said. "Calm down, we're all set now.

"No, this time I'm really sure. Yes, I promise! What am I, twelve? Now listen, what's this new case, I thought I was going to Edinburgh with the others?

"Egypt, what the hell is in Egypt?" he asked, completely bewildered.

In the distance, he could hear several sets of sirens. Closer still, however, was the pounding rhythm of a helicopter's rotors.

"All right, look . . . no, no, wait. Yeah, my ride's here. Fill me in when I get back to the office."

As the helicopter landed in the parking lot, Hellboy stooped and ran to pick up his gun. He holstered it, then hoisted himself up into the chopper's cargo bay.

"Jesus," the pilot said, glancing over his shoulder as they took flight once more. "Remind me never to piss you off."

Hellboy smiled.

"Come on, Kevin," he said. "I'm not the temperamental type."

"Uh-huh," the pilot responded.

"Well now, what the hell is *that* supposed to mean?"

CHAPTER ONE

In the brightness of late morning, with the air still touched by the previous night's chill, the office building's mirrored windows sparkled with sunlight. The landscaping around the building revealed a significant Asian influence, an attempt to merge the creations of man with the creations of God. Trees and shrubs surrounded glass and cement, embraced the office building so that its presence there, on the hill, seemed a natural one.

A carefully crafted illusion. A pleasant façade, like the day itself. It was beautiful, warm and dry, and birdsong filled the air. As a whole, the picture made a powerful deceit.

The building was located in Fairfield, Connecticut. Even for those who had never set foot in the city, it conjured images of country clubs and horseback riding, of wealthy, conservative America. And the office looked conservative enough, in its way.

There was no sign on the building. No sign in the smallish parking lot. No sign on the glass door, nor any logo or similar design in the lobby or foyer of the building. The receptionist would happily guide visitors to meetings, but anyone without an appointment was escorted out the door by a squadron of security guards, most of whom had once been Secret Service or Marine Intelligence.

There was no sign.

But if you knew what you were looking for, you couldn't miss it. If you were sensitive to such things, you would have felt its presence throughout the long ride up into the hills.

The Bureau for Paranormal Research and Defense.

Bureau employees, from researchers to support staff to field operatives, knew that, no matter how conservative their headquarters, no matter how idyllic their surroundings, no matter how beautiful a day might seem, there were always layers of corruption beneath the superficial reality.

Such knowledge put them in constant danger.

Dr. Tom Manning hurried down a long hallway decorated in earth tones which, despite their reputation to the contrary, did nothing to calm his nerves. The Bureau had limited resources, particularly when it came to seasoned field agents. It was one thing to research the paranormal. It was another thing entirely to investigate it in person and, if necessary, to combat it.

When he arrived at the conference room, his nerves received another jolt. An argument was in progress.

"Listen, Professor, if you don't want me along, that's your problem," Elizabeth Sherman stated curtly. "Dr. Manning asked me to take part in this investigation, and I fully intend to do so, whatever your personal feelings on the subject."

The object of her ire was Professor Trevor Bruttenholm, the greatest and also the oldest field agent the BPRD had ever employed. Mainly because Professor Bruttenholm would rather have died than move into management and sit behind a desk until they forced retirement upon him. Which nobody was prepared to do, for a number of reasons not the least of which was that, without the professor, there might never have been a Bureau.

"Miss Sherman," Professor Bruttenholm said reasonably, "I'm not sure what you think I said, but I most certainly did not express displeasure at having your company during this investigation. Rather, I merely wondered if you were prepared for field work, since . . ."

"Two years, Professor!" Liz Sherman shouted. "It's been two years since I lost control of the fire! Doesn't that count for anything with you?"

"Indeed, it does," the professor agreed. "It means you have controlled your innate abilities for two full years, longer than you were ever able to exert such control in the past. It does not mean that you have mastered those abilities, however."

Dr. Manning stood just outside the door, taking in the exchange but not wanting to interrupt. The argument should be solved by the operatives, if possible. If he squelched it, it might flare up and jeopardize them in the field.

But it seemed as though Liz was done with the conflict, at least for the moment. She retrieved a cigarette from her jacket pocket and sat down in one of the conference room's soft, black leather chairs. Liz pointed her index finger at the end of the cigarette, and her flesh caught fire. Flame jumped up from her finger. She lit the cigarette, then shook her hand once and the flame was gone.

Neither Professor Bruttenholm nor the attractive young pyrokinetic woman spoke another word. The only other person in the room, the operative called Abe Sapien, was slumped over the conference table with his head on his folded arms, apparently asleep.

Showtime.

"All right, people, here we go," Dr. Manning said as he hustled into the room.

As Director of Field Operations, Tom Manning was perhaps the most powerful individual within the BPRD. Much to his dismay, that meant he was also the person whose job it was to send people into situations of great danger. In his career, he had sent two men and four women to their deaths. Those souls haunted him, but not in any way that the Bureau could detect.

Dr. Manning sat at the head of the conference table and began sliding information kits detailing the mission and its objective to the three operatives present. When the white folder bumped against Abraham Sapien's hands, the man looked up. Tom struggled not to react, as he did every time he got a good look at Abe.

In truth, Abraham Sapien was not a man at all. Rather he was an amphibian, the only known humanoid able to breathe water. The Bureau suspected genetic engineering, but Abe's true origins were still shrouded in mystery. He had been discovered by plumbers working in the basement of St. Trinian's Hospital in Washington, D.C. They had broken through a sealed door and discovered an abandoned laboratory.

Within a fluid-filled glass cylinder, apparently lifeless, floated the amphibious man. A label on the cylinder classified the "experiment" as an Icthyo Sapien. It was dated April 14, 1865, the day Abraham Lincoln was murdered. Hence his name, Abe Sapien.

As Liz had once said, "It's better than calling him 'Icky.'"

Liz. Elizabeth Sherman, twenty-four years of age. Her powers were no less disturbing. Their initial manifestation thirteen years earlier had decimated a city block and incinerated thirty-two people, her entire family among them. Looking at her, Dr. Manning thought, it was easy to forget her history, her power.

Abe was not so lucky.

"Okay," Dr. Manning said. "Let's get down to business."

"What of Hellboy?" Professor Bruttenholm inquired. "Shouldn't we wait for him? He is our point man on this mission, after all."

Tom nodded slightly, about to respond. He was grateful when a familiar, heavy tread in the hallway relieved him of the responsibility.

All three operatives assigned to the Edinburgh investigation looked around toward the door. Only Professor

Bruttenholm was smiling. It occurred to Dr. Manning that the observation was uncharitable: it was possible Abe Sapien was not capable of smiling.

The heavy oak door swung open, and Hellboy ducked slightly to enter the room.

"Glad you could join us," Abe said with friendly sarcasm.

"Up late," Hellboy replied. "I had to get a few hours sleep."

Hellboy regretted the words as soon as he spoke them. He glanced guiltily at Liz, then looked away. Sleep was a difficult subject for her. She was never able to sleep undisturbed by horrific dreams. Hellboy often wondered what effect that deprivation might have on her over time. He wasn't certain he wanted an answer.

"Glad to see you emerged unscathed from your encounter with the Crittendon family," Professor Bruttenholm said kindly.

"Thank you, sir," Hellboy said, as he took a seat next to the professor.

Bruttenholm gave Hellboy an affectionate pat on the shoulder, and turned his attention back to the meeting.

The two were extremely close. Professor Bruttenholm had been among those present on a night in December 1944, just before Christmas, when the Second World War had proven to be a conflict on many levels. The Nazis were seeking paranormal weapons. They tried to summon something, something powerful to fight for them.

What they had called looked for all the world like a demon child.

". . . Hellboy . . . ," Professor Bruttenholm had whispered.

That was the only name they knew to call him.

Dr. Manning had not yet been born, but he knew the details well enough from the dozens of times he had studied the file. Hellboy was an extraordinary creature, an extraordinary person.

Since the American government had been in charge of the operation that had resulted in Hellboy's discovery, they laid claim on him as if he were property. Despite Trevor Bruttenholm's furious protests—he felt quite protective of their strange visitor—the Americans brought Hellboy back from England with them.

Fortunately for all, the professor's persistence and influence finally forced a compromise. Bruttenholm and a group of other paranormal experts founded the BPRD, with funding from the American government. They were granted custody of Hellboy. Bruttenholm raised him. Educated him. Trained him. And, of course, studied him. They still didn't know precisely what Hellboy was.

Professor Bruttenholm had been like a father to Hellboy for more than forty years. Tom Manning had asked himself many times who, or what, Hellboy's real father might be. The question never failed to disturb him.

But there wasn't an operative he trusted more.

"Hellboy will not be joining you in Edinburgh," Dr. Manning said, then held up a hand to halt the questions and protests he knew would be forthcoming.

"This is preposterous," Professor Bruttenholm said, before Dr. Manning could speak again.

"I agree," Liz Sherman added. "We have no idea what's waiting for us inside MacGoldrick Castle. We need a point man who knows the ropes. Hellboy's the best."

"Or at least the most durable," Abe said dryly, and glanced over at Hellboy, who smiled thinly.

So much for halting their protests, Dr. Manning thought.

"Listen, you guys, I appreciate it, really," Hellboy said. "But the investigation Tom's pulling me out of the Edinburgh trip for is important to me."

"Not just to you," Dr. Manning said, grateful for Hellboy's intervention. "The British, American, and Egyptian governments are in an uproar over the whole thing. We have to send somebody in, and it just so happens that Hellboy was specifically requested by the . . ."

"So who's our point man?" Liz asked, her doubt and disappointment almost palpable.

"Mister Johnson," Dr. Manning replied.

"He'll do," Abe muttered.

"Seems he'll have to," Professor Bruttenholm sniffed, obviously put out that Hellboy would not be on his team.

"I'm a big boy, sir," Hellboy said. "I can take care of myself."

"Since when?" Abe asked.

Hellboy smiled again but didn't reply. Dr. Manning realized that, despite Abe's apparent inability to smile, Hellboy seemed to know when he was joking.

"So where *are* you going?" Abe asked.

"Egypt," Hellboy said. "Apparently they've lost a bunch of archaeologists."

Abe popped a new cassette into his portable cassette player. A few moments later, Dire Straits' "Walk of Life" began to pipe from the tiny speakers. The song had been a hit earlier in the year, and radio had played it to death. Hellboy was sick of the song. Sick of Dire Straits. Sick of MTV. But Abe couldn't get enough.

They were friends, so Hellboy did his best to ignore it. They'd be landing soon, anyway, the main team staying behind in Scotland while the plane's crew took Hellboy on to Egypt.

In the belly of the refurbished cargo jet the BPRD always had on call, Hellboy massaged his temples. The hum of the plane and the happy pop posturing of Dire Straits had begun to give him a headache.

"I still don't understand why they didn't send us on different planes," Hellboy complained. "Not that I don't enjoy the company, but it would have made a lot more sense."

Professor Bruttenholm frowned.

"How do you mean?" he asked. "You would have had

to fly over Europe or the Mediterranean anyway. We're close enough that sending two planes would not have been practical, even if it was within the budget."

"I don't get it," Hellboy admitted. "Why do we have to fly over Europe to reach Egypt? There must be some more direct . . ."

"Apparently, you haven't seen the news," Professor Bruttenholm said.

Hellboy heard disappointment in his mentor's voice. Though he knew it might only be his imagination, still it disturbed him. The man was the only father he had ever known, and like any son, he wanted to make his father proud. Sometimes it seemed to Hellboy that he was a constant disappointment, but the old man loved him anyway. He knew that, without reservation. Most of the time, it helped.

Despite his age, Trevor Bruttenholm had resisted all of the BPRD's attempts to limit him to a desk job. He took great pleasure in research, in the obtaining of knowledge, but it was in the field where the professor truly lived and thrived. Hellboy had always tried to live up to Professor Bruttenholm's example, but he was a creature of action. Books and research, current events and reports, these

things were dry and boring to him. He wanted to be like the professor, to be among dusty, ancient things, to find the face of evil and stand fast beneath its gaze.

But he hated to study.

This last had a tendency to get him into trouble. If he'd been human, his almost chronic lack of preparedness, the very thing which most disappointed his mentor, would have cost him his life dozens of times.

Fortunately, Hellboy was pretty hard to kill.

He ran his left palm over the black stubble of his scalp and his tail waved slightly back and forth on the floor of the airplane.

"The news? No, I guess I haven't," he admitted. "What did I miss?"

"Only that we're on the verge of war with Libya," the professor responded.

"Libya?" Hellboy asked, incredulous. "With that moron, Khadafy, or whatever his name is? You're kidding. Why?"

Professor Bruttenholm sighed. Hellboy couldn't blame him. Nor could he defend himself. He lifted his hands in a halfhearted, helpless shrug, then shot a glance at Liz Sherman, who had been listening to their conversation despite the roar of the plane's engines.

"A club filled with German civilians and American servicemen was bombed in West Germany yesterday," she said, in an attempt to explain that was lost on Hellboy.

"I still don't . . . ," he started to say.

"Libya is a breeding ground for terrorists," Professor Bruttenholm interrupted. "They've all but admitted their involvement, spitting in President Reagan's face with every speech Khadafy makes. We may not be on the verge of war, but I sincerely doubt the Americans will let this go by without some sort of retaliation. Even ol' Maggie Thatcher wouldn't let that go."

"Jeez," Hellboy cursed. "The dig I'm headed to is only a couple of miles from the border. That could get pretty hairy."

"Just make sure you stay out of Libya," Professor Bruttenholm said. "All we need is an international incident."

"No problem, sir," Hellboy promised. "Libya isn't exactly a tourist mecca. No theme parks. No good restaurants."

Liz smiled and Hellboy felt a bit better.

"Let's hope Anastasia has more than military rations out in the desert," Liz said. "Maybe she'll make you that shepherd's pie you liked so much."

Hellboy winced, let out a breath, looked anywhere but at Professor Bruttenholm. Abe hummed along to his music and tried to pretend he wasn't listening. He was smart enough to stay out of these conversations.

"Anastasia?" the professor asked. "Anastasia Bransfield? What's she got to . . . Don't tell me she's the one who called in the BPRD on this!"

"Well . . . ," Hellboy started.

"Come on, Trevor, give Hellboy a break," Liz defended him. "He can handle himself. She's just a woman, for God's sake."

"There's no such thing as *just* a woman, my dear," Professor Bruttenholm sniffed.

He looked disapprovingly at Hellboy. Professor Bruttenholm had never liked Anastasia, had blamed her for what had happened five years earlier. Hellboy had never faulted Anastasia. He had never expected things to turn

out any differently. That just wasn't the way things were
meant to be.

"Be careful, Hellboy," Professor Bruttenholm said,
more gently.

Of what? Hellboy wanted to ask, but thought better of
it. Whatever had happened to the archaeological team that
Anastasia was searching for, whatever went down between
the U.S. and Libya, the one thing Hellboy was anxious
about at the moment was seeing Anastasia Bransfield's face
again.

"Careful's my middle name," he finally said, and forced
a smile.

Turbulence jostled Hellboy awake. He yawned
wide, scratched his head, and shook off the phantom weight and heft of his amputated horns, the way a
man who has lost a limb must force himself to ignore
phantom pains. Hellboy often dreamed he still had horns.
These weren't nightmares, but when he woke, he never
liked the way the dreams made him feel.

They had stayed in Scotland only long enough for the
plane to refuel. Hellboy had slept quite a bit of the second
leg of the journey, from Scotland to Egypt. Now he just
wanted solid ground beneath him, and the hum of the engines gone from his head.

He twisted quickly to look as the navigator ratcheted
open the cargo door. Heat and wind tore through the plane.

"What's going on?" Hellboy asked.

Redfield, the copilot, tossed a large parachute on the
floor in front of him.

"Put this on," the man said.

"Look," Hellboy snapped. "Just because I'm durable doesn't mean I like getting shoved out of airplanes!"

"You have two choices," Redfield said. "You can parachute, or we can land in Cairo, two days' ride by jeep from where you need to be. If you're not in a hurry, then . . ."

The copilot let his words trail off, but Hellboy got the gist of it. If anything had really happened to the archaeological team, he could not waste any more time than he already had. He sighed and buckled on his parachute.

"Got your gear?" Redfield asked.

Hellboy patted the massive belt that was cinched around his waist, the many compartments of which held all manner of charms, talismans, instruments, weapons, and some rations as well. He nodded.

"Check your homing beacon?"

Hellboy tapped a red sigil on his belt buckle, and a steady beep filled the transformed cargo hold. Redfield held up a small monitor and glanced at it.

"We're good to go," he said.

Hellboy turned toward the open door, the wind buffeted his face. He took three steps to the door, and dove out into the superheated desert air. Skydiving had never been fun for him. He had never imagined it was fun for anyone but lunatics. Whoever thought jumping out of a plane thousands of feet above the Earth was a good idea, he wondered.

"Not me," he grumbled, but the air whipped past him so quickly it stole the words away. He could only hear them inside his head.

Hellboy fell. He'd seen the illustration of equal gravity

many times, but he could not dismiss the feeling that his
heavy right hand was pulling him faster and faster toward
the Earth. No matter how tough he was, without the parachute . . .

Below and slightly to the west was an encampment that
had to be Anastasia's group for the simple reason that there
were no others. Still farther west was a large depression in
the desert floor, almost like a massive oval footprint. Hellboy knew it must be the basin within which the oasis of
Ammon flourished, a large lake at its center. As he fell, he
even thought he could see the sun reflecting off the surface
of the lake.

Otherwise, all he saw was sand. Speeding rapidly toward him.

Hellboy pulled the ripcord.

Nothing happened.

"Son of a . . . ," he cursed, and pulled it again.

The ripcord snapped off in his hand, his strength too
much for the thin line. Frantically, he searched for the secondary cord, a precaution all parachutes had for just that
kind of emergency. Problem was, in all of his previous

jumps, he had never had to find the secondary cord, and so, hadn't bothered to pay attention to where it was located.

He glanced down.

"Yaaaa!" he thundered. "Don't look down. Good idea."

But he couldn't help it. As Hellboy searched for the secondary cord, the ground lurched toward him with nauseating speed. Seven hundred feet to go, as he searched the parachute restraints at his lower back. Six hundred as he ran his hands up and down the straps at his chest.

Five hundred.

Four hundred.

At two hundred feet, he found it. Pulled.

Nothing.

CHAPTER TWO

Hellboy took a deep breath, and pulled the ripcord again. The cord came off in his hand . . . but the chute opened. One hundred feet above the ground, Hellboy was jerked back with extraordinary force by the opening parachute. A human man might well have had his neck broken from that jolt alone. A human man could never have survived hitting the ground if his parachute had opened one hundred feet in the air.

His eyes were squeezed tight, waiting for impact. Hellboy opened them at the last moment to see two Bedouin guides and half a dozen camels immediately below him. There wasn't a thing he could do but pray, and he'd never been very good at that. Hellboy wasn't sure if even he could survive the impact. But he was lucky.

A camel broke his fall.

"Uhnff!" he grunted as he hit the ground, the shriek of the camel barely registering through the haze of shock.

"Hey!" he said in amazement. "I'm okay!"

Hellboy stood and brushed himself off. His hands came away from his calves sticky, and even as he lifted them to his face, he caught the scent of blood. He whirled in horror to see the shattered, bloody corpse of the camel he had landed on. The two Bedouins were staring at him, pointing in gape-mouthed horror.

"Oh, jeez," Hellboy said, biting his lip. "I am so sorry. I didn't even see him until the last minute."

The Bedouins ran, screaming in terror, spouting epithets in Egyptian, a language Hellboy had never even thought of studying.

He looked around at the surviving camels, who glared balefully back at him. Hellboy shrugged.

"I said I was sorry."

At the edge of the Great Sand Sea, Anastasia Bransfield stood atop a dune and wiped sweat from her brow. Squinting her ice-blue eyes against the sun, she removed the elastic that held her strawberry-blond mane in a ponytail. Anastasia ran her hands through her hair, and let the wind blow it across her face for a moment before tying it back up again.

Exhaustion had begun to settle into her bones, and it was only the second day of the search. The very idea of a search was laughable, she thought. The desert was constantly in motion, evolving, folding in upon itself. It would swallow its secrets in moments, and only give them up when it desired.

But search they would. That was their job, after all. Anastasia only hoped war did not break out with Libya while they were camped scant miles from that nation's border.

Idly, she wondered how long the British government would continue to search the shifting sands before calling the whole thing off and chalking it up to good old unexplained phenomenon. This investigation stank of weirdness and mystery. Two of her favorite things. But there was nothing Anastasia hated worse than a mystery she couldn't solve.

"Stacie!" a voice called from behind her. "Dr. Bransfield!"

Anastasia turned. A man stood on the dune behind her, his words being stolen away by the wind. She recognized him despite the linens he used to shield his balding scalp and dark-skinned face from the sun.

"What is it, Arun?" she cried.

Arun Lahiri, the expedition's historian, pulled the linen veil away from his face. Anastasia could see the anxiety etched into the man's features.

"It's the bloody MI5 again, Stacie," Arun shouted as he trudged closer to her. "A couple of Bedouins stumbled into camp, raving about a sand demon or some such. The gits from Intelligence jumped in a jeep and off they went, without any comment as to where they were headed."

"Rude of them, eh?" Anastasia commented, smiling broadly.

"Make fun if you like," the British-born Indian man sniffed. "But I don't trust those bastards a bit."

"They're MI5," Anastasia explained. "You're not supposed to trust them."

Arun didn't return her smile. They'd known one another for several years, their relationship lingering somewhere between acquaintance and friendship. Although at one gala museum benefit, Professor Lahiri had had the bad taste to drunkenly proposition her. He had smiled that night, but now that she considered it, Anastasia wondered if she'd ever seen him smile since.

"All right," she surrendered to his paranoia. "Let's get a jeep and check it out."

"Already done," Arun replied. "Bottom of the dune."

Anastasia slipped on the New York Yankees cap she had received many years earlier as a gift from an American friend. She pulled her ponytail through the back and fitted the cap snugly on her head. As long as they didn't get a bad sandstorm, it would stay on.

She squinted and stiff-legged it down the dune behind Arun. Across the endless stretch of sand she could see the investigative team's base camp. More than a dozen large tents, seven trucks, two jeeps, and what she considered to be a herd of camels. And the people. Archaeologists, British Intelligence agents, geologists, translators, and an ever-changing staff of Bedouin guides, cooks, and supply couriers.

Her team. Her expedition. Or at least, it was supposed to be. The whole lot of them answered to her, but that didn't include the morons from MI5. They weren't even officially there, or at least that was the word from the Prime Minister. They were ghosts.

But they had to be fed, and quartered, and they didn't take orders from what the MI5 commander, Michael Creaghan,

called "some upstart little tart thinks a Ph.D. makes her queen of the bloody universe." Anastasia smiled at the memory. She'd been called worse, but never in so colorful a manner.

Creaghan was a Neanderthal. Anastasia couldn't wait for the Cold War to end so people like Michael Creaghan would cease to be necessary. She wasn't fool enough to think such people wouldn't find work, but then at least she wouldn't have to deal with them.

Arun fired up the jeep and motioned for her to hurry.

"Keep your pants on, Lahiri," she grumbled, but knew the words would be stolen by the wind before they reached him.

With a foot on the front tire, Anastasia pulled herself up into the jeep.

"All right," she said, "let's go see our Bedouin sand de . . ."

Anastasia blanched. She spun on Arun and grabbed his arm.

"Sand demon?" she cried. "The Bedouins saw a sand demon?"

"That's what they said," Arun replied, glaring at her as though she were insane. "But I don't think we've anything to be afraid of."

"Jesus!" Anastasia barked. "Step on it, Arun, before they start shooting at him!"

"Shooting at . . ."

"Drive!" she shouted.

Arun gunned the engine and the jeep tore off across the desert. Anastasia stood up on the passenger seat and held a hand above her eyes, trying to see over the rolling plains of sand.

"There!" she cried. A funnel of dust blew up into the air, the trail left behind by Creaghan's jeep.

"We'll never catch him," Arun observed.

"Just try!" Anastasia shouted.

Hellboy trudged across the desert in the general direction of the camp he'd seen from the sky. He held a tether from which three camels trailed. He'd had to leave the dead one behind, which was a shame because he thought the people in camp might want to eat it. He didn't know if people ate camels. The idea had never before occurred to him. But he supposed that out in the desert, you might eat just about anything after a time.

It was hot. But he'd known worse.

Every once in a while, the camels became stubborn and held back for no apparent reason. Twice, he nearly left them. Let those idiot Bedouins come back and get them, he thought. But that wouldn't be practical or responsible. Sometimes doing the right thing was a pain in the ass.

It wasn't long before Hellboy saw the trail of sand dust pluming into the sky ahead. Seconds later, a second plume appeared in the distance behind the first. After half a minute or so, he could see that the sand cloud was caused by a jeep that bounced across the desert toward him.

"Hey!" Hellboy shouted, and waved to get the attention of whomever drove the jeep. "Hey!"

The jeep rocketed toward him over the sand. Its engine buzzed like a chainsaw, a disconcerting association, given the barrenness of the desert. Hellboy could see it better now, an open vehicle with at least four passengers.

With a whine of its engine, the jeep took air off a small dune and its tires spit sand as it landed. Hellboy squinted against the sun's glare. Something about the approaching vehicle didn't seem right to him. He looked more closely at the passengers.

Then he saw the guns.

"So much for the welcome wagon," he muttered under his breath.

As the vehicle slewed sideways in the sand and choked to a halt fifty yards from where he stood, Hellboy thought about going for his own gun. He decided against it. Guns bothered him. Of course, they bothered him most when they were pointed at him. But he had no way of knowing what the men in the jeep were up to.

What was that old saying? he thought. Hope for the best, and expect the worst, and you'll never be disappointed. But Hellboy had always had a problem with expecting the worst. No matter how grim he thought a situation might become, the world never failed to surprise him with something far beyond his capacity for pessimistic imagination.

When the jeep's driver killed the engine, the four passengers leaped out and leveled their weapons. They wore black jumpsuits without insignia. Each carried the new British SA80 rifle, with tele-optic sights. Hellboy had read about the SA80—so much for me not doing my homework, he thought—in a pile of documents about new weaponry Dr. Manning had given him the week before. The assault rifles were gas-operated, and fired about a dozen rounds a second.

"Not another step!" one of the gunmen shouted.

Getting shot had never appealed to him. Getting shot with that particular gun appealed to him considerably less.

The driver climbed out of the jeep and signaled two of the men forward. Apparently, he was the leader. As they moved to box him in, Hellboy lost his patience.

"You guys got some kind of problem?" Hellboy barked angrily, and took a long stride forward, leaving the camels behind.

Bullets punched the sand inches from his hooves.

"Perhaps you're a bit deaf?" the leader suggested. "Or a bit daft."

"Yeah, that's it," Hellboy agreed. "I'm a little deaf. Why don't you come a whole lot closer so I can hear what you're saying?"

The man smiled. He had blond hair and sparkling blue eyes. If not for the British accent, Hellboy might have thought somebody thawed out one of the SS troopers the *Schrecksturm* had put on ice back in '49. The idea made him shiver. Nearly all of Hellboy's childhood nightmares prominently featured Nazis. He hated Nazis.

"Okay!" Hellboy snapped. "I'm getting a little cranky standing out here doing nothing."

"You're trespassing, Hellboy," the blond man said.

"Oh yeah, prime real estate you've got here. I know you, pal?" Hellboy asked, uncertain.

"No, but I've heard of you, of course," the man responded. Weaponless, he moved cautiously toward Hellboy. "Though I always assumed you were a hoax, or some genetic mutation, or perhaps just tragically ugly. No offense."

"Sorry to disappoint you, Mr. . . . ?"

"Captain Michael Creaghan, British Intelligence," the man said. "And I'll ask you again, sir, what you are doing here?"

MI5, Hellboy thought. Great. And the guy was a real charmer, too.

He started toward Creaghan. The four other agents who accompanied Creaghan brought their weapons to bear on him, but Hellboy kept walking. A sudden breeze blew sand in his face, and he wiped the grit from his eyes.

"Captain?" one of them asked, obviously waiting for orders to perforate their target.

Creaghan unholstered his pistol and pointed it at Hellboy's forehead. Hellboy did not break his stride. Creaghan cocked the pistol and tilted his head slightly. That gesture might have indicated curiousity regarding Hellboy's choice of action. Or the man might simply have been concentrating on his aim. Either way, it gave him pause. He'd been shot before, plenty of times. But point-blank in the head? That might be a problem.

"I was invited," Hellboy said.

"Why is it nobody told me you were on the guest list?" Creaghan asked.

"Maybe it was supposed to be a special surprise," Hellboy suggested, his deep voice sharp with sarcasm. "This your birthday or something?"

"You aren't funny," Creaghan said. "I thought you should know that. Normally, I would have shot you already. But since I don't believe anyone could impersonate you, I am certain you are who you say you are. All I want to know is, why are you here?"

Hellboy sighed.

An engine roared suddenly, and a second jeep took air off a dune behind Hellboy. He half-turned to see it land, wheels throwing up sand. The jeep shuddered to a halt, and Hellboy recognized the woman in the passenger's seat immediately.

"Dr. Bransfield!" Creaghan shouted. "I must insist you remove yourself from this area immediately. You are compromising a . . ."

"Oh, sod off, Creaghan," Anastasia snarled.

She jumped from the jeep and stormed angrily over to Creaghan.

"Just what the devil do you think you're doing, anyway?" she demanded. "I find it hard to believe that you

wouldn't recognize Hellboy, Captain. It isn't as if there are a lot of enormous red gentlemen with cloven hooves and tails running around, is there?"

"You're out of line, Miss Bransfield," Creaghan began.

"No, it's you who are out of line, sir," Anastasia said coldly. "I am in charge of this investigation. As such, I asked Hellboy to lend us his services as a personal favor . . ."

"Told you I was invited," Hellboy said, and smiled. "Moron."

"You ought to have informed me of his impending arrival, then," Creaghan sniffed. "We might have avoided . . ."

"I didn't know when or even if he would arrive, Captain," Anastasia explained. "Now, if you're through pointing guns at my guest?"

Hellboy watched the faces of the men from MI5. Their eyes flicked from Anastasia to their commanding officer. They lowered their weapons slightly, illustrating their confusion, their hesitation.

"We will discuss this at length when you return to base camp," Creaghan stated.

He waved his men back to their jeep and they all climbed in. The jeep coughed into life and Creaghan drove them off across the desert, back the way they had come.

Hellboy and Anastasia watched Creaghan's jeep disappear over a dune. The sun felt much warmer, suddenly. Uncomfortable. Or perhaps it wasn't the sun at all. Hellboy glanced at Anastasia's jeep, and the thin, bespectacled man behind the wheel. The man gaped at him in astonishment.

"Your friend thinks he's at a sideshow," Hellboy said.

"Well, you are quite unique, after all," Anastasia replied.

He felt her staring at him, but for a moment could not turn and face her. Every day they spent together in the short time they had shared played itself over again in his head. In his heart. All the things he had faced in his life, all the horrors he had witnessed, and he couldn't meet the eyes of a woman he cared for.

Well, he thought, I'm only human.

"Why the smirk?" Anastasia asked.

Hellboy hadn't been aware that he had smiled, much less smirked. Of course, Anastasia was likely one of only two or three people in the world who might have been able to tell the difference.

"Just thinking about your MI5 buddies," he lied. "They're getting pretty punchy out in the desert, I think."

"Well," she said, "you could have made all of our lives easier and explained to them what you were doing here."

"I don't think they would have listened," Hellboy replied. "What are they doing here, anyway? I thought, what with the whole Libyan crisis, that there might be troops here. But MI5?"

"It's a long story," she said vaguely.

Finally, he turned to look at her. Their eyes met, and for a moment he thought he could see pain in hers. Then they were only blue. Anastasia smiled, and stepped toward him, arms open.

Hellboy took her in his arms and held her tight.

"Jeez, it's good to see you," he confessed, trying his best to make the words harmless.

"You too," she said. "Though, as usual, I think you've cracked a couple of my ribs."

"Sorry," he muttered, and let her go.

"That's okay," Anastasia replied, taking a deep breath and letting it out. "I'm just not used to it anymore, I guess."

That led to a protracted moment of silence.

"You haven't changed at all," Hellboy finally said.

"You have," Anastasia countered. "You're a lot quieter than I remember you."

Hellboy ran a hand over the stubble on his head. He scratched his skull absently, then shrugged.

"I guess I'm more careful of what I say," he explained.

Anastasia smiled. "Oh, I doubt that," she said.

The man in the car beeped. Anastasia took Hellboy by the arm and walked him back to the jeep.

"Arun Lahiri, I would like you to meet Hellboy. Arun is an historian from the British Museum," she explained.

Lahiri held out a hand and Hellboy shook it.

"We met very briefly back in '79 in Cameroon," Lahiri noted. "I was on Jim Powell's third Mokele-Mbembe expedition. You probably don't remember, but I'm honored to meet you again. Also, of course, your reputation precedes you."

"Thanks, I think," Hellboy said. "But don't believe everything you hear."

"Why don't we head back to camp?" Anastasia suggested.

"What about the camels?" Hellboy asked.

"Well, they can't ride with us, and it's quite a walk. I'm sure the Bedouins will come out and get them once I tell them what happened. Once I explain to them that you aren't a sand demon," she said, and grinned.

"Sand demon," Hellboy sniffed. "What's wrong with these guys?"

Hellboy climbed into the back of the jeep, and Anastasia followed, leaving the front passenger seat conspicuously vacant. Lahiri gave Anastasia an angry, rather proprietary look.

"What am I, a chauffeur?" the professor asked, then smiled weakly.

Despite his words, Hellboy wondered if the man's thinly veiled anger was based more on Anastasia's forsaking the seat next to him, and less on feeling like a servant.

Lahiri cranked the engine over, and they began to roll across the sand.

"I guess I should tell you why you're here," Anastasia began, not even bothering to address her associate's sarcasm.

"I was wondering when you would get around to that," Hellboy admitted. "I don't fly halfway around the world and jump out of an airplane over the desert just for anybody, you know."

Anastasia smiled. In that moment, it was as if they had never been apart.

CHAPTER THREE

"Thanks for coming," Anastasia said warmly. "I was afraid you wouldn't."

"That's a lie," Hellboy replied. "I could never say no to you."

"Well, that's only because my logic is flawless," she boasted.

"Actually, it's just that I hated the way your lip quivered whenever you were disappointed," he said.

Hellboy noticed Arun settle himself more firmly in the driver's seat of the jeep. He suspected that the man was attempting to listen to his conversation with Anastasia, but if so, his efforts were in vain. The wind tore their words away so quickly that they could barely understand one another in the back of the vehicle. Arun could not have heard them.

Hellboy was pleased. Anastasia's complete lack of discomfort regarding their relationship, despite her awareness that most people could not understand it, had always impressed him. But other people weren't always so understanding. Even now, Anastasia appeared not the least bit uncomfortable with their minor flirtation—a conversation that implied past intimacy—despite Arun's presence and surreptitious attention.

That nonchalance had been one of the things that

made Hellboy love Anastasia from the very beginning of their acquaintance.

"But enough about my irresistible nature," she joked. "And back to business. I asked you to Egypt to join my current investigation."

"Which is?" he asked.

"Five weeks ago, the British Museum sent an archaeological team here," Anastasia explained. "One of the team members was a third cousin or some such to the Royal Family."

"That explains why Creaghan and the other James Bond wannabes are here," Hellboy noted. "But I still don't know why *I'm* here."

"The team had Bedouin couriers deliver supplies and mail once a week," Anastasia continued. "Last week, when the couriers arrived, the team was gone."

"Gone?" Hellboy asked. "Okay, so a half-dozen people get lost in the desert, can't find their way home, and wind up walking until they drop. Tragic, but not exactly my area of expertise."

Anastasia sighed.

"I'm afraid you misunderstand," she said. "I mean they were gone."

"Yeah, I got that part,"

Hellboy insisted. "I don't see a mystery. If they didn't get lost, then some desert bandits killed them or something."

The jeep bounced over a small dune and rolled into the investigative team's base camp. The sun was brutal, and every time the wind kicked sand up from the desert floor, Hellboy shielded his eyes. Several Bedouins pointed at him and hid in their tents. Others merely stared.

"Are these people going to mutiny if you bring me into their camp?" he asked.

"First of all, it's my camp," Anastasia said. "Secondly, I've told my people about you. Creaghan will probably have told the rest of his team about you by now. Word should spread fairly quick. Then they won't bother you anymore.

"As for your getting-lost-or-attacked-by-desert-bandits theory, this wasn't a half-dozen people wandering about the desert," Anastasia insisted. "We're talking about twenty-seven people, eight vehicles, and an enormous amount of equipment. Look around at this camp, and you'll understand the kind of undertaking we're talking about here."

Hellboy squinted and nodded as he looked around. Tents and trucks and equipment and camels and people.

"I know what you're saying," he admitted. "It would take a lot of people a lot of time to evacuate a camp this size. But the thieves would have had all the time in the world. No one around, no rush. I still say desert bandits."

"And it's a nice fantasy," Anastasia replied. "But you've been asking why I called you here, and I'm trying to explain it to you. When I said they were gone, I meant everything and everyone. Twenty-seven people disappear in the Egyptian desert without a trace. No tents. No food or garbage or equipment. Not a scrap. Even if somebody took everything, like the bloody Grinch, there would still be some sign that people had been here. The desert covers everything, but it's like the ocean tides. Things get thrown back to shore after a while. We've found refuse from geographical surveys twenty years ago, perfectly preserved.

"It's as if they were never here at all," she concluded.

"Well, that's more like it," Hellboy nodded. "Now I know why you asked me to come."

Arun Lahiri climbed out of the jeep. Hellboy and Anastasia both followed.

"That's not all," Anastasia said. "It gets weirder."

Hellboy was about to reply when Creaghan appeared from within one of the tents. He scanned the camp, spotted them, and strode across the sand in their direction.

"Here comes my fan club," Hellboy grimaced.

But Creaghan barely glanced at Hellboy. He marched up to Anastasia with a grim set to his jaw.

"Miss Bransfield," he began. "I thought you would want to know that the Americans have commenced bombing Libya."

"Wonderful!" Anastasia cried. "That's just what we need!"

"How close are we to the border, again?" Hellboy asked.

"Just a few miles," Arun responded, and Hellboy glanced at him curiously. He had almost forgotten the man was there. He seemed to hang back, to skulk as if frightened or ashamed. Hellboy didn't trust him. At least with someone like Creaghan, he was dealing with an eminently predictable nature.

It was midafternoon. The camp seemed busy already,

and Hellboy didn't want to consider how cramped it would get when the search teams who must be out in the desert returned to their tents.

Spicy cooking scents filled the air.

"Do you guys think we could talk about this while we eat something?" he asked. "I'm starved."

"I don't know if we've got enough food to feed you," Anastasia joked. "Not the way you eat."

"Is this a time for humor?" Arun asked in alarm. "We've got a damned war coming down on our heads, and you make jokes?"

"There won't be a war," Anastasia insisted.

"You sound sure of that," Creaghan said skeptically.

"Fairly," she answered. "The American President, Reagan, wants to make a stand against not only terrorism, but the arrogance of the Libyans. They crow about their involvement in such acts. They'll come in and bomb the shit out of Libya's military and industrial targets, then go home. Khadafy will run away with his tail between his legs."

"I hope you're right," Hellboy said, but Anastasia's logic seemed sound to him, as usual. "But just in case, I guess I'd better eat now if I'm going to get anything at all."

"All right," Anastasia surrendered. "Let's go fill your stomach. I can't worry about things I can't control. War is one of those things."

A short time later, Hellboy sat with Anastasia and Arun while a Bedouin cook made them plates of falafel, cheese, and roasted pigeon. A basket of figs sat not far from the fire.

"I don't know about this," Hellboy complained. "I mean, pigeon?"

"Don't be so narrow-minded," Anastasia chided him. "It tastes just like chicken."

"That's what they say about everything," Hellboy mused. "I kind of have a feeling pigeon will taste like pigeon, though. No matter what you say."

Anastasia sighed and tore into the bird on her plate. Arun chewed in silence and Hellboy glared doubtfully at his plate. He bit off a piece of falafel and nibbled on a small hunk of cheese. Finally, he gave in and tasted the pigeon.

"Not bad," he admitted with a shrug. Then he gave Anastasia a skeptical sidelong glance. "Doesn't taste a bit like chicken, though."

They ate quietly. When the cook offered them figs, Hellboy took several gratefully. He pondered the ease with which he and Anastasia had fallen back into the rhythm of patter that had once been so familiar for them. As if it had been five weeks since they last saw one another, not five years.

None of which meant anything in the end. They had ended their intimate relationship and maintained a carefully balanced friendship in its place. No matter how bittersweet it might be, he would do nothing to jeopardize that friendship, and he knew Anastasia felt the same, though they had never discussed it.

"So, Hellboy, what do you think?" Arun asked, interrupting his musing.

"Tasty," he confessed. "Even the pigeon. But it could have used some cayenne."

"I meant about our conundrum," Arun said, smiling broadly. "I wondered what you thought of our Saharan Triangle."

"Like Bermuda," Hellboy noted. "I like that. But a couple dozen people disappearing in the middle of the desert is no comparison to the Bermuda Triangle, where boats and planes have been vanishing for years."

Arun and Anastasia stared at him.

"What?" he asked.

"I'm sorry," Anastasia said. "Creaghan interrupted us and I never got to finish the story. Remember I said it got weirder?"

"Oh, yeah," Hellboy nodded, though he had, in fact, forgotten.

"There have been a number of minor disappearances in this area over the years," she said. "Which is to be expected in the desert, right? People get lost, they die of dehydration or starvation. It happens."

"Okay," Hellboy agreed, unsure where Anastasia was leading. "There's a 'but' coming up, right?"

"Arun can tell it better," Anastasia said, and glanced at Lahiri, who sat a bit straighter now that his knowledge and expertise as a historian was in the spotlight.

"The year was 525 B.C.," Arun began. "Egypt was at war with Persia, and they were losing. The Persian king, Cambyses, was an extraordinary military leader, among other things. But it wasn't enough for him to have Egypt's metropolitan areas, to have the pyramids and the Nile. He wanted it all, the greedy bastard.

"That year, Cambyses sent fifty thousand soldiers on a trek across the Sahara to claim an oasis city. According to the

Greek historian Herodotus, near the end of their six-hundred-mile trek, a hurricane-force sandstorm blew up and swallowed the army. Fifty thousand men, their supplies, their armorers and animals. Vanished.

"In two thousand years, no one has ever found a single trace of the lost army of Cambyses," Arun concluded.

"Fifty thousand men, huh?" Hellboy asked, mulling it over. "Are we sure this happened?"

"As sure as we can be," Arun replied. "It could be historical hyperbole, but after that, Cambyses never seemed to be quite so in command of his empire."

"Let me guess. We're sitting on the spot where the army disappeared?" Hellboy asked.

"As near as we could determine, yes," Anastasia confirmed.

"Of course," Hellboy sighed.

He thought about what Arun had told him, and considered the disappearance of the archaeological team as a factor. Finally, he shrugged.

"I don't know what I can do, really, to help you out," he said. "But the way I see it, you've got only two options."

Anastasia looked at him expectantly. He glanced at Arun and saw that the man wore an identical expression.

"Well, it's just my opinion, remember. But either that

story is all crap and we're all out here for no reason whatsoever except to find some poor saps that wandered off or committed some mass suicide or something. Or, there actually was an army that got swallowed up by the desert," he explained.

"You actually believe that's possible?" Arun asked. "I mean, I know the history, but I don't know what to believe."

"I've seen some things that made a believer out of me, Professor," Hellboy said. "And as for you, well, you've seen me, haven't you?"

"Indeed," Arun answered thoughtfully.

"Nothing is impossible," Hellboy declared. "That's the first thing I learned when I started to do fieldwork for the Bureau. Nothing is impossible."

"So what could have done that, some enchantment or something?" Anastasia asked.

Hellboy winced at the skepticism in her voice. She had seen her share of weirdness when they had been together. But such things were always hard for people to accept at first.

"Maybe," he answered. "Or maybe giant sandworms like in *Dune*, but I doubt that.

"Look, the way I figure it, if anything paranormal happened here, it comes down to annoyance," Hellboy said. "Your friends probably stuck their noses where they didn't belong and somebody got pissed off. Why don't we start looking at it from that angle?"

"So, you believe we could find them?" Anastasia asked.

"No," Hellboy admitted. "Look, your lost army was fifty thousand guys and nobody ever found any of them.

When you take that into consideration, our chances don't look too promising."

The three of them fell silent, watching as the cook twisted four more pigeons on spits over the open flames. After a moment, they heard a commotion coming from the edge of the camp.

"Anastasia!" somebody yelled.

"That's Larry Scott," she explained. "One of our search squad leaders."

"He sounds excited about something," Hellboy observed.

Larry ran to Anastasia, tripped in the sand, and fell face first on the desert floor. He looked up at them, and recoiled slightly when he saw Hellboy. The man shook it off quickly, and Hellboy remembered that they had all been warned to expect him. All but Creaghan and his bonecrushers.

"What is it, Larry?" Anastasia asked. "Why are you so out of breath? Where did you run from?"

"From the oasis," Larry replied, still breathing heavily.

He stared up at Anastasia.

"Stacie," he wheezed. "We found them."

Just under a mile northwest of camp, even closer to the Libyan border, lay a freshwater oasis several hundred yards in diameter. It was almost a crater in the middle of the desert, a deep depression with stone and earth walls that sloped steeply down from the sand to the edges of the small forest that surrounded the lake at the center of the oasis.

"Wow," Hellboy mumbled.

"Indeed," Anastasia said. "Intellectually, you may know

that they exist, but seeing an oasis, particularly one of this size, is still nearly a surreal experience."

"It just doesn't look like it belongs here," Hellboy observed, glancing around at the arid desert as they began their descent into the oasis depression. "It's like somebody planted this huge garden in the middle of nowhere."

"And yet you find them all across the desert. Few and far between, true, but there nonetheless," Professor Lahiri said.

Their jeep bounced down the steep incline, tires tearing into dirt, finally getting traction after weeks on the sand. Hellboy gazed out across the blue expanse of fresh water and nodded slightly in amazement as he realized the extent of the oasis. The land around the lake for forty or fifty yards was truly verdant, almost lush. Where the green stopped, the soil began. He was amazed the desert didn't simply overtake it all. Apparently the high walls around the oasis protected it from the Sahara.

Something distracted him far off to the left. He glanced in that direction and searched the hillside for some sign of movement. Nothing moved, but after a moment, Hellboy identified what had drawn his attention. The side of the hill seemed stained with several dark spots. Then he realized what the spots were.

"Are those caves?" Hellboy asked.

"Your eyesight is incredible," Arun commented. "As far as we can tell, there was once a clan of cave dwellers that lived on the banks of this oasis. It isn't on any map I've seen, but I believe it's probably the oasis of Ammon, which was previously considered to be merely a myth."

"But nobody lives here now?" Hellboy asked. "Why?"

"That's an excellent question," Anastasia replied. "It certainly could sustain a small village or town. But few people, even among the nomads, would be hardy enough to make the trip to the nearest settlement for trade or communication without modern transportation. Which the desert people just don't have access to."

"So, of course, we're out here in the middle of nowhere, where not even an Egyptian would want to be," Hellboy said sarcastically.

"It's the desert," Anastasia said, and shrugged.

They reached the bottom of the slope and Arun turned left to follow the outer perimeter of the oasis. The jeep rattled and wheezed and Hellboy began to wonder if they would be able to make it back up the hill.

Anastasia turned to glance back, and Hellboy followed her gaze. Creaghan and several of his men had followed them in another jeep, guns at the ready.

"You know, I'm beginning to feel a bit useless here," Hellboy admitted. "You people seem prepared for just about anything, and more than capable of coming up with any strategy that might occur to me."

"That's where you're wrong," Anastasia said. "You're far more familiar with the paranormal and how to combat it than anyone on my team. I don't know what we might run into, but I definitely want you around. Your instincts may be all we have to go on."

"I'm all fuzzy inside," Hellboy mused. "But at this point, you don't even know that there's anything paranormal happening around here."

A little more than forty feet ahead of the jeep, a black woman shot from the trees and stood in their path. She waved at them frantically, and Arun swerved the jeep to the left and jammed on the brakes. The jeep shuddered to a halt.

"What happened to Larry?" the woman asked, staring at Hellboy so vacantly that he could not even decide if she really were staring, or just shell-shocked by what she had found.

"He's resting, Jenny," Anastasia responded. "He really didn't want to see it again, he said."

"Can't blame him," Jenny said. "Soon as you guys have had a look, I'm going back to camp. I don't even want to be near this oasis again. Not after today."

Hellboy got out of the jeep and stood with Arun and Anastasia as the men from MI5 leaped out of their own jeep and ran up to meet them. Unlike most people, who would run at the first sign of something supernatural, Hellboy had made a career out of hunting down and investigating such things, and often enough beating them senseless. That was his job. Yet, despite that such investigations often came to violence, the BPRD held the acquisition of knowledge as its main goal. The defense part was easy: some paranormal being got out of line, the BPRD was there to take it down, hard.

But soldiers had a tendency to shoot first. Hellboy was always uneasy around any kind of military personnel; no matter how hard he was to kill, it didn't make him immortal. To send a numbskull like Creaghan up against something paranormal was just asking for trouble. Hellboy didn't want to get caught in the crossfire.

"Let's go," Anastasia said, and tugged lightly on his arm.

Her touch sent a wave of feeling through him, a protective affection that she had chastised him for in the time when their relationship was still intimate. She could take care of herself. He knew that. But it didn't mean he wasn't going to make absolutely certain that, no matter what else happened, no matter the cost, Anastasia would be safe. While he was at her side, it was the least he could do.

Creaghan was at the head of the group as they cut through the trees and Hellboy glared at his back. Captain

Creaghan was a dangerous man. But he'd never met anyone like Hellboy before.

Ahead, several more members of Anastasia's team were
gathered at the edge of a small clearing. They stood in a
tight group, speaking softly to one another. When
Creaghan arrived, they moved aside, and Hellboy felt Anastasia stiffen next to him.

She might be in charge, but Creaghan had the authority of his position, and of the Crown, behind him. Their
conflict was bound to continue.

Creaghan and his men froze at the entrance to the
clearing. Hellboy could smell the water from the oasis,
which likely sprang from an underground reservoir or
river of some kind. It was a sweet, fresh smell, and welcome. But it was tainted. Tainted by blood.

"Oh dear God," Anastasia cried.

Across the clearing, the upper limbs of dozens of trees
were strewn with gory decoration, red streamers that might
once have been the viscera of human beings. Half bodies
hung from trees, leaking crimson ichor on the tall grass.

Behind him, Arun Lahiri turned and vomited profusely
between two tall trees. Hellboy ignored him, and started

across the clearing. After a moment, Anastasia began to follow. He did not turn, but he sensed her approach, and was proud of her.

Creaghan went with them, in silence.

They stood several feet from where the green grass was sprayed with blood and bone and other human matter. The bodies appeared to have been mutilated horribly, slashed to ribbons, and their remains strung about the trees with a revoltingly gleeful abandon.

"How long ago did you say these people disappeared?" Hellboy asked.

"Come now," Creaghan huffed. "How can we be certain this is even the team we're searching for?"

Hellboy frowned and turned to regard the square-jawed blond man as though he were an idiot.

"Now who else would it be?" he asked. "I guess you can tell the Queen her cousin won't be summering at Buckingham Palace this year."

"You disfigured, simian oaf!" Creaghan cried. "How dare you speak of Her Majesty with such disrespect."

"Put a sock in it, pal," Hellboy snapped. "You're not even supposed to be here, remember? You're invisible, a ghost. Why don't you start acting like one?"

Creaghan appeared to consider his response, but in the end said nothing. Part of Hellboy felt disappointed. He wanted to pummel the Captain. But the BPRD frowned on him causing international incidents. So it was all for the best.

"Several weeks at least," Anastasia said, and the tension between Hellboy and Creaghan dispersed. At least, temporarily.

"What?" Hellboy asked.

"The team disappeared several weeks ago," she repeated.

"But this massacre just happened, a few hours ago, no more," Hellboy observed. "They weren't anywhere that we could find them, but they were alive, and well fed until they were brought here and slaughtered."

"How can you know all that?" Anastasia asked.

"Trust me," he responded. He didn't think she would want him to point out the stomach and intestines he had spotted several trees over, their contents spilling out through a vertical slash.

"So you think whoever abducted these people, desert pirates or aliens or what-have-you, murdered them just to warn us off?" Creaghan demanded, his voice filled with testosterone-supplied bluster.

"Well the British government doesn't hire men who frighten easily," he continued. "Your job is over now, Dr. Bransfield. But I'm going to find these terrorists and show them what kind of justice a man might expect for perpetrating such monstrous acts!"

"Are you through?" Hellboy asked quietly.

"What?" Creaghan snapped.

Anastasia looked at Hellboy curiously. Across the clearing, the rest of the people who had witnessed the carnage watched, unable to determine what, exactly, was being said. Hellboy ignored them, but he gave Anastasia a confident look, meant to reassure her. He hoped that it worked.

"I asked if you were through, Creaghan," Hellboy repeated. "I think you're way off on this one. I don't think this massacre was meant to scare us away. I think that whoever did this wanted us to find these corpses so we would know exactly where to start looking. This is their way of shouting, 'Hey, here we are, come and get us!' They want to be found."

"But why?" Anastasia asked. "Why not just kill us, if that's their goal?"

"I don't know," Hellboy confessed with a shrug. "It's all just hunches, you understand. But then, why didn't they kill all these poor bastards until now? What were they keeping them alive for?"

There was a moment of silence, then. None of them really seemed to want an answer to that question.

"Well, you seem to be the expert on savagery, Hellboy," Creaghan sneered. "Where would you suggest we start looking for whoever did this horrible deed? They can't have gotten far."

Hellboy raised his eyes above the tree line and stared at the dark holes in the hillside.

"Let's check those caves first," Hellboy said. "There's nowhere else to hide around here."

Nobody spoke. Hellboy turned, curious at the lack of response. Anastasia and Creaghan were staring across the clearing toward the lake at the center of the oasis. Hellboy followed their line of sight through the trees.

Something moved at the edge of the lake. Lumbered up from the water and shambled into the trees, headed toward them. Not just one thing, but several.

"What are they?" Anastasia whispered as she stared at the lurching things that glistened in the harsh desert sun.

"I can't make it out, but I think they're carrying swords," Creaghan said.

Hellboy could see them just fine.

"They're soldiers," he said. "Persian soldiers."

Creaghan and Anastasia turned to stare at him. Hellboy strode grim-faced toward the lake.

"Maybe we can finally get some damn answers around here!" he snarled.

CHAPTER FOUR

Low branches stung Anastasia's face as she set off after Hellboy. He wasn't running, but his strides were long enough that she had to jog to keep up. Captain Creaghan and the pair of MI5 agents that always accompanied him followed close behind her. Some of the others might have followed as well, but Anastasia didn't bother to look.

It was insanity not to simply flee, and let those trained for such things deal with the monstrous men dragging themselves up the lakeshore. But Anastasia kept running. The horror she had witnessed in the clearing left her numb and nauseous. The fear was nearly overwhelming. But she forced herself to ignore it. Hellboy was there, just ahead, and she had faced the unknown with him before and survived. In truth, she had been far more afraid nearly six years earlier, when the Obsidian Danse were preparing her for sacrifice, than she was now. Perhaps that experience had desensitized her. Her fear now was more for him than for herself.

Ahead, Hellboy strode purposefully between trees toward the lake. The sun splashed on his flesh and made it seem to glow with vitality. The deep red of his skin had always seemed to her so healthy. He still wore the small tuft of hair at the base of his skull tied in a knot, as she had suggested long ago when he had wanted to shave it off. The rest of his skull was covered with a dark black stubble, the harsh feel of which she remembered well.

As he stalked toward the killers, his tail curled stiffly, clenched with anger and purpose as surely as he clenched his fists where they hung by his sides. His duty was to question the unknown, but as long as Anastasia had known him, Hellboy had shown himself far more likely to beat it into submission. If Anastasia had the power, she had always told him, that was how she would have dealt with her fears as well.

Hellboy moved to the left for a broader opening in the trees, and Anastasia stumbled to a halt on the path. She could see the men moving up the shore now, and knew without question that they were exactly what Hellboy had said they were: Persian soldiers.

Soldiers who had died two thousand years earlier.

Hellboy emerged from the trees forty feet from the water. His hooves stabbed the firm ground. After only a handful of hours on sand, he was grateful for solid footing.

The surface of the oasis lake shimmered in the sunlight, and Hellboy felt the temperature difference immediately as he left the cool tree shade. Behind him, he heard several people come to a halt at the tree line. He didn't have to turn around to know they were staring. And not at him.

Halfway between Hellboy and the water, three horrifying forms shambled stiffly up the shore. They were garbed in soiled linens, their flesh wasted away, dried and cracking upon their bones. Where once the soldiers might have had eyes, now there were only deep pits glowing with an arcane green light visible even in full sun. Their mouths had rotted away, leaving their decayed teeth bare in an eternally corrupted smile.

While once they might have worn some covering for their heads or chests, nothing was left but thin, wispy, dark hair and papery skin. The metal glint that Hellboy and the others had seen through the woods was not armor after all, but weaponry.

The ghoulish soldier closest to Hellboy wielded a double-headed iron axe with a handle at least three feet long. The walking corpse held the weapon with both hands. Behind it, the other two staggered forward. They seemed burdened by their own weight, but not at all by the weight of the heavy iron and bronze swords each held at the ready. They all wore daggers strapped to their bony hips.

"Not another step, zombie-boys!" Hellboy barked. "I want some answers."

The Persian warriors paused, apparently taken aback by his presence. Green light glowed ever brighter from their shriveled eye sockets. Hellboy wondered if that meant they were actually looking at him.

The axe-wielding leader opened its mouth. The flesh around the teeth, or what remained of them, cracked and peeled back like a snapped elastic. Then it spoke.

"Our quarrel is not with you, demon," the warrior said, but its voice seemed more an echo of a voice. An echo of words spoken from the depths of a dank, crumbling well, or through muffled cemetery earth.

"We are bound to obey our master, himself the slave of

Mar-Ti-Ku," the creature declared. "Stand aside, and you will survive the day."

"Yeah, like that's gonna happen," Hellboy muttered. "Look, I've got a better idea. Why don't you guys tell me who your master is, and where he's hiding. Then we'll get to the bottom of this. I'd like to know what happened to the archaeological team whose remains are decorating the trees back there."

The rotting soldier turned slightly, as if to stare off into the forest despite its lack of eyes. When its head swiveled back toward Hellboy, the green light in its eye sockets had diminished to a pair of furious pinpoint embers.

"They were trespassing," the thing said simply, in that hollow, faraway voice. "Now, will you stand aside?"

"No," Hellboy answered. "Why don't you take me to your master? Maybe he and I can . . ."

Faster than Hellboy would ever have imagined, the desiccated walking corpse hefted the battle-axe and swung it at him.

"Hey!" Hellboy cried, ducking under the blow that was meant to sever his head. The axe glanced across his brow, metal clanging on the stumps of his horns, and the warrior began to bring the axe around again.

Hellboy unholstered his gun, thumbed back the hammer on the old weapon, and blew a massive hole through the Persian soldier's chest. It staggered back, axe faltering in its hands, and stared down momentarily at the ribs protruding from its torso.

It glared at Hellboy.

"Damn," he muttered.

The other dead warriors moved to join the first. They

held their swords at the ready and moved to either side, trapping Hellboy between them. In front of him, the corpse with the axe hefted his weapon and moved in, more cautiously this time.

"Hellboy, look out!" Anastasia screamed behind him, but Hellboy didn't dare look around.

He was in trouble. Creaghan and his men could probably take down one or two of the dead men with their weapons, but they would just get up again. Whatever he did had to be a bit more permanent.

The axe fell. By instinct, Hellboy swung his right arm up and blocked the blow with his stone hand. One side of the double-edged axe shattered on that hand. With his left, he reached out, grabbed the axe-wielder by the throat, and spun the soldier to the left, impaling it on its comrade's sword.

Hellboy glared over the warrior's shoulder into the glowing eye sockets of the swordsman. The axe-wielder spat orange bile and writhed, impaled on the other's sword, which jutted from its stomach. The swordsman tried to slide the blade out, but Hellboy snagged the razor-sharp point with his invulnerable right hand and pulled. The swordsman's arm burst through its comrade's back as if the entire body were made of rotten fruit.

A blade slashed across Hellboy's back and he cursed loudly. He had not forgotten the third dead Persian soldier, merely lost track of the dead thing's location in the course of battle.

"Damn!" he snarled, cursing the pain.

He tore the blade from the first swordsman's hand, lifted it high, and used all his strength to bring it down in

a slashing arc, hacking the heads from the two interlocked
corpses. The heads tumbled to the packed earth, and the
dead men fell to the ground, their bodies cracking open
like piñatas, spilling desert sand instead of gore.

"What the . . . ?" Hellboy began.

A sword pierced his back and he grunted as it first
stretched, then tore the skin of his abdomen. Its point
dripped with blood and Hellboy looked down at it in
amazement. Behind him, the dead soldier gripped its
sword with both hands, and twisted it within Hellboy's
body, with strength far more than human.

Hellboy fell to the sand. Above him, the last of the
three Persian warriors towered over him, dagger in hand,
and moved in for the kill. Hellboy looked up to see that all
but Creaghan, his two lackeys, and Anastasia, had fled the
scene.

Hellboy and Creaghan locked eyes, and Hellboy saw
the fear there.

"What the hell are you waiting for?" he demanded
weakly. "Shoot him!"

Creaghan blinked once, and signaled to his men. Their
SA-80's exploded in a torrent of bullets which literally tore
the third dead soldier apart. Sand flew everywhere, and

when it was over,
nothing remained of
the dead soldiers
other than their
weapons.

Hellboy tried to
move, but the point
of the sword had
embedded itself into
the dirt when he fell. The pain was excruciating.

"Got to take this out," he groaned.

He looked up at Anastasia, who stared down at him in
horror and sympathy.

"I'm so sorry," she said.

"Dead guys," Hellboy mumbled as unconsciousness
began to claim him. "There's just no talking to them."

The immediate danger was over. Anastasia forced
away the fear that had nearly overcome her moments earlier. Hellboy needed her, and she wasn't going to
let him down.

She scanned the people assembled on the lakeshore.
Creaghan was flanked, as always, by two MI5 agents who
might have been his bodyguards. Anastasia knew their
names, Burke and Carruthers, but the two men were so
emotionless and devoid of personality that she could never
recall which was Burke and which Carruthers. One of
them, whose dark hair was slightly lighter than the other's,
wore a canteen strapped across his shoulders. It was the
desert, after all.

"You!" Anastasia snapped and pointed at the canteen. "Give that to me!"

The agent's eyes widened and his eyes darted quickly to Captain Creaghan for some indication as to how he should proceed. After a moment's hesitation, which Anastasia believed the man feigned merely to establish his authority, Creaghan nodded.

The MI5 agent held out his canteen and Anastasia snatched it from his hand. She heard gasps from the tree line and glanced up to see that some of the members of her investigative team had returned. She didn't see Arun Lahiri there, and mentally cursed him for his cowardice.

Hellboy lay on his stomach, the sword protruding from his lower back. Its point had penetrated through his torso and into the ground below. His head was turned slightly to one side, so the left side of his face was visible.

Anastasia upended the canteen, splashing water on Hellboy's head, neck, and face. He spluttered and his muscles tensed.

"Don't move," she barked, and he froze.

Hellboy grunted, winced. His eyes flickered open, and relief flooded through Anastasia. She had seen him in far worse conflicts, seen him sustain more devastating injury, but she had never seen him pass out before. The twisting of the sword, and the impact as it hit the ground while still inside him, must have overloaded his pain receptors, Anastasia reasoned. But it had been quite alarming, no matter the cause.

"You had me worried for a minute, there," she said.

"I'm still worried," he replied, and forced half a smile. "Somebody want to help me with this sword?"

Anastasia stared at the spot where the iron blade entered the crimson flesh of a man she cared deeply for.

"I can't do it," she confessed, and looked up at the MI5 agents. "Creaghan?"

Without hesitation, Captain Creaghan stepped forward. He gripped the sword two-handed, as the dead soldier had.

"Why don't you count to three," Creaghan suggested. "Prepare yourself. This is going to hurt."

"No kidding?" Hellboy said. "So far it feels kind of good. Just pull the damn thing out before . . ."

Creaghan yanked. The sword slid out, followed by a six-inch-high spurt of blood.

"Jeez!" Hellboy growled, and sucked in a deep breath.

He let it out slowly, then brought his knees up under his body and climbed painfully to his feet. "That's much better," he groaned.

"Hellboy," Anastasia warned. "Maybe we should just try to get you back to camp. We'll get a bunch of people to carry you."

"Thanks, 'Stasia, but I weigh nearly a quarter ton," he replied. "I don't think you'd have much luck. I'll be okay in a few hours."

Hellboy turned so Anastasia could get a good look at the wound in his back. Her eyes widened. Though the dead soldier had nearly bored a hole in Hellboy's body with his sword, the wound had closed to a one-inch puncture already. A small trickle of blood seeped from it, and Anastasia knew that, too, would soon be closed.

"Christ," one of the MI5 agents, the one she thought was Carruthers, whispered. "What the hell is he?"

"That's quite enough," Creaghan snapped.

Anastasia smiled. Apparently MI5 agents had emotions after all.

Hellboy glanced around the shore at what remained of the Persian soldiers. Anastasia followed his gaze. All that remained of the dead men was sand and ragged clothing, and their weapons.

"Sand," Hellboy muttered. "Just sand."

"Have you ever seen anything like that before?" Anastasia asked.

"Never," he answered. "I once saw a zombie transform into a kind of humanoid albino alligator, but I've never fought anything that disintegrated into bits of sand right in front of my eyes."

"It's almost as if they became the desert," Creaghan commented.

Anastasia glanced at him. For the first time, she realized something had changed about the man. It seemed that the strangeness of the situation had instilled in him a far greater interest in cooperation. It was about time, as far as she was concerned. He would probably always be condescending, but it would make life much simpler if they could at least work together instead of at cross-purposes.

"Or the desert preserved them this way, somehow," Anastasia offered.

Hellboy only stared at the ground, at the clothes and small piles of sand. Anastasia began to pick up the dead warriors' weapons.

"Jenny, grab the rest of these, will you?" she called.

Three people, including Jenny Marcus, approached the

spot where Hellboy stooped to examine the remains of the dead soldiers. He sifted the sand through his fingers as Anastasia made certain her team handled the ancient weapons carefully.

"What do you think you're doing?" Creaghan asked. "Those are evidence."

"Evidence of what?" Anastasia asked, bewildered. "Mass murder? The killers have been dead for two thousand years. They're dust now. Meanwhile, these are probably the best preserved weapons from the ancient world ever discovered. I'm sure the Prime Minister would agree that the British Museum ought to have something for its losses."

Creaghan did not respond. Hellboy stood up and looked around, his eyes darting from face to face.

"We've got to figure out who this 'master' is they were talking about," he said. "Whoever made them this way has got a lot of power."

"What do you mean, 'They were talking about'?" Creaghan asked.

Anastasia frowned and stared at Hellboy. The same question had been on her mind as well.

"The lead zombie, or whatever they are," he explained. "The guy said they were slaves to some guy who's also a slave to some guy named Mar-Ti-Ku. Come on. Are you guys as confused as I am?"

"Ah, sorry to tell you this, old friend," Anastasia said, "but all we heard coming from those dead things was some kind of disturbing gibberish. No words. Or at least no words in any language I understood."

Hellboy looked at Creaghan, who nodded his agreement with Anastasia.

"Well," he shrugged, "that's not terribly surprising, actually. One time the BPRD sent me to check out a possession in Tennessee. Little kid named Eric Powell. Spit blood, swore at his mother, all that *Exorcist* crap. He babbled on in what everybody else heard as gibberish. It sounded like English to me.

"When I touched the poor kid's forehead, he opened his eyes, took a look at me, and screamed. His mother comforted him, and he was fine after that. But the Baptist preacher that was supposedly going to do the exorcism tried to kill me, because he said I could 'hear the voice of evil.'"

There was silence for a moment. Anastasia didn't know what to say. The story disturbed her. Apparently, it disturbed the others as well, because nobody would meet Hellboy's eyes. Even Creaghan shuffled his feet nervously.

"Jeez, will you guys lighten up," Hellboy complained. "I kind of thought it would come in handy, you know, my understanding arcane languages. And anyway, the most overwhelming question isn't how these guys got this way or who did what to whom."

"What is it then?" Creaghan asked.

"Well, according to Professor Lahiri, there were fifty thousand of these guys, right?" he asked.

"Yes," Anastasia agreed, and her stomach lurched as she realized where Hellboy's logic was leading.

"What I want to know," he said, "is where are the other forty-nine thousand, nine hundred, and ninety-seven missing Persian soldiers?"

Creaghan blanched.

"Maybe it's time we head back to base camp," Anastasia suggested.

CHAPTER FIVE

A t dusk, the desert horizon to the west seemed to glow with a magical golden light that, for a brief moment, overcame the chilling effect of the day's events. Even when it was gone, and night had fallen, and the memory of the dark and evil workings of the day seemed all too real and threatening, the denizens of Anastasia Bransfield's camp were relieved.

Night meant that work was over. They had taken enough photographs of the massacred archaeological team, investigated the site of the slaughter, and the area where the undead Persians had fought Hellboy, in great detail. Anastasia had brooded about it, and finally ordered that the significant and recognizable body parts must be recovered from the trees if possible.

Her team refused. She didn't have the heart to force them, and thought that even if she tried, they might simply quit. They weren't made for that kind of work, hadn't been sent to Egypt to climb trees filled with rotting gore and human limbs.

Creaghan's men didn't have a choice. They searched the trees until they found the head of Lady Catherine Lambert, a daughter to a second cousin of the Queen. They bathed afterwards, of course, and burned the clothes they had worn. But all of the MI5 agents were quiet later on. Anastasia thought she heard Carruthers—or was it Burke?—retching behind his tent just before dusk.

But finally, the day was over. When the sun disappeared, the desert grew extremely cold quite rapidly. Fires were lit, and burned warmly but without any real comfort. Most of her team retreated into their tents, some for the kind of warmth they could only get from one another, others merely to sleep. To sleep, and try to keep the nightmares at bay. Even those who had not witnessed the atrocity in the clearing had heard enough of it to sicken them.

Creaghan posted a guard. Two men on at all times. Whatever was happening, they were all agreed it wasn't over.

When all but the guards were asleep, Anastasia still sat with Hellboy around the dying fire. She moved close to him for warmth, confident that neither of them would assume any other motive. Their split had been too definite, their knowledge of one another too profound, for such games.

"Getting sleepy?" he asked in a gruff voice, the closest he could come to a whisper.

"Yes," she admitted. "But I don't want to sleep. I'm afraid to dream tonight. You're lucky you don't need much rest."

Their eyes met. His were strong and calm, loving, and contemplative. They were what had drawn her to him all those years ago. Now they were a comfort she sorely needed.

"Don't worry," he said, the fire flickering off his red skin, turning it orange. "I'll keep watch over you."

"Thanks," Anastasia said, and smiled. "You always could keep the nightmares away."

"Hey," Hellboy brightened, "that's my job."

They sat in silence then, but a comfortable one. The quiet familiarity of old friends satisfied with the mere presence of one another. Conversation was unnecessary. Despite his outward appearance and his sometimes brusque manner, she had never met a man more attuned to human emotion, never met a man as honest and good.

That's what he was, after all: a man. Many would argue with her, and their arguments might be sound. But to her, Hellboy would never be anything but a man. Once upon a time, he had been *her* man. Now, he was only her friend. But the truest friend she had ever had.

The fear and the numbing horror from earlier in the day lingered somewhat. But with Hellboy there, she was able to push it away. She had faced the unknown with him before and survived.

She had been afraid for Hellboy as much as she had feared for her own life. His temper was the only quality she did not admire in him. But even that rarely surfaced outside of life-threatening situations. And she could not take him too vehemently to task for that. After all, that temper had saved her life more than once.

Anastasia was contemplating how their relationship had changed, warmed by the fire, lulled and sleepy. Hellboy put his arm around her protectively, and pulled her close. The movement caused him to wince in pain. She looked up at his face in alarm, realizing his wound had not yet completely healed.

"It's all right," he said. "I'll be fine in the morning. I'll be . . . what was it you used to say?"

"Right as rain," she answered.

"Yeah," he smiled. "Right as rain."

Then the sky lit up around them and the night exploded with sound. Two flares burst above their heads and began their unnaturally slow descent toward Earth. A thunderous rumbling came from beyond the dunes not far from camp. Seconds later, the first tank appeared. It was followed by many other vehicles: tanks and trucks and jeeps.

"Look!" Hellboy said, and pointed into the sky.

 Anastasia saw dark shapes blotting out the stars. She shivered, but wasn't sure if it was the cold or dread that gave her such a chill.

"What are they?" she asked.

"Parachutes, would be my guess," he answered. "Supplies for the troops, weapons and such. Easier to airlift them than carry them overland."

They watched as the vehicles approached, dozens of headlights and spotlights arcing toward their camp. Anastasia felt a tightening in her stomach unlike anything she had ever felt before.

"Is it war, then?" she asked quietly.

"I don't think so," Hellboy answered. "They're awfully conspicuous for it to be war. But let's go find out, just to be sure."

Hellboy was tempted to lead by a few steps, to protect Anastasia should anything unexpected occur. But she was a capable woman, and in charge of the investigation. Instead, he held back and allowed her to lead him through the scrambling MI5 goons and archaeologists who scurried from their tents to see what the commotion was about. Still, he brought himself up to his full height, and held his tail stiffly up behind him.

It seemed like macho bullshit. Hell, it even felt like macho bullshit. But he couldn't help it. He wanted anyone who saw her coming to know Anastasia had serious backup.

They set out across the desert for the jeep that had broken from the military pack to take the lead.

"Are we sure these aren't Libyan troops?" Hellboy asked.

"The Libyans aren't that stupid," Anastasia answered. "Invading Egypt would not be a good idea right now."

An engine revved behind them and Captain Creaghan pulled alongside with Burke and Carruthers in his jeep.

"Would you care to join us?" Creaghan asked.

Carruthers squeezed into the backseat with Burke so Hellboy and Anastasia could pile in front.

"Thank you, Captain," Anastasia said with what Hellboy considered to be remarkable restraint. "But aren't you supposed to be keeping a low profile?"

Creaghan sneered at her, but said nothing.

The jeep lurched forward, and a few moments later, came to a stop once more, directly in front of the convoy's lead vehicle. Even as they all climbed out, two armed soldiers leaped from the vehicle, to be followed very grandly by a man in the dress of an American military officer.

"I'm looking for Stacie Bransfield," the officer said.

Hellboy raised an eyebrow. Only Anastasia's close friends called her Stacie. He himself had always preferred her full name, which suited her. She didn't really like Stacie, especially not from strangers.

"I'm Anastasia Bransfield," she said stiffly.

"My apologies, Miss Bransfield," the man said. "That was the name I was given to ask for. I'm Colonel Jack Shapiro, United States Army. We have a coordinated effort here with the British and Egyptians."

"Actually, it's Dr. Bransfield," she corrected. "So, are we at war, or aren't we?"

"No, no," the Colonel said. "Not at all. We're merely here to make sure that war never happens. The Libyans aren't going to start anything. They're little more than a warehouse for worldwide terrorism. President Reagan gave them a spanking, and we're here to be sure there aren't any tantrums as a result."

"Don't you think any backlash would probably be through other terrorist actions?" Hellboy asked.

He had been standing behind the rest of them, near the back of the jeep. Now he took a step forward, and Colonel Shapiro's eyes grew wide with astonishment.

"My God!" the Colonel said. "What the . . ."

"This is Hellboy," Anastasia interjected quickly. "Of the BPRD. I'm sure you've heard of him, Colonel."

Shapiro colored and executed a curt nod. "Indeed I have," he said sternly. "My apologies, sir, I was unaware of your presence on this dig. I meant no offense."

"None taken," he lied.

Anastasia shot him a questioning look, apparently curious as to the Colonel's deferential treatment of Hellboy. Most people treated him like a celebrity, but here the Colonel was treating him like a superior officer or visiting dignitary.

"I have a Presidential commission," he explained softly, so that only she and perhaps Burke of MI5 could hear him. "I guess I'm the ambassador to the paranormal realm, or some such thing that gets Ronnie a photo op with me once or twice a year."

She smiled at that. Politics, particularly American politics, were about as paranormal as anything Hellboy had ever encountered. She'd given up trying to understand government years ago.

"In any case," Colonel Shapiro continued, obviously irked at the rudeness of their private conversation, "I have been instructed to suggest that you withdraw your team and discontinue your dig until the present crisis has passed."

"What?" Anastasia snapped, her voice echoing across the desert in the darkness. "Do you know what you're suggesting? The research that will be lost, the time and money squandered?"

"I'm only repeating the instructions I was given by the United Nations when they became aware of your presence here," the Colonel said. "I'm to suggest that you withdraw."

"We might ask the same of you," Creaghan said archly. "We don't need babysitters, Colonel."

Colonel Shapiro smiled in a patronizing fashion.

"Ah, I was wondering when MI5 would speak," the Colonel said.

Creaghan blinked twice rapidly, taken aback by Shapiro's statement.

"You are MI5, aren't you, sir?" the Colonel asked.

"Sorry, Colonel," Creaghan said, cracking an adversarial smile as he recovered from his surprise. "You don't have clearance for that information. Suffice to say that whatever we want to do here will get done. After all, if the Prime Minister had been interested in taking the U.N.'s advice about our withdrawal, we'd already be gone.

"I'll make you a deal, you stay out of my way, and I'll stay out of yours," Creaghan concluded.

The Colonel's eyes flicked from Hellboy to Creaghan and finally to Anastasia. He seemed to be contemplating what else he might say, but in the end, turned away without another word.

"Well, this is going to be cozy," Anastasia said as they

began to climb back into the jeep. "You make friends so easily, Creaghan."

"In my line of work, friends are a liability," the Captain responded.

"I'll remember that when the time comes for me to haul your butt out of the fire," Hellboy grumbled.

"What makes you think I'll need your help?" Creaghan asked, his tone more arrogant than ever.

"Just a feeling I get," Hellboy replied. "A feeling that today was only the beginning."

The jeep started across the sand. When they pulled into camp moments later, the army constructing their own base camp in the desert nearby, one of the MI5 goons ran up to meet them.

"Captain Creaghan!" the man shouted. "Good God, sir, come on. You must see this!"

"It can wait, Agent Rickman," Creaghan insisted. "It can . . ."

"No sir," Rickman responded. "No sir, it really can't!"

Rickman glanced nervously at Hellboy and Anastasia, then raised his eyebrows. His interest piqued, Creaghan began to accompany the man, with Burke and Carruthers bringing up the rear.

"What about them?" Rickman asked, gesturing toward Hellboy and Anastasia.

"What *about* them?" Creaghan sneered.

"I think we're going to need him," Rickman explained, and pointed at Hellboy.

"Say, what is this all about?" Creaghan demanded.

"You won't believe me if you haven't seen it first, sir," Rickman declared. "Really."

Simultaneously, they all realized that Rickman wasn't nervous. Not at all. The man was terrified.

"Okay," Creaghan relented. "Let's go. But this stays here in this camp. I'll not have the Americans sticking their noses into our business. Bloody assholes."

Agent Rickman led them all to a tent where several people, including two MI5 agents, and Jenny and Larry from Anastasia's team, waited outside.

"What are all these people doing here?" Creaghan demanded.

"She . . . she asked for them, sir," Rickman stammered.

"Who? Who in the bloody hell are you talking about?" Creaghan barked. "What in Christ's name is wrong with you people?"

Rickman stared at the sand beneath his feet.

"It's Lady Catherine, sir," Rickman said. "She wants to speak with Hellboy."

Silence. Hellboy and Anastasia stepped warily forward, and Creaghan stood his ground, staring at the tent in front of him. Burke and Carruthers watched their superior officer a moment, but then they stepped aside. In that moment of silence, Hellboy thought Creaghan would shout and berate his men for what he would consider their foolishness. The Captain even opened his mouth, as if to question or clarify his subordinate's words.

But before he could speak, they all could hear another voice. The delicate, feminine voice of a woman, speaking in soft, slow, dreamy cadence.

"Is he here yet?" the voice asked. "Is Hellboy here?"

"Good God," Creaghan whispered.

Hellboy pushed past him, and then Creaghan followed. A moment later, Anastasia joined them.

Professor Lahiri crouched in the center of the tent, eyes wide as if he were enchanted. He did not react at all to their entrance, and Hellboy assumed that the man had, indeed, been put into some sort of trance.

"Hellboy?" the voice said again.

Hellboy stepped around Lahiri. On the floor, propped up on the black rubber body bag in which it had been kept, was the head of Lady Catherine Lambert. Several inches of spinal column protruded like a useless limb from the bottom of her neck and lay like a lizard's tail on the black surface. There was a huge bite out of one cheek and teeth marks on her forehead.

But Lady Catherine's eyes were bright and intelligent, and her mouth curled into a smile as Hellboy appeared in her line of sight.

"Good," she said to herself. "And Captain Creaghan and Dr. Bransfield as well."

Hellboy was aware that the others would be completely unprepared for this. He had spoken with the dead many times, but even a woman as extraordinary as Anastasia, or a man as formidable as Captain Creaghan, could not help but be horrified and probably revolted at the mere idea.

"Stay back," he warned them, but more for their peace of mind rather than their safety. After all, Lady Catherine's reanimated remains were nothing but her head. What could a head do?

"Why did you call for me?" Hellboy asked. "And why for the others?"

"I called for the others because each of them had friends and associates amongst the archaeological team that died

with me. I am the only way in which they might communicate with their friends, to put them at ease. I was performing a service," she said kindly, with none of the haughtiness Hellboy might have expected from a British royalty, even twice removed.

He didn't point out that speaking to a disembodied head would not necessarily ease the minds of those who had seen friends murdered.

"But it was most important that we speak," the head continued. "You must speak with Dr. Bransfield and Captain Creaghan. They hear me now, but I doubt they are truly listening. You must insist that everyone leave now."

"Where are you now?" Hellboy asked, curious. Lady Catherine was a spirit. Her head was lifeless, but being controlled by the woman's essential force, or soul, if you believed in such things. Which Hellboy did.

"We are in the oasis," Lady Catherine explained. "All of us. Hazred's magicks trapped us here, but we have one another for company, and so will not be lonely."

"You're damned to stay there forever?" Anastasia asked from behind him, and Hellboy marveled that she could even bring herself to address the savagely mutilated head.

"Until Mar-Ti-Ku has been defeated," Lady Catherine answered.

"Okay, you're going to have to give me a little more to go on, ma'am," Hellboy insisted. "Who is Hazred? Who is this Mar-Ti-Ku that the Persian soldiers referred to? Are there any more of those zombie guys? Where were you kept after you disappeared from camp? What . . ."

"Please, Hellboy, I cannot keep up this communication for very long. Already we have spread our essences very thin to reach you. I will answer what I can, but the shroud of death has clouded life. Much is even now lost to me. Hazred is a sorcerer, and leader of the oasis people. He worships Mar-Ti-Ku, an ancient Sumerian magician who was banished from our world eons ago, but yearns to return. I do not know if there are any more soldiers.

"Now, you must go," she urged. "You are not safe here."

"I don't think so," Hellboy said. "I'm sorry, but I want to have a little talk with this Hazred guy. You can't just go slaughtering people and not expect some repercussions."

"I plead with you to change your mind, but if you persist, I will say only this: be careful of the spiders. Besides the hideous and sadistic face of Hazred, they are all I can recall of my captivity. That, and water," she said.

"Watch out for spiders," Hellboy repeated. "Got it. You can't remember anything else?"

"Nothing, and now my slaughtered comrades call to me from the oasis of Ammon. I must return or risk the dissipation of our souls," she said. "Please go, for all your sakes."

"Lady Catherine?" Hellboy asked.

But Lady Catherine's eyes rolled back in her head. Her tongue lolled out of her mouth. The remnant of her spine twitched once and then was still.

"Christ, I think I'm going to be sick!" Creaghan muttered, and pushed past the tent flap out into the night.

Arun still crouched on the ground by Lady Catherine's severed head. His eyes were wide and vacant, and he crooned a haunting melody so low that none of them had noticed it before.

"Professor Lahiri," Hellboy said. "Professor, hello? Can you hear me?"

"What?" Arun mumbled as his senses returned to him. "What happened?"

"Why don't you cover her up?" Hellboy suggested, and gestured to where the bloody head lay on top of the body bag.

Arun looked down at the head, shrieked in horror, and scrambled away from it as far as the tent's confines would allow. He panted for a few moments and then mumbled, "She . . . she called to me. I remember it all now. Oh, my dear God."

"Why you?" Anastasia asked.

"I was just passing by the tent, and I heard her whispering to me," Arun explained, trembling. "I want to go now. I want to leave Egypt."

"How could you have heard her whispering if her head was still inside the body bag?" Anastasia inquired.

"I want to go home," Arun said again. He stood and pushed past them, then stepped out of the tent.

"Give him until morning," Hellboy advised. "He'll be a lot more reasonable when the sun rises. His education could be helpful in getting to the bottom of this."

"I think he's out of his depth," Anastasia explained. "Even the most detailed history books only refer very generally to the lost army of Cambyses. Many people believed it a myth, though obviously we now have proof that it wasn't. If he wants to go home, I'm inclined to let him. What help will he be in searching out this Hazred person Lady Catherine mentioned?"

Hellboy searched Anastasia's eyes for some sense of the revulsion and, more than likely, fear that he expected to find there. He found none of it.

"You're awfully calm, considering what we just witnessed," he observed. "I've been doing this for decades, and I still get creeped out talking to dead people."

"Maybe you've forgotten," she replied. "This is hardly the strangest night I've spent with you."

Hellboy smiled. "Ah, yes. Corfu. Now that was weird."

"Don't get me started," Anastasia said, and shivered. "Okay, I'll try to talk him into sticking around. But I wouldn't bet on it. So what now?"

"Now?" he repeated. "Now we try to get some sleep. Tomorrow morning I'm going for a swim in that lake. That's where those zombie soldiers came from, right?"

Anastasia frowned.

"What, you didn't expect us to leave, did you?" Hellboy asked.

"No," she confessed. "I've known you too long for that. It's just that this is my investigation. I ought to be with you wherever you go."

Hellboy wanted to argue. The idea of Anastasia in any kind of jeopardy had always disturbed him. But he had learned a long time ago that she was a resolute and capable woman. And this was her show, after all.

Still . . .

"You don't have any scuba gear handy, do you?" he asked.

"Of course not," she said, and smirked. "We're in the middle of the desert."

"Well, no diving for you I guess," he said. "Sorry."

Anastasia opened her mouth as if to reply, then shook her head and slowly let out a breath.

"Be careful," she warned.

"Hey, careful's my middle name."

"You don't even have a last name!" she pointed out. "Big, silly bastard. Come on, then. Let's get some sleep."

Anastasia turned to go, but Hellboy didn't follow her. Two steps from the tent's flap, she stopped.

"What is it?" she asked.

"Lady Catherine," he explained.

Hellboy turned, his tail sweeping through the tent. His hooves punched the ground, and in one place, tore the canvas tent floor. He knelt by the severed head of Lady Catherine Lambert. As gingerly as possible, he lifted the woman's gory head and slid it back into the body bag from which Professor Lahiri had removed it.

When he stood, he lifted the body bag and carried it with him. Anastasia looked at him strangely.

"We may need her help," Hellboy explained.

CHAPTER SIX

They exited the tent and found Captain Creaghan standing outside.

"Did you want something?" Anastasia asked him.

"Want something," he sneered. "Well, it's my bleedin' tent, isn't it?"

"Oh, I guess it is," Anastasia replied.

They began to walk away.

"Hey!" Creaghan called. "What the hell do you think you're doing with that?"

Hellboy and Anastasia turned. It was obvious what Creaghan meant. But the man couldn't bring himself to refer to the severed head in the bag as Lady Catherine. He couldn't even describe the object in the body bag, not after what he had seen inside his tent.

"Those remains must be returned to England, Hellboy," Creaghan declared. "Dr. Bransfield should know better."

"Before you leave for England, I'll give Lady Catherine back to you," Hellboy vowed. "But for now, she stays with me. We may still need her help."

"You're out of your fucking mind!" Creaghan cried.

"Really?" Hellboy asked. "Well, if you insist, I could just put her back in your tent. But you never know when she's going to have something else to tell us."

Creaghan stared at him, eyes narrowed with fury. He turned his hateful gaze on Anastasia, who remained expressionless.

"Don't lose it," Creaghan finally said.

"My head?" Hellboy replied, and could not fight back a wide grin. "I'll do my best not to."

Anastasia cracked up at his side, and the two of them walked back toward her tent, laughing. It was in poor taste, certainly, but after all they'd been through, the absurdity of it all was too much for them.

As they walked away, Hellboy heard Creaghan muttering behind them.

"Goddamned bloody asylum, this is," the man said. "What next?"

Which Hellboy thought was an excellent question.

An even better question, of course, was where he was going to sleep that night. He didn't have a tent or even a bedroll. The obvious answer was that he would spend the night with Anastasia. He knew she would offer. He simply wasn't certain how comfortable either one of them would be with that arrangement. No matter how happy they were with the relationship as it was, lying together in the dark silence of the night, sweet memories would surely resurface. Such things could lead to more physical sweetness that would likely be regretted in the morning.

Love, in all its forms, was a dangerous thing.

They reached the opening of Anastasia's tent and he began to follow her inside. She turned and held out a hand to stop him.

"I don't think so," she said sternly.

"Oh," he fumbled, "I'm sorry. I just thought . . ."

She laughed. "Not you, silly. Just leave the head out-side."

Anastasia lay on her side and watched Hellboy sleep. They had talked for nearly an hour about old times, and more importantly, about what had occupied their lives in the five years since they had last been in one another's company. Then they had stretched out on the floor of the tent, she in her thermal sleeping bag, he on a couple of extra blankets, with one thrown over him for good measure. It was very cold outside. Even though Hell-boy wasn't very susceptible to these climate changes, Anas-tasia knew that such small human acts, like curling up under a blanket, were a great comfort to him.

In truth, that had been the fundamental reason for the failure of their relationship: no matter how much they cared for one another, their intimacy served to constantly remind Hellboy that he was not, in fact, human. It was debilitating for both of them.

But as she watched him now in the innocence of sleep, she missed those times. His heavy brow, usually so stern with determination, was smooth with serenity. With each breath, his nostrils flared and she could hear a rumble deep in his chest, a profound purring from a lion in repose.

Hellboy exhaled warm air, with the faint scent of some-thing spicy and exotic. Anastasia inhaled at the same mo-ment, and the sensation of warmth and intimacy was very sensuous for her. She was happy he was asleep. If he were not, the moment might have led her to break through the wall of friendship they had so carefully constructed.

Instead, she remained content just to watch him and remember. They had spent more than a year gallivanting around the world from dig to dig. He had been her constant companion, her teacher and student. They learned from one another as they loved. But the scrutiny their relationship earned had been too much for both of them.

Anastasia bit her lip with regret. She watched Hellboy's chest rise and fall, recalled so well the feel of that massive chest beneath her, his red flesh always hot to the touch, like laundry fresh from the dryer. During their time as lovers, even in midwinter, Anastasia had never needed a blanket or spread. Hellboy had been her own personal furnace.

The memory brought a smile to her face and temptation to her heart. She reached out to where he lay, his eyelids flowing with REM motion, and wondered what Hellboy dreamed about. He never talked about his dreams.

Gently, she stroked his face and the stubble on his head. She ran a finger over the rough surface of the stump of one of his horns, and shivered. Hellboy kept them filed down, and apparently had done so for forty years. Horns didn't fit his self-image. Of course, neither did a tail, or hooves, but the horns he could actually do something about. Still, Anastasia would have liked to see what he would look like if he allowed his horns to grow back.

Finally, she lay back down and tried to sleep. But the moment she closed her eyes, the fear washed over her. Anastasia had masked her terror and revulsion upon seeing Lady Catherine's reanimated head. Her explanation was real — she had experienced much worse with Hellboy. But that did not mean the fear went away. The horrors of her time in captivity at the Obsidian Danse still haunted her, and each new experience with the paranormal only served to heighten her terror.

But she was no coward. She would not succumb to the urge to flee. Hellboy was determined to discover precisely what happened to Lady Catherine's archaeological team. Anastasia would not allow him to go into such danger alone. Not to mention that, it was, indeed, her job to investigate the slaughter.

She denied her fear, but it lingered.

When Anastasia finally drifted off, she did not sleep well at all.

Dawn swept rapidly across the desert. A short time later, it became too hot to sleep within the tents, and even the most exhausted members of Dr. Bransfield's team roused themselves and trudged out into the arid Sahara morning.

Anastasia ran a hand through her strawberry-blond hair, tied it back with a rubber band, and pulled her baseball cap snug onto her head. She blinked back the harsh light before donning a pair of dark aviator sunglasses. They were a disadvantage at times, distorting her visual perception in ways she didn't really understand. But in the early morning, with the sun reflecting off the sand at a vicious angle, they were necessary.

Hellboy had risen at least an hour earlier. Despite his efforts at silence, she had been sleeping lightly enough that he woke her as he left. She fell back to sleep immediately, but missed his warmth. Until the sun rose.

She scanned the desert
for him, and saw Hellboy
standing with several members of her team, drinking
coffee. Anastasia looked
around her tent, curiously,
for the body bag contain-
ing Lady Catherine's head,
but it was nowhere to be
found. Smoothing the
wrinkles from the clean
shirt she'd pulled on this
morning, Anastasia walked
over to join them.

"I don't remember you being a coffee drinker," she observed.

Hellboy raised his mug and nodded. "Good morning,
sleepyhead," he greeted her. "Actually, it's decaf. I'm agi-
tated enough as it is without adding caffeine to my diet."

"Well, I'll take some of the strong stuff, thank you," she
replied. "If there's any left, that is."

After Larry Scott had poured it for her, Anastasia
glanced around the immediate area, looking for the body
bag again. She turned back toward her tent and still saw
nothing out of the ordinary.

When she had stopped darting her head around, Hellboy stepped closer and said, "What are you looking for?"

"Your oracle," she explained quietly. "I thought it might
be pretty conspicuous, and I don't want to upset the team
any more than they already have been."

"You mean Lady Catherine?" he asked. "She's right over there."

He pointed to a cloth drawstring bag that was cinched at the top. It sat on the sand next to a very large machine which was, essentially, a high-powered metal detector. The massacred archaeological team had used a similar machine to search for the lost army. Of course, they had never found the lost army, Anastasia thought morbidly. Instead, the army had found them. Or at least, a handful of Persian soldiers had.

Which reminded her of Hellboy's plans to dive the oasis lake that day.

"Still going swimming?" she asked.

"Just waiting for you to wake up," he answered. "Didn't want to do anything without your say-so. Figured you'd want to bring some of your team, maybe notify Creaghan and his groupies."

The idea of Hellboy diving in that lake alone filled her with anxiety. But she knew he was determined to do it, knew that it made perfect sense. In truth, it was the only logical next step. And, after all, there weren't a lot of things that could do him any real damage.

"Well?" he asked, pushing for her authorization.

It was her investigation. Her team. She had fought over her authority with Creaghan ever since they departed London. And she wanted to get to the bottom of this. Needed answers, closure, and even, perhaps, vengeance of some kind.

A ripple of self-loathing flowed through Anastasia. She hated herself for her indecisiveness. She was strong, independent, and sensible, and she'd been proving that all her life. To act in any other fashion would be to betray herself, and she'd worked too hard to start doing so now.

She sucked back the last of her coffee and then gave Hellboy a slight nod. Without any hesitation, she turned to her team.

"All right, ladies and gentlemen, pay attention please," she began.

Sand flew into her face on a sudden breeze and she sputtered, but otherwise ignored it.

"We've all seen some terrifying and inexplicable things in the past day or so," she said. "Well, I suspected as much when we began this investigation, thanks largely to the legend of the lost army. That's why I asked Hellboy to join our team.

"Now we know what happened to Lady Catherine and her dig crew, but we don't know how or why or who did it. I'm not going to be satisfied if we leave here without those answers. I'm not leaving without them, and neither is Hellboy. If any of you would like to return to England now, it will not be held against you in the choosing of teams for future investigations, digs, and expeditions.

"Anyone?"

Larry Scott, who had been the first to discover the slaughtered archaeological team, stepped forward immediately.

"I'm sorry, Stacie," he said, "but I'd love to go home. And I hope I'm not out of line in saying that I think you all should go home as well. Whatever is responsible for yesterday's atrocity is . . . well, it's evil. I'm going."

"Godspeed, then, Larry," Anastasia said warmly. "I don't blame you a bit. Anyone else?"

Several people stepped forward and, in the end, they were left with a team of just over a dozen members, including Jenny Marcus and Arun Lahiri. Anastasia thought that left somewhere between twenty and twenty-five people in camp, including the MI5 agents and their captain.

The army was another story entirely. Their convoy had deployed itself into a huge armored camp at the crest of a large dune. Now it simply sat there, an unforgiving metal and cloth monolith, a war machine more than one thousand men strong.

But the army didn't even know about the oasis. The army didn't know why they were here, only that they had the sanction of the highest possible authorities. Anastasia wasn't about to tell them, and she knew Creaghan wouldn't either. He obviously hated the commander of the joint allied forces.

When those who had decided to leave departed to begin packing their things, Anastasia addressed her dwindled team once more.

"All right, we haven't had a bath in days, so we're going to get one now," she explained. "The . . . soldiers which attacked Hellboy at the oasis yesterday came out of the lake. That's where we'll start our search. Hellboy's going to dive the lake while we wade along the shoreline, seeking underground access tunnels or some such. In the meantime, wash up. We don't know how frequently the opportunity will arise.

"Now, Arun, find our copy of that aerial map Lady Catherine's team was using. And Linda, please ask Captain

Creaghan to see me as soon as possible. Let him know our plans."

There was a moment of inaction, as the entire team looked to Anastasia for something more. She wasn't sure what they wanted: reassurance, confidence, some words of comfort. Anastasia didn't have them to give.

"Let's go!" she said, and clapped her hands, exuding the kind of urgency that the confusion of the past few days had not allowed her to feel. Until now.

As the team scattered to their appointed tasks, Hellboy stepped over to the metal detector and picked up the cloth sack which held the head of Lady Catherine Lambert.

"Oh, Christ," Anastasia said, staring at the sack.

Hellboy looked at her with a mixture of concern and amusement on his face.

"What in God's name are we getting ourselves into, here?" she asked, though she was still resolved to continue.

"Nothing," Hellboy replied. "We're already so deep into this thing that it's too late to go back. Hazred, whoever he is, is powerful enough to prevent us from leaving if he feels like it. Going ahead is the only way now."

"I know," she answered.

"You know, 'Stasia," Hellboy said warmly. "You're something else."

The blue oasis water shimmered in the sun, the wind creating ripples on the surface. Anastasia and her team had first bathed, and then began to wade the circumference of the lake in search of some visible clue. Something to hint at the manner in which the archaeological team was abducted, where they were kept, or where the Persian soldiers had come from.

Hellboy watched them for several minutes, then walked along the lakeshore to the spot where he had battled the dead soldiers the day before. He checked to be certain all the pouches on his belt were snapped closed. Most everything he carried was waterproof, or otherwise unaffected by cold or moisture. Charms, talismans, and the like would probably not be damaged, and the few weapons he had, tiny flare and concussion grenades, for instance, were self-contained and waterproof.

On the other hand, there was his gun. He unstrapped the holster from his hip, and laid it on the ground. He thought a moment, then removed his flashlight as well. It was supposed to be waterproof, but he didn't trust the manufacturer's claim and didn't want to test it for no reason.

Without further hesitation, he stepped into the water. His hooves sank into the soft, sucking sand beneath the surface of the lake. Though the water was only slightly cool, the superheated desert air made the lake seem quite cold indeed. When Hellboy had waded out until the water reached his upper thighs, he began to dread going any further. He knew the chill water would be like a vise grip on his privates.

"Only one thing to do," he sighed.

Hellboy filled his lungs, then dove into the oasis lake, spearing the calm surface and sending huge concentric ripples spiraling outward. He kept his eyes wide open. It was bright above water, and the sand was white beneath the surface. There was quite a bit of light available. But the deeper he swam, the darker it became. As he approached the center of the lake, it was deep enough that he could not even see the bottom.

Nearly seven minutes after he submerged himself, Hellboy finally surfaced for air. He scanned the banks, trying to situate himself. Anastasia and her team were still wading along the shore in search of some clue, but they were on the other side of the lake, more than one hundred yards away. Nevertheless, Hellboy waved to let her know that everything was all right thus far. When she waved back, he smiled to himself. She was concerned for his safety, and was watching him like a hawk. There wasn't a lot Anastasia could do if he got into serious trouble, but he felt comforted just the same.

He breathed deeply, and went under again. Straight down, he swam, sweeping the water up and behind him with extraordinarily powerful strokes. Digging himself a hole in the lake water. As it grew darker, his eyes adjusted rapidly. Still, he concentrated on his hands as he drew himself down, expecting at any moment to touch bottom.

His fingers dug into featureless sand before his eyes recognized that he had reached the bottom of the lake. Kicking his hooves did not provide as much propulsion as human feet might have, but Hellboy made do. Pulling himself along the sandy floor of the oasis lake, he grabbed hold of several unusual stone outcroppings. Underwater flora swayed as he passed, and he scanned the lake bottom for some clue.

The soldiers had come from the lake. No question about it. But from where? There was no sign of anything out of the ordinary—as far as Hellboy would have recognized such an indication. It simply didn't make sense.

His lungs began to burn and his eyes to bulge. The pressure had built up within him and he knew it would be only moments before he had to take another breath. Ignoring his body's distress, Hellboy continued his search. He pulled himself along toward shore, clawing the sand, his stone hand throwing up a swirling cloud.

But he was only putting off the inevitable. Hellboy decided he must surface before he endangered his life. He planted his hooves on the lake bottom and pushed off, rocketing himself toward sun and fresh air.

Hellboy grunted with pain as something clamped around his ankle, digging into his flesh, and dragged him back down. With his stone right hand as ballast, he flipped around in the water. Metal glinted in the little light that reached down to the floor of the lake, then something stung his side. He felt a cool rush and looked down to see blood mixing with water, hanging like red liquid spider webs in the water then floating away.

A sword. A face almost bare to the bone but for scraps of rotting flesh and one pale, white eyeball as gelatinous and colorless as a boiled scallop. Yet it stared at Hellboy with malevolent fury.

Finally, his hooves dug into the sandy bottom and he got his bearings. The Persian soldier was half-buried in the sand. Apparently it had been burrowed there beneath the lake bottom until his own passing had disturbed or awakened it. Now it wanted to kill him. Whether it was attacking of its own instinctual volition or if it was driven by the sorcerer Hazred's commands, Hellboy didn't know.

But at the moment, he didn't much care, either. His air was running out and he didn't have time to fight dead men at the bottom of an oasis lake.

The soldier's sword slid through the water toward Hellboy's throat. Hellboy grabbed the Persian warrior's wrist with his left hand, stopping the sword from finding its mark. He tore the arm from its socket, a deadly, slow-motion, underwater dance.

Hellboy reached down with his right hand, clamped the stone fingers around the dead man's skull, which he crushed in his palm like ancient plaster. The lake water suddenly swirled with sand as the dead man dissolved to nothing.

The veins in Hellboy's head were throbbing, near to bursting with the pressure and the lack of air. He shoved off the bottom and pulled himself toward the surface with powerful strokes of his arms. He was near unconsciousness from oxygen deprivation when he shattered the surface of the lake.

Heaving great gasps of air, he lay on the water's surface for a moment before he registered the sound of someone shouting in the distance. Hellboy glanced around and saw Anastasia, much closer now than she had been, waving her arms to get his attention.

She didn't need his help, though. That was his first thought. Rather, she had been anxious for him and wanted to make sure he was okay. Suddenly, he realized that he still held the zombie soldier's dead arm, undisintegrated, in his

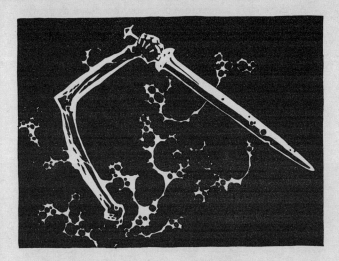

left hand. With his right, he plucked the gleaming sword from the dead hand, and the arm swirled away to nothing, leaving him holding a scrap of torn cloth.

Hellboy looked back up at Anastasia, who was still waving, apparently awaiting some sign that he was all right. Squinting against the shimmer of sunlight off the water, he held up the sword in his right hand and gave her a thumbs up with his left. He wanted her to know he'd found something, but that he was okay.

A light breeze feathered the surface of the lake, and Hellboy inhaled the scent of the oasis, the trees, and the lake. He forgot, for a moment, that he was in the middle of the Sahara desert, that war loomed just over the horizon. Then the moment had passed, and he became dreadfully aware of the horrors that might lurk below him, in the darkness at the bottom of the lake.

So there were some more dead soldiers down there. But that didn't explain where Lady Catherine's archaeological team had been taken after their abduction. All he had discovered thus far was more questions.

Hellboy wanted answers. He took several deep breaths, held the last one, and went under once again.

CHAPTER SEVEN

Up to his waist in the lake, Arun Lahiri stared into the water in search of some sign or clue. They had already covered the shoreline, without finding any indication that Lady Catherine's expedition had been transported or marched along—or in or out of—the lake. And Arun didn't think they would find any.

It didn't make sense.

On the other hand, there were several odd things about the lake itself, and the oasis.

"Any luck, Arun?" Anastasia asked.

She stood in the water several yards behind him. While he scanned the lake bottom just about where his feet dug into the loose sand, Anastasia was examining the shore more closely.

"It's a mystery," he replied. "One of several."

"Oh?" Anastasia asked, and looked at him quizzically. It was the first time they had paid any attention to one another in at least fifteen minutes.

"What are the other mysteries?" she asked.

"Well," he began, "I could be reading more into this than is really there, but my observations indicate that there was once a village or at least a long-term encampment here at the oasis."

Anastasia nodded. "We've thought that all along," she

agreed. "The perfect roundness of that clearing, the crude tools we found. Why, given the size of the oasis alone, it would be folly to believe there had not been some kind of civilization here."

"Indeed," Arun responded. "But where did they go, and why?"

When Anastasia raised her eyebrow and cocked her head to one side, Arun felt suddenly very insecure. She had the power to do that to him, a woman of her beauty and intelligence. But he would not be cowed by her skepticism. He found the whole situation exceedingly odd.

"They died out," Anastasia replied. "Or they moved on, became nomads, or settled somewhere else."

Arun looked across the lake to the other side of the oasis, scanned the water for some sign of Hellboy, then went back to wading along the shore.

"If you say so," he muttered noncommittally.

"What's the problem, Arun?" she asked. "I've known you too long not to know when you're being insincere."

"Have you?" Arun asked, amused at the thought. If Anastasia knew even half of what he was thinking at any given time, she'd probably have him arrested. Especially when those thoughts were about her.

"Spill it," she demanded.

He tried to see her eyes past the dark sunglasses she wore. The breeze momentarily buffeted both of them, plastering Anastasia's button-down cotton shirt to her body for a moment, then billowing it out instead. It was a distraction, but Arun had learned to live with the distraction that was Anastasia Bransfield. Every moment with her was distraction, and temptation.

"Okay," he sighed, and rubbed the back of his neck. He'd been leaning over in direct sun for nearly an hour, and his neck was already beginning to burn.

"If the lost army disappeared—or at least most of them, since some of them are now accounted for—and Lady Catherine's expedition disappeared for a time, it only stands to reason that the same thing happened to the oasis people."

He looked at Anastasia, who held up her palm to urge him on.

"Well, if there was a village here, we haven't found any real physical evidence of it. Still, there had to be, right? Without any animals, they had to eat the fruit of the oasis, as well as whatever they could grow. But that wouldn't be enough. There had to have been fish."

As Arun watched, Anastasia blanched.

"Dear God, I hadn't even noticed," she confessed, then turned and scanned the lake. "There are no fish."

"You would think there would be a lot more fish now," Arun explained. "Instead, there are none as far as we can tell. Of course it's possible that the lake was fished out, and the village had to move on because of it. But these were not foolish people. To move a whole village hundreds of miles across the Sahara would be suicidal."

"So, then, what happened to the fish?" Anastasia asked.

Arun shrugged. "I wish I knew. As I said, just another mystery we have to solve."

Anastasia was still looking at the calm surface of the water.

"Just another piece of unexplained phenomena," she said quietly. "I'm sure Hellboy will be thrilled."

"He's been down there a long time," Arun observed.

"He can take care of himself," Anastasia explained. "Hellboy can hold his breath an awfully long time."

"You never did tell me how you two first became acquainted," Arun pointed out.

"You're right, I didn't," Anastasia replied, then turned her attention back to searching the shoreline, walking away from Arun.

"I didn't mean to intrude," he said, but his curiosity was piqued. He couldn't help but wonder why Anastasia was so sensitive about her association with Hellboy.

"Anastasia, I'm sorry," he said.

She took several more steps away from him without acknowledging that he had spoken. Finally, she turned around and gave him a hard look.

"That's okay," she replied. "I've just had to deal with too many bloody morons in this world, and a lot of them because of my relationship with Hellboy."

They looked at one another. In that moment's pause, Arun knew what Anastasia was going to say.

"He used to be my boyfriend," she said, and smiled. "He's the most loving man I've ever known."

Arun was at first astonished, and then disgusted. He had pined for Anastasia since the day they first met. She was everything he could ever dream of in a woman: brilliant, beautiful, witty, and confident. Now, Arun didn't dare close his eyes for fear his subconscious might conjure an image of the woman he had secretly longed for in the arms of . . . Christ, he didn't even know what to call Hellboy!

"He isn't even human!" Arun finally said.

Anastasia blinked, and he expected her to recoil with the insult. She did not. Rather, she breathed deeply and shook her head very slowly. Her lip curled up with the only visible sign of her anger, and she spoke with severity and finality.

"You are an historian, Professor," she said. "You are not a physician, or a biologist, or an anthropologist. It is not for you to judge who is and is not human."

"I'm . . . I'm sorry, Stacie," he stammered. "I didn't mean to . . ."

"We've known one another a long time, Arun," Anastasia said grimly. "I hoped a man of your academic stature would be more open-minded. Now I see you're just another judgmental asshole."

"Stacie, I . . ."

"Hush now, Arun," she said. "Before I decide to hate you."

Arun was torn. He had made a mistake, stepped over a line that he had known existed despite its invisibility. And yet he could feel little remorse. The idea of Anastasia and Hellboy together as lovers was repulsive to him. Not merely because Hellboy was so bizarre, in Arun's mind as freakish as the Elephant Man or Siamese twins, but because it was Anastasia Bransfield.

A sudden, terrible, and nearly overwhelming urge came over him. He opened his mouth to ask the current nature of Anastasia's relationship with Hellboy. But she turned and splashed away down the lakeshore toward the spot where Shelby Claremont, their preservation expert, searched for clues.

He was relieved when she had gone. If he had opened his mouth again, he knew their relationship would have been severed forever. Regret overwhelmed him. Arun admired Hellboy and enjoyed his company. But so much mystery surrounded him that it was impossible not to wonder what he truly was. And the idea that Stacie could choose a . . . beast like Hellboy over a normal man, over Arun himself, simply nauseated him.

Distracted, he turned his attention back to the work at hand: the search for the madman who had slain or ordered Lady Catherine and her team to be slain. He had sublimated his feelings for Anastasia as best he could for years. He would simply have to add his reaction to this new knowledge to the long list of emotions and urges he did not dare reveal publicly. Particularly to the primary object of those emotions.

He continued along the shore. Sunlight glinted off something in his peripheral vision. Arun looked down at the sand, scanning it for something that might have reflected the sun. He found nothing, shrugged, and was about to move on, when he saw that glimmer again. A tiny sparkle of sunlight. Right at his feet, now. Jutting from the sand was the edge of some kind of golden disc.

Arun knelt, excited by this discovery. It could have been anything, the pocket watch of some archaeologist, he thought. But somehow he knew it wasn't. Somehow he knew it was important. He had the inescapable feeling that it was meant exclusively for him. As if it were his own pocket watch, or some other treasure that had always belonged to him.

The professor reached out with his right hand, touched his fingertips to the metal, and a jolt ran up his arm. The air expelled from his lungs with a gasp and he nearly fell on his face in the sand.

"Arun?" Anastasia called from behind him. "Are you all right?"

He wanted to respond. Desperately wanted to tell her that no, he was not all right. That he'd been stricken by some kind of seizure, or electrocuted, if that's what it was. But he didn't say anything of the sort. For the moment he thought of Anastasia; all of his feelings for her and about her relationship with Hellboy boiled up within him again.

His fingers seemed to jitter where they made contact with the metal disc. And then all of those thoughts and feelings inside him roiled like acid in his stomach, bilious and sickening.

Remorse became disgust. Guilt became anger. Affection became a punishing lust. He was no longer capable of thinking about Anastasia Bransfield as his friend. The only term that came to mind along with her image was "slut." Filthy slut.

He tried to push the words away from his mind, but he could not ignore the pulse of those three syllables.

Filthy slut.

Nearly in tears, Arun could not understand the vehemence of his reaction. No matter how often he had fantasized about Anastasia, he had never truly believed he would have her. Particularly not in the disgusting ways he now imagined.

And yet now it occurred to him that for a woman who would lie with a creature more animal than man, many of his darkest new fantasies might be entirely possible. That such things could be real had never occurred to him. And the very idea drove Arun Lahiri into a moral abyss.

Filthy slut!

He could barely control the urge to turn, to chase Anastasia down and savage her with pain and pleasure. A grin spread across his face.

"Filthy slut," he whispered to himself through that painful smile.

Something happened then. Hearing his own words, Arun recoiled. Whatever moral regulator existed within him to stem the tide of such violent, perverse, irrational thoughts, finally and belatedly intervened.

He drowned in guilt, and it saved his sanity. He bit his lip, drawing blood, to keep himself from weeping openly.

"Arun?" he heard Anastasia call again behind him. "Arun, what's the matter?"

There was splashing, as she came toward him. Part of him panicked at the idea that she might see and desire the object buried just beside his right knee, and he yanked it free of the sand. It came away with hesitation. An engraved bronze medallion on a long chain.

He was entranced by it.

Filthy slut! The words came into his head again, but now it almost seemed

as if somebody else had said them. Arun glanced around
quickly, but there was only himself and Anastasia approaching him from behind, splashing, coming nearer.

Coming nearer and he could do whatever he wanted to
the filthy slut!

He shook his head, and bit into his lip again, but
not to keep from crying this time. Arun's mind cleared
for a moment, and he stared at the medallion again.
It was etched with unfamiliar symbols and the image of
a jackal, infamous scavenger of Egyptian history and
mythology.

Without another thought, he slipped the medallion in
his pocket. He ought to have presented it to Anastasia immediately. It was, after all, the first significant artifact they
had found in their investigation. But the urge to pocket it
was uncontrollable.

It felt warm in his pocket, with only light cotton separating the medallion from his flesh. Arun smiled again,
but felt more in control than he had moments before.
Stronger.

"Arun?" Anastasia said softly, her hand on his shoulder
sending a shock through his entire body. "What happened? Are you all right?"

He stood, turned to face her. The words, the terrible,
hateful words, lingered in the back of his mind. But now
he felt as though he controlled them as well. They were
under his power now.

Arun studied Anastasia's face. She had taken off her
glasses and her features were creased with concern. He felt
the heat of the sun on his neck, a minor distraction, and
he wished it away. He would not allow his neck to burn. A

breeze, cool and innocent, rolled off the lake. He smiled.

"I'm okay," he said. "Just stumbled on something, maybe my own feet. I've always been a bloody oaf, Stacie. You know that."

Anastasia frowned, and tilted her head as she looked at him quizzically.

"Are you sure you're all right?" she asked.

"I'm perfect," he answered. "And I'm sorry for what I said. I never meant to offend you. We've known one another too long for that."

Anastasia smiled warmly. "That's okay. I know it seems odd. Odd for anyone to imagine that Hellboy is as human as you or I, no matter what he looks like."

"Not at all," Arun replied, still smiling that confident smile. "He's warm and kind and fabulously sincere. I've dealt with prejudice in my own life. Now I've got to learn not to allow appearance to come before character in my own judgment of others."

"Still friends, then?" Anastasia asked.

"Never more so," Arun answered.

"I'm glad," she said, and gripped his shoulder with her hand, affirming her words. "It's crazy enough out here without conflict between us. We've got to work together or this thing is going to drag us down."

Anastasia turned to splash back toward Shelby Claremont. The medallion pulsed warmly in Arun's pocket. Completely in control of his faculties, he watched Anastasia move away, watched the way her flesh moved beneath her clothes.

A grin split his face and he became aroused.

"Filthy slut," he whispered.

It was a hassle to carry the sword underwater. Hellboy slashed it back and forth several times, and was surprised at how slow and unwieldy it seemed. Even more so than an underwater hand-to-hand confrontation would have been, he believed. Still, he held on to it as he made his descent. No way to tell how many other members of the lost army might be lurking below.

When he had found what he believed to be the place where he was attacked, Hellboy swam south. He was certain he had seen some dark shapes in that direction. Now, he believed he could hear some kind of noise underwater. A high-pitched sound, almost like whale song.

Sword in his left hand, destruction in his right, he moved forward swiftly. A little more than a minute after he had touched bottom, he saw the lake begin to slope up toward the shore.

Then he saw the caves. A warren of black depressions in the ground, just like those he had seen pitting the hillside which ringed the oasis. Once more, he was intrigued. These must have been the dark shapes he had seen. It was only logical to think that the dead soldiers might have come from there. Though it didn't seem likely the archaeological team had been transported that way. They would have drowned long before reaching whatever their destination was.

On the other hand, if the caves under and above the water were the same complex, that was an entirely different story. It was possible, even likely, that Lady Catherine and the others were taken through the hillside, and the soldiers, already dead, traveled beneath the lake. After all, he thought, they had yet to discover any other unexplored territory in that godforsaken desert.

Hellboy surfaced quickly to draw another, deeper breath. Then he dove again, ready to explore. Sword in front of him, he ventured several steps into the darkness of the cave. The squealing he had heard before was even louder, thrumming in the water that pressed in on his eardrums.

As he moved further into the cave, his eyes began to adjust to the darkness. After a moment, he realized that not all the light within the cave was refracted from the surface of the lake. A strange luminescence glowed dimly much deeper in the cave.

His right hoof struck something solid, and Hellboy glanced down. He blinked, attempting to see the object more clearly. It seemed to be a tablet of some kind, perhaps exactly the kind of artifact Lady Catherine's archaeological expedition was meant to discover. It was about four inches wide, and perhaps three inches poked out of the sand, but he had no way of telling how long it might be. There was some kind of etching on the tablet, miraculously not worn away by the water.

Driven by curiosity, Hellboy momentarily forgot his search and the light ahead, and bent down to get a better look at the tablet. The noise in the water seemed to fade as he crouched and brushed sand away from its base, where it was embedded in the floor of the cave. Aware that he had perhaps three minutes before he must again surface, he traced the engraved lines with a finger.

Some kind of sea monster was depicted on the stone. Its tentacles whipped in a frenzy above water, lashed out at small human figures scurrying on the shore. Around and beneath the monstrous scene were glyphs and symbols which Hellboy assumed were some ancient language.

He brushed away more sand, then looked up in alarm. It might have been his imagination, but he thought that the eerie sound from deep in the cave had become louder. And either his eyes had adjusted even further, or the weird glow from the cave had grown brighter.

Still, no matter how strange things got, he needed to know what that tablet was. Hellboy brushed more sand away from the base of the tablet. It was buried quite deep. With several more lines of ancient writing, he still could not decipher any of it.

Perhaps Arun or Anastasia would be able to read it, he thought. It wasn't as if he had put the necessary time into studying languages of the ancient world. He knew what Professor Bruttenholm would say. "Train the mind as well as the body, my boy." Hellboy knew the professor was right, but that didn't help him now.

Hellboy put down the sword and dug his fingers into the sand around the tablet. Beneath the loose granules was hard-packed sand and earth. The tablet went down into the ground. He said a silent prayer that he wouldn't break it—of course with his luck, he could hardly avoid it—and pulled with all his strength.

Nothing.

He had perhaps a minute more before he would have to fill his lungs, with air or lake water, whichever was available. Already his lungs burned and his pulse beat loud in his ears.

Driving his hooves into the ground on either side of the tablet, he gripped it as tightly as he was able. He was careful not to clamp the fingers of his stone right hand too tightly, lest he crush the tablet to powder in his grip.

Then he pulled. At first he didn't think anything was going to happen. Then the tablet gave slightly, and he was encouraged. He barely noticed the growing glow in the deep cave, or the heightening pitch of the wailing he could still hear under water.

Suddenly, the tablet came loose in his hands. Only eight or nine inches long, he was amazed it had been such a struggle to uproot.

Yes! he thought.

The green phosphorescence in the cave flashed like lightning up toward him, striking the tablet and playing harmlessly over its surface. The noise that had been buzzing in his ears through the water abruptly ceased.

The ground began to shake.

What the hell is . . . ? he thought. And then he realized he had made a terrible mistake.

Hellboy knelt and tried to jam the tablet's pointed end back into the sandy floor of the cave. It couldn't be done. The rumbling inside the cave increased and the light grew even brighter. He used his right hand to claw a hole in the ground, but even when he stabbed the tablet into it, nothing changed.

The glaring green light was blocked for a moment. In the shadows thrown by the luminescence, long protrusions whipped back and forth like Medusa's hair. And those were only the shadows. He didn't want to see the real thing.

But it was coming. The water ahead in the tunnel churned, and then the green light was extinguished entirely.

Time to go, he thought.

With the tablet under his left arm like a football, Hellboy pushed off the ground with a mighty kick, propelling himself out of the cave. With his huge right hand, he pulled for the surface.

He was running out of breath, and running out of time.

Behind and beneath him, half a dozen caves in the gentle slope of the lake bottom erupted with dozens of massive red tentacles, raw and trailing gore as if newborn from a timeless womb.

Hellboy glanced back once, cursed himself and the tablet he had unwisely removed.

Crap! he thought.

Then the first of the tentacles twined around his waist. The thing could easily have dragged him down and drowned him then. But so ecstatic was the creature from its newfound freedom that it kept coming. The side of the lake erupted as the creature bulled its way out of the earth.

It continued to rise. Wrapped in its tentacles, Hellboy burst into the open air and gasped for breath. He was barely able to suck in a lungful before the creature began to squeeze. It continued upwards, holding him dozens of feet above the ground.

He tore at the thing with his stone right hand, and kept the tablet from being crushed with his left. He wished for the sword he had dropped below, but wasn't sure what good it would have done.

In distress, he searched the shore for Anastasia, praying she would be all right. He found her where she stood with Shelby Claremont, not far from Arun Lahiri and several other members of the team.

Tentacles lashed out for them, but most were able to scurry to safety. Karl Idelson was not so lucky. A red, bleeding tentacle lifted him off the ground and beat him mercilessly against the sand. After the second blow, Hellboy could see by the way Karl's body moved that his spine was broken, and perhaps his neck as well.

Then he saw that another tentacle has lashed around Shelby's leg and pulled the poor woman into the lake. She went under in an eyeblink, and Hellboy knew if he did not free himself immediately, Shelby was dead. They all might be dead, if the creature didn't need water to live and could go after the others. He didn't know anything about the monster, save for its murderous intent.

"Uhnnf!" he grunted, as the thing squeezed even tighter. Another tentacle whipped up, going for his head. Hellboy had a momentary flash of his head being popped off like a sadistic child's doll. It chilled him.

"I don't think so!" he shouted.

When the tentacle whipped toward him, Hellboy grabbed it with his right hand and held on. With no idea how to combat the thing, and with its hundreds of tentacles snaking across the land, Hellboy was at his wit's end.

The beast surged up out of the water and Hellboy looked down. From nearly one hundred feet in the air, he stared into the single, cyclopean eye of the beast from the oasis caves. Whatever it was, prehistoric monstrosity or other-dimensional god, it had an eye. It had to see. It could be hurt.

In his experience, anything could be hurt.

Switching the tablet to his right hand, Hellboy tried desperately to slide his left under the tentacle, to get to his belt. He had another moment to wish for the sword he'd left beneath the lake, or even his gun. Then he sucked in his stomach and slid his hand between his flesh and the tentacle before it could tighten.

In seconds, he found the right pouch and pulled out a magnesium flare. He didn't dare drop the tablet, not after all he'd gone through to keep it. Instead, he brought the flare to his mouth, closed his eyes, and pulled the pin with his teeth. It flashed in his face, scorching his skin.

Then he dropped it, straight down. He had timed it perfectly. When the flare struck the creature's single eye, it exploded with a flash of fire. The eye burst and the creature screamed.

It dropped Hellboy, who plummeted to the lakeshore and struck the sand painfully. When he looked up, the creature was gone, disappeared beneath the surface and back into its lair.

Whatever else they had to face to finish this investigation, he prayed they had seen the last of the lake monster.

CHAPTER EIGHT

In the heat of late morning, wind-whipped sand grated lightly against Creaghan's tent. He had become so used to the noise that he ceased to notice it, the way people who lived near the ocean sometimes lost the ability to hear the crashing of the surf.

The surf. What he wouldn't have given to be at the shore just then. The south of France would have been nice, but Creaghan would have been happy to swim in the testicle-crushing frozen waters off Scotland's northern coast. He missed water. He missed civilization.

He missed sanity.

Creaghan didn't know what the hell was happening at the oasis, but he knew two things for certain. The first was that it was paranormal. Disembodied heads didn't often speak to him. And as far as he was concerned, nothing human could have done what had been done to those poor bastards on Lady Catherine's archaeological team. Otherwise the killers would have been in the British government's employ during the Falklands War.

The second thing of which Creaghan was certain was that he, himself, was not crazy. His thoughts were perfectly clear and rational. That was what disturbed him the most. To deny what he had seen would mean to question his own unshakable sanity. Creaghan wasn't prepared to do that.

The Captain lifted a ceramic mug and took a long draft of tepid water. There was a slight metallic tang to it, but he didn't question the taste. It was water. That was all that mattered.

With a snap, one of the long flaps at the entrance to his tent folded back, and Agent Rickman stuck his face inside.

"We're all here, Captain," Rickman announced.

"Very good," he replied. "Bring them in."

Rickman's eyes widened. "All of them, sir?" he asked. "There isn't much room inside your tent."

Creaghan didn't even look up at Rickman again. "Bring them in. We could all do with being out of the sun, even if only for a few minutes."

Rickman nodded. A moment later, the men began to file in, filling the tent on either side so that their heads poked at the material and they had to crouch a little.

Captain Creaghan looked around at the expressionless faces of the ten MI5 agents in his command. Burke, Carruthers, Rickman, and the others were all deeply tanned and visibly exhausted.

"I'm sorry, gentlemen," he said honestly. "Like it or not, we're going to stay on here until we have some answers for the Prime Minister. It isn't as if we can stroll into Buckingham Palace and tell the Queen her cousin's little girl got beheaded by some paranormal force and have that be the end of it. We've got to get to the bottom of this."

None of the men would meet his gaze. Creaghan didn't like that at all.

"What?" he barked. "What in bloody hell is the problem today?"

Most of them glanced up nervously, then looked over at Carruthers. Creaghan stepped around the table upon which were spread maps of the nearby desert and the oasis of Ammon. He moved in close to Carruthers and stared at the man until he was forced to lift his eyes.

"Carruthers?" Creaghan asked.

"Well, sir, it's only that none of us are trained for this kind of thing," Carruthers explained. "We're not cowards, Captain. We're MI5, by God. But we've searched miles of desert by land and by air. If there's . . . well, magic involved, Captain, how are we to even begin a proper investigation now that we know that Lady Catherine's party are all dead?"

Creaghan stared at Carruthers, eyes narrowed with disapproval. But it was that the men had doubted him that bothered their Captain, not their uncertainty. That, he could most surely understand.

"You're right," he said finally, and a small smile crept across his face.

Carruthers's expression of astonishment was comical. "I'm sorry, sir?" he asked, apparently not believing what he had heard.

"As you should be," Creaghan snapped, his smile gone. "Don't question your superior officer. Any of you." He turned and strode to a corner of the tent, so he could address them all at once.

"You're trained better than that," Creaghan told them. "Whether it's covert ops in Liverpool and Hong Kong, or in this godforsaken, inhuman place, you're MI5, and you answer to me. Are we clear on that?"

"Yes, Captain!" the men responded in chorus.

"Fine," he said quietly. "Now, let's get down to it. Just so we have no argument about it later in case one of you boys doesn't have the bollocks to admit what he's seen, whatever's happening here is not earthly. Call it sorcery, or whatever you like, but it isn't natural. Still, somebody's responsible, and it's our job to find out who and eliminate the bastards."

There was no argument. Nor would he have accepted any. Creaghan took two steps toward the center of the tent and brushed all of his maps and geological surveys onto the ground.

"Right, then," he announced, "this stuff's useless, isn't it? So what do we do now, gentlemen? What is our next move?"

Rickman opened his mouth, then closed it quickly. Creaghan narrowed his eyes and glared at the man. Of all his team, Rickman had always seemed the least reliable. He was a slight man, and apparently nervous by nature. His thin goatee and round wire-rim glasses gave him a boyish look. But, after all, Rickman was MI5, which meant he was a skilled soldier and capable killer, if it came to that.

"Don't be so damned hesitant, man," he scolded Rickman. "Let's have it, then."

"Well, Captain," he said anxiously, "it seems to me that Hellboy is sort of drawn to these sorts of things. Or them to him, I'm not sure. But, either way, sir, I believe our best chance is to keep close watch over him."

"And just wait until the answers present themselves, eh?" Creaghan asked, apparently skeptical.

"Yes, sir," Rickman replied. "Whatever's out there, it's more likely to show itself to him, or even to attack him, than us, I should think."

Creaghan nodded grimly. "Unfortunately, gentlemen, that is our plan. That's why I've gathered you here. Burke, Carruthers, and Meaney, you're to watch Hellboy and Dr. Bransfield at all times. The rest of you will stay here with me to deal with the regular army wankers we've got breathing down our necks."

"Captain, I . . . ," Rickman began. Creaghan held up a hand to prevent him from saying anything more.

As far as he was concerned, Rickman was a little bit too much in awe of Hellboy. It could get the man killed. If he thought that was unfair, so be it. Fairness was hardly a part of Creaghan's job description.

"You have your orders," he said.

"And I have mine," came a voice from just outside the tent.

Creaghan looked up, and blinked as the tent flap was lifted and the sun shone in. The darkened silhouette wore a uniform. After a moment, he recognized the voice. Then the man came further into the tent and he could see precisely who it was.

Colonel Shapiro. The American was filled with that brusque brand of Yank confidence that had always grated on Michael Creaghan. But MI5 were trained to shake anybody's confidence.

With a ratcheting of safety catches and a chambering of rounds, ten automatic pistols were leveled at Colonel Shapiro. The American knitted his greying eyebrows together, but otherwise showed no reaction. Creaghan was impressed. Shapiro had cold blue eyes that did not waver even for a moment from their focus.

"Can I help you, Colonel?" Captain Creaghan asked.

"I've consulted with my superiors and I'm afraid you'll have to withdraw yourselves and Dr. Bransfield's team well away from the border, Captain," Shapiro said blandly.

"Really? Consulted your superiors, did you?" Creaghan noted. "That must have taken quite some time."

None of his men smiled at the barb. They were MI5. They weren't allowed to smile.

"In any case, your superiors—as I'm quite sure you realize—are not my superiors," Creaghan continued. "My orders come from the Prime Minister of Great Britain. From him, and him alone."

"Your defiance is imprudent, to say the least," Colonel Shapiro observed. "We won't be able to defend you properly. You are all in grave danger the longer you remain here."

Creaghan almost smiled at that. If he bothered to tell the American just how much trouble they all might be in, the man would think him certifiably insane.

"Yet you can't force us to go without causing an international incident, and a possible exchange of weapons fire that might well cost civilian lives," Creaghan said. "We have a job to do, Colonel, just like you. You don't get in our way, we'll do our best not to get in yours."

The two men stared at one another for several moments. None of Creaghan's men cleared his throat, or scratched his head, or wavered his aim even the slightest bit.

"Out of courtesy, I would expect at the very least that your men would lower their weapons," Colonel Shapiro said. "We are allies, after all. Your countrymen are under my command out there."

Creaghan did not instruct his men to lower their weapons. They did not. Ten barrels pointed at Shapiro's head, ten bullets prepared to shatter the American's skull on his order.

"I apologize for your discomfort, Colonel," Creaghan said insincerely. "You've intruded upon a meeting you Americans might call 'top secret.' My men are merely following protocol for such an intrusion."

They stared at one another.

"You may go now, Colonel," Creaghan said sternly. "Your concern is appreciated. I'll pass it on to Dr. Bransfield when she returns from today's expedition."

Shapiro pushed his left hand through the silvery grey hair on his head, and smiled. It was a hateful smile, but Creaghan had become familiar with such reactions over the years. Maybe it was MI5, or just him, but he seemed to bring such joyous fury out in people.

"If war happens, Captain Creaghan, I will assume that you and your people have evacuated the area," Colonel Shapiro said. "If this camp is vaporized by the Libyans, or even friendly fire, well, even your countrymen under my command will not be able to report that you were not warned."

Creaghan smiled back, then replied: "And if your troops wake up one morning to find that someone slipped in during the night and slit your throat, Colonel, you can rest easy knowing that my men will find the Bedouin camel driver responsible." He had never reacted well to threats.

Shapiro seemed about to speak, then swallowed hard. "Just so we understand one another," the Colonel said.

"Oh, I believe we do," Creaghan responded.

Finally, though he was obviously loathe to leave and appear to have backed down, Colonel Shapiro turned and strode from the tent, unmindful of the weapons pointed in his direction.

"Former CIA, sir?" Rickman asked.

Creaghan watched until Shapiro had disappeared from the tent entrance. "Former?" he asked. "Current CIA, I'd say."

Anastasia was shaken. Whatever that lake monster had been, it had killed Shelby Claremont and Karl Idelson in seconds. When Hellboy blinded it, the thing had retreated, taking the corpses of her friends with it. They wouldn't even be able to bury Karl and Shelby. And when they returned to London, Anastasia would be the one to have to tell their families.

God, she was tired.

Hellboy stood up a few yards from the lakeshore, and shook his head a few times as if disoriented. He took a step toward her, paused, then continued on with a more confident stride. His tail, which usually bobbed along behind him, trailed in the sand. That was her only indication that he might be injured.

"Are you all right?" he asked as he came closer.

"Christ, no," she answered. "Just look around."

Her comment was rhetorical, but Hellboy did take that moment to glance along the shore. What little remained of

Anastasia's team was slowly making its way around the lake to converge upon the spot where she stood.

"I'm going to send them home," she said.

"They're lucky," Hellboy replied. "What about you, are you going home?"

Anastasia searched his face for some clue as to what he was feeling at that moment. She saw nothing. He was grim as ever, but Hellboy always looked grim when he wasn't smiling. There were lacerations on his face just as  there were all over his body, but they would heal quickly, she knew.

"I'm not going anywhere," she said finally. "Not until I have some answers."

There was a red spark in Hellboy's eyes when he smiled. Sometimes Anastasia believed it was there, and other times she thought it was a trick of the light. But she saw it just the same. There had been times when the brightness in his eyes had been quite intimate. As if, somewhere in his mind, a fire burned just for her.

"That's what I figured," he said. "Let's head back to camp and grab some supplies. Then we'll start checking out those hill caves."

"Wait," Anastasia said, startled by Hellboy's abruptness. "You mean you're not going to try to talk me into staying behind?"

Hellboy glanced at her, a quizzical expression on his face.

"Would you?"

"Not bloody likely."

"So what's your point?" he asked.

Hellboy tied the canvas bag containing Lady Catherine's head to his belt and cinched it tight. He hefted a pack with canteens of water, rope, several flashlights, and six cans of Spaghettios, among other food items.

When he ducked out of Anastasia's tent, she and Arun were sitting cross-legged on the sand, studying the tablet Hellboy had ill-advisedly retrieved from the underwater cave. Everyone else had left. Some with great relief, others with tearful reluctance. But Anastasia had insisted, threatening one or two with termination if they did not relent.

"Anything?" Hellboy asked.

Anastasia was tracing her fingers along one of the tablet's inscriptions, and Arun seemed to be staring at her face. Neither of them responded.

"Hello?" Hellboy said. "Earth to wherever the heck you guys are?"

They both looked up, Anastasia apologetically, and Arun rather guiltily, Hellboy thought. If he'd had any question as to whether the professor was attracted to 'Stasia, that look resolved it. In fact, Hellboy thought it went a bit further than mere attraction.

"Ready to go?" Anastasia asked.

"Almost," Hellboy replied. "What have you got?"

"Not much, I'm afraid," she said. "Arun?"

Arun glanced up at Hellboy, then looked down at the tablet somewhat anxiously.

"Well, I can't really decipher most of these figures, but they do seem to be a combination of Persian and Egyptian languages from the second or third century, B.C.," Professor Lahiri explained.

"Obviously, part of the text is a warning not to remove the tablet or else face the wrath of . . . I think this says 'the Ancient One' or 'the Elder Beast,' something like that."

They both looked up at him and Hellboy flushed with embarrassment. He wanted to smile, to pass it off with a joke, but he couldn't. People had died because of his carelessness. It wasn't funny, and he vowed to himself to be more careful in the future.

"I'm sorry," he said, directing his apology to Anastasia.

"You couldn't have known," she said, trying to soothe him. And it worked, a little.

"The tablet also says something about opening a doorway, or passage, made of black flame, or some such, perhaps a reference to sulphur?" Arun suggested.

He shrugged, then. Obviously, that was as far as he'd gotten.

"Don't sell yourself short, Professor," Hellboy said. "I can't read the Sunday funnies without a decoder ring. Just keep working at it. Whatever we learn from that slab of granite might save our lives."

Hellboy squinted in the noonday glare. He shielded his eyes a moment, and scanned the now nearly empty camp.

"I guess it's just the four of us," he observed.

"Four?" Anastasia asked.

Hellboy pointed to the sack that jostled against his hip as he walked.

"Don't forget Lady Catherine," he reminded her.

Anastasia made a sickened face. "How could I?" she asked.

"Here comes the Captain," Arun noted, staring up from his work and across the barren camp at four figures approaching.

The heat rippled the air above the sand, and sand stung Hellboy's bare chest and back. The wind had picked up, and the flying grit had become more of a nuisance. He wondered if anyone had seen a weather forecast lately.

"Can we do something for you, Captain?" Anastasia asked, as she stood and brushed off her pants.

"I see the rest of your team has withdrawn," Creaghan noted.

The three MI5 agents who accompanied him stood silently by. Two of them Hellboy knew by name, Burke and Carruthers. Though, like Anastasia, he had trouble telling them apart. They both had curly brown hair and dark eyes. One was older and his hair had more grey in it, but Hellboy could never figure out which one it was.

The third was a black man who was always quiet. Hellboy didn't know if he had ever heard the man speak. Or even heard anyone else refer to him.

"I instructed my team to return to London," Anastasia explained.

"Colonel Shapiro will be pleased," Creaghan noted. "Meanwhile, where are the rest of you off to, now? Another expedition today?"

Anastasia lifted her chin defiantly.

"We're going spelunking, if you must know, and you and your men are not invited," she informed the Captain.

"On the contrary," Creaghan said pleasantly. "Agents

Burke, Carruthers, and Meaney will be accompanying you. For security purposes, of course. None of you is well armed, and if I were to allow you to meet the same fate as Lady Catherine's expedition, I would be terribly remiss in my duties."

"Great," Hellboy mumbled. "Moe, Larry, and Shemp. We don't even get Curly on our team."

"Yes, Captain," Anastasia said with great suspicion. "While we appreciate your concern, and the accompaniment and protection of your men, why aren't you joining us? Certainly you can't hope to find the answers you seek right here in camp."

Creaghan raised an eyebrow. Hellboy suspected the man was surprised that Anastasia had not argued about bringing MI5 agents along with them. The Captain couldn't know that had been part of their plan all along. They had no weapons other than Hellboy's own gun. Three soldiers with SA-80's could come in handy against undead Persian warriors, or whatever else they might find within those caves.

"Since you've asked," Creaghan finally replied, "I've determined that some of us need to remain behind to secure the camp against . . . outside interests."

"Do you mean Libyans, or Colonel Shapiro?" Anastasia asked.

"I mean outside interests of any kind, Dr. Bransfield," Creaghan answered. "In the meantime, as long as your instructions do not contravert the orders I myself have given to my men, I have commanded them to obey you."

"What a guy," Hellboy said. "The question is, what are their orders from you?"

Creaghan looked at him directly for the first time. The

Captain smiled amicably. Which Hellboy knew meant the guy believed he was pulling one over on them. Good, Hellboy thought. Let him.

"I'm sorry, Hellboy, but you don't have the clearance for . . . ," Creaghan replied, before Hellboy interrupted him.

"I have the clearance for anything I want to know, Captain," he said. "But don't worry, I won't push it. Besides, if I need to know anything, I can always ask Lady Catherine."

Hellboy patted the heavy sack which hung at his hip, and Creaghan's eyes widened. His lip curled in disgust, but he said nothing. The paranormal created new rules for any situation. Creaghan had obviously realized that, or he never would have allowed them to carry Lady Catherine's head around in such a manner.

"Good luck," Creaghan said.

CHAPTER NINE

T here were more than two dozen caves in the oasis hill-side. In teams of two, they searched them all. Most of them, even the largest, went in no more than twenty feet and then ended either in a small cavern dwelling or a simple dead end. There were markings on the walls, some in the same odd glyph language that was inscribed upon the tablet Hellboy had discovered in the lake.

Three of the caves, each a distance from the others, did not end so simply. These they determined to investigate as a group. One wound quite deeply into the hillside before the passage was blocked by a cave-in. Hellboy believed it had been intentionally blocked, as the mountain of rubble barring their path did not appear to have come from the ceiling of the cave.

A second tunnel led up through the hillside and ended abruptly where it opened into a huge cavern. The ground fell away into a darkness so profound that their three high-powered flashlights combined could not cut it deep enough to see the bottom or the other side.

Finally, two hours after beginning their search, they entered the last cave.

"This has got to be it," one of the MI5 men declared, and Hellboy noted that the man's voice had more hope than certainty in it.

But after several minutes of following the winding tunnel down through hard-packed earth and stone, and into the very foundation of the desert, they arrived, once more, at a dead end.

"Well," Anastasia said as they flashed their lights around the cavern. "What next?"

Hellboy shrugged. It just didn't feel right to him. If there was some passage underwater through the caves, it only made sense that there must be some passage from aboveground as well. He tried to remember what Lady Catherine had said.

"Come on," Arun said. "It's getting kind of cramped

in here. I feel . . . strange. My body aches."

"Wait," Hellboy said.

He untied the top of the sack that held Lady Catherine's head, reached in, and pulled the lifeless thing out by its hair.

"Jesus, that's disgusting," Agent Meaney hissed.

"It's blasphemous is what it is," added one of the others, Burke or Carruthers.

Hellboy held up the decapitated woman's head so that he could look into her eyes. "Lady Catherine?" he prompted. "Lady

Catherine, we need your help, now. We're trying to avenge you, but we're not having a heck of a lot of luck here. Any suggestions?"

There was no response.

"Thank you," Hellboy said. "You've been helpful."

He turned to the others. "The head isn't helping. I guess we should go back."

"Avenge us?" a weary voice said.

"Bloody hell!" one of the agents shouted.

Hellboy lifted the head and shined his flashlight at Lady Catherine's face. Her eyes, now open, winced at the glare.

"Lady Catherine?" Anastasia began.

"Who are you?" Lady Catherine asked. Now that she was talking again, fresh blood dripped from the shattered vertebrae that hung from her ragged neck stump.

"Dr. Anastasia Bransfield, madame, at your service," she replied.

"Ah, yes, Dr. Bransfield," Lady Catherine sighed, and her eyes seemed to die again for a moment, staring off, unmoving, into nothing. Then she coughed slightly, and a bit of blood drooled out the side of her mouth. There were insects in it, some kind of sand chiggers or something, Hellboy thought.

In the darkness of the cave, he heard one of the MI5 men retching.

"I'd . . . forgotten," Lady Catherine said. "Will you avenge us, those of us who died in that oasis clearing?"

"We're trying, Lady Catherine," Anastasia replied. "But we need more information. We're in the caves now, the caves that I believe were used to bring you all to Hazred's domain. But we can't find our way in. We've searched them all and . . ."

"The entrance is near," Lady Catherine said, and her eyes rolled back in her head, revealing white pulsing orbs lined with red veins as her face was lined with slashes. "I remember now, just a bit. We walked through the wall, as if we were already ghosts. Dead and gone. But we were alive then, so alive and radiant and . . . oh, you must destroy him. Destroy the sorcerer."

Then Lady Catherine was gone.

"Looks like our oracle is less help than expected," Hellboy said. "Now I wish I'd left the head back in Creaghan's tent."

"Don't be such a pessimist," Anastasia said. "She said the entrance was near. Let's look around again."

"They 'walked through the wall,'" Arun noted. "We're assuming she doesn't mean literally. So if there wasn't magic involved, perhaps there's some kind of passage."

Hellboy had excellent vision. Despite the cave's dim flashlight illumination, he could see that Arun was sweating profusely. The man looked awful, sickly.

"Are you all right, Professor?" he asked.

Arun jumped as if he'd been goosed.

"What? Oh, yes, yes. I'm fine. A little stuffy in here is all."

"Do you want to go back outside?" Anastasia asked. "One of the others can accompany you."

Arun glanced over at Burke, Carruthers, and Meaney, who were standing in the corner looking rather lost, and shook his head.

"Right, then," Anastasia announced. "Let's look around. Spread out and do a circuit of the cavern, sticking close to the walls. Run a hand along the stone and examine it carefully."

The six of them fanned out around the circumference of the cavern. Hellboy estimated that it was roughly twenty feet in diameter in most areas, and a little wider where the tunnel they had followed opened into the cavern. The ceiling was about twelve feet from the floor, and he had already taken a good look at it to be certain there were no obvious openings.

Hellboy ran his left hand along the stone wall and focused his flashlight on it a foot or so at a time. Every step he took, the click of his hooves echoed eerily within the cavern. It was a hollow, inhuman sound that he had to keep reminding himself originated with him. He had become so used to the sound that it did not normally even register to him. But in such a small, enclosed space, and with that horrible echo, he could not escape it.

Self-consciously, he wondered if it bothered the others half as much as it was bothering him. After a moment's consideration, he forced the thought away and concentrated on the task at hand.

He had covered several feet of cave without any luck, and began to think they were going to strike out.

"Here," Agent Meaney said. "Over here, have a look at this."

Hellboy pointed his flashlight at the man's face; shadows reflected obsidian on his dark skin.

"Where?" Anastasia asked, as they all converged in the corner where Meaney stood.

"Right here," he said, pointing to a depression in the rock wall that none of them had noticed before.

"Is it some trick door or something, then, Paul?" one of the other agents asked Meaney.

"Can you not see it, then?" Meaney asked. "It's an optical illusion. Look."

Meaney walked straight into the recessed corner of the cavern and the wall seemed, for a moment, to bend around him. Then he had passed through, and it was clear.

"My God," Anastasia gasped. "Could that be a natural formation, do you think? Could nature have formed such a perfect illusion?"

Hellboy studied the wall closely. Or rather, the walls. There was an opening from floor to ceiling, a passage right in front of them. It was a shadowy corner of the cavern, so that at first it had only seemed to be a natural depression in the wall. They would have noticed it sooner, but the passage was only about five feet deep, with a large stone obelisk standing at the end, as if someone had cut a huge door in the wall and shoved it backwards. If one walked into the gap and stepped forward to the recessed stone, there were openings to the left and right leading out of the cavern.

"Let's go," was Hellboy's only reply. The day was passing quickly outside, and he wanted to investigate as much as possible before the others grew too tired to function properly. Already he had serious concerns about Professor Lahiri. He wondered whether he ought to have left the man behind.

"Which way?" Burke asked. Or it might have been Carruthers.

"Agent Meaney, Hellboy, and I will go left," Anastasia decided. "You two take Professor Lahiri and go right. We all walk fifty paces, then turn around and report back. At that point, we'll decide upon one path or the other."

"No!" Arun snapped.

Hellboy stared at him. They all did. The professor was behaving more and more oddly.

"What's wrong, Arun?" Anastasia asked. "Come on, man, if you've got claustrophobia or something, now is the time to tell me."

"I just think I should go with you," Arun said, his voice almost a whimper. "You might need me."

Anastasia frowned. "I'm a big girl," she said. "I can take care of myself. Besides, Arun, we're going to meet back here in just a few minutes. Why don't you restrain yourself until then."

At first Hellboy assumed this was just another example of Arun's infatuation with Anastasia. But then another, more disturbing thought entered his mind. Hooves clacking on stone, he stepped over to where Arun stood with the MI5 agents.

"Listen, Professor," he said, "if you've translated more of that tablet, you'd better say so. If we're in danger . . . or at least, any more danger than we already know, you'd be a fool not to say so. Not to mention pissing me off. You're at risk here, too. So what do you say? Got anything you want to share?"

"Not at all," Arun said stiffly, his old self again for a moment. "Why, the very suggestion is an insult."

"Okay, then, let's move on, shall we?" Anastasia asked, but it wasn't really a question.

Hellboy took the lead on his side, and one of the MI5 agents led the other group. They set out at the same time.

About twelve paces into their tunnel, Hellboy held up a hand and motioned for Meaney and Anastasia to stop. There was a green glow ahead that he found very familiar. He had seen it before, underwater.

And far off in the tunnel, he thought he heard an odd singsong melody that might have been that weird noise he'd heard in the lake that reminded him of whale song.

"Careful now," he said, and moved on.

His flashlight cut the darkness, but barely. It illuminated a path in front of them scarcely three feet wide. A few more paces and he began to notice that the tunnel seemed to have a small luminescence of its own. A green, sickly glow.

Then he stopped. Several feet ahead, the tunnel ended. Or rather, the ceiling did. The cave path opened up to the right and above, becoming a rocky ledge along a sheer cliff.

"What on Earth is that glow?" Anastasia asked softly.

"We'll know soon enough," Hellboy replied. "But it damn sure isn't Kryptonite."

A scream cut the darkness behind them, then voices, shouting, and the pounding echo of footfalls. Without a word, Agent Meaney set off back down the tunnel the way they'd come. Anastasia and Hellboy followed.

"Meaney, look out for that big . . . ," Hellboy began to say.

But Meaney was not stupid. Though he had no flashlight of his own, he instinctively sidestepped the obelisk in their path and dodged into the cave. He was already around it and starting down the right-hand leg of the tunnel before Hellboy cleared the huge stone.

He stopped in his tracks. Meaney stood over Arun, who was crumpled up on the ground, hysterical. One of the other two agents leaned against the tunnel wall, heaving in great gasps of air from having run in terror.

"What happened?" Meaney demanded.

"It's Burke, Paul," the other agent said. "He's dead."

"What?" Hellboy asked. "How in the hell did that . . ." He stomped past them and started down the tunnel. Agent Carruthers grabbed his arm.

"No, sir, don't go down there," Carruthers said. "Or, at least, keep your flashlight aimed at the ground. Where it starts to slope, even gently, don't take another step."

It occurred to Hellboy that now he knew which man was which. But it had been a horrible way to learn to tell them apart. Carruthers was alive, and Burke was dead. Their former similarity didn't seem quite so amusing anymore.

Hellboy started down the tunnel, training his flashlight on the stone floor in front of him. A dozen or so paces later, the path did indeed begin to slope just a bit. Heeding Carruthers' warning, he stopped there.

"What is it?" Anastasia asked, and Hellboy was slightly startled. He'd been so focused on where he was going that he had paid little attention to other noises in the tunnel.

Now he stopped and listened carefully. Other than human sounds, the clearing of a throat, the scuffing of a boot sole, knuckles cracking, he heard absolutely nothing. Except there was something else. Something moving. The sound of . . . friction?

Hellboy held the end of his flashlight between his teeth. The light bounced along the walls as he searched through

the many large pockets of his belt for the one thing that
might be useful to him at that very moment.

"Hellboy?" Anastasia asked. "What are you looking for?"

He ignored her. Had he responded with the flashlight
between his gritted teeth, the words would have come out
as grunts anyway. After several frustrating moments, the
fingers of his left hand brushed a long, thin stick that was
his objective. Grimly, he removed it from his pocket. Hellboy hated to waste it. It might have come in very handy
later. But a man was dead, and he deserved to have people
know how he had died.

In fact, they had an obligation to return his body to his
family, if it could be retrieved.

Hellboy held the long object in both fists. He gave it a
powerful twist, and it erupted in sparking flame.

"A flare?" Arun cried in disbelief. "You had a flare all
this time? Why didn't you use it in the cavern before?"

Hellboy shook his head. He was beginning to tire of
the little professor.

"If I'd used it before," he replied, "we wouldn't have
had it now, would we? It isn't as if I brought a case of
them, pal. Even I don't know what other crap I've stored
up in the pockets of this belt. But I knew I had at least
one of these."

He tossed the flare down the tunnel ahead of him, and
it dropped lower than the floor they were standing on. Finally, it hit stone and then skittered down a slick decline
as smooth as a child's slide. Where it came to rest, Agent
Burke stared up at them with bulging, dead eyes.

And things moved. Slithered over one another. Asps,
anacondas, cobras, dozens of other breeds, thousands of

them down there, dragging the man's body down among them, burying him in their leathery hides.

"Snakes," Hellboy said with great disgust. "I hate snakes."

"Jesus! Burke," Meaney cursed. "He walked right into it."

"You're all going back," Hellboy declared. "Right now. Back to the cave and then out of here. I should have come alone to begin with. I don't know what I was thinking. I never work well in a group situation. Let's go."

"Just a moment," Anastasia said, annoyed. "I'm in charge here, and I say nobody's going anywhere."

Hellboy pushed past Arun to take both of Anastasia's hands in his own. In the dim glow of their flashlights, he looked into her eyes and saw fear and determination at war.

"'Stasia," he said softly. "I know you have a lot of courage. You're a tough woman, and you've been through a lot. But being down here is just asking for trouble. I know you think this has all been just like old times. I feel that way, too. But it isn't really. It's a lot more risky."

"Well, why should we go back and you stay?" she asked.

"I'm a lot harder to kill than you are," Hellboy answered.

Anastasia chuckled. "Lucky for you, or I'd have killed you long ago."

Hellboy smiled, but behind him, Professor Lahiri grunted some noise of disapproval. That was enough for him. Obviously, Arun had feelings for Anastasia, but that was no reason to . . .

"Have you got something you want to say?" Hellboy snapped angrily.

Arun seemed fearful, but when he said, "No," Hellboy knew he was lying. Professor Lahiri was a terrible liar.

"Let's go," Anastasia ordered, then turned to Carruthers and Meaney. "You know we can't go down and get him. Is there anything you want to say about him now, or a prayer he might have liked?"

"Indeed," Carruthers said softly. "An old Welsh blessing that Chris Burke particularly liked. 'May you be in heaven a half hour before the devil knows you're dead, old friend.'"

"Now, madame, if it's all the same to you, I'd like to stay with Hellboy," Carruthers noted. "I've got a score to settle with whomever is responsible for this."

Hellboy was about to argue, to insist that Carruthers go topside with the others, when he felt a sudden warmth and wetness at his hip. There was a muffled noise, as if someone were speaking through a gag. And in the canvas bag tied to his belt, something moved.

"Oh, I think I'm going to be . . . ," Arun said. And then he was. Hellboy found the stench rather nauseating.

He opened the bag and before he could even pull out Lady Catherine's head, she shrieked, "The door is disappearing!" and then the head was still. She was dead again.

"The door is . . . ," Hellboy repeated.

Then he ran, hooves chipping stone, sending shattering echoes through the tunnel. Fifteen paces. Twenty paces. Thirty paces and he could see the green glow up ahead again.

"Wonderful," Agent Meaney said behind him. "The entrance is gone, sealed up somehow. It's like somebody slid that huge stone into the doorway, closing it up. But that's ridiculous. Nobody's that strong."

"I guess somebody doesn't want us to leave until after coffee and dessert," Hellboy joked, scanning the tunnel ahead and behind for either threat or clue.

"We're trapped here now," Arun whined. "We're going to die here."

Then his voice changed a little, became almost perverse in its glee. Hellboy didn't have to look at the little man to see the lascivious grin on his face.

"Together," Arun said, glaring at Anastasia.

Hellboy clapped a hand on Arun's back, and the professor went down painfully on one knee. Sometimes Hellboy forgot his own strength.

"You need to calm down, Professor," he said. "I have a feeling there are at least a couple of other ways out of here. Dangerous, maybe, but we knew that before we came down here. Whatever kidnapped and slaughtered Lady Catherine and her friends wasn't selling Girl Scout cookies."

He had their attention. Good.

"I'll take point. Meaney, you and Carruthers bring up the rear. Professor, there's a ledge up ahead and we're going to have to be very careful. Stay calm, and everything will be fine. Now, just follow me."

Hellboy moved along to where the tunnel opened up into the main cavern. To their left, a sheer rock wall climbed high above the ledge upon which they stood. To their right stretched a chasm some fifty feet across.

"What in the world is that green glow?" Agent Carruthers asked. "It seems almost . . . diseased."

Hellboy had to agree. The green light emanating from what he assumed was the bottom of the chasm seemed somehow rotten, vile. Even evil, and Hellboy had enough experience with evil to know that not only did it exist, but it spread like a virus.

"Stay close to the wall," Anastasia said. "Steady yourselves with your hands, if necessary. Just be careful. This must be the way Lady Catherine's people were brought, for they most certainly did not go through those snakes."

Hellboy stepped carefully. Every time he put his foot down on the ledge, he feared it might crumble beneath him. He did not know the thickness of the rock outcropping on which they walked, or how much weight it would support.

Anastasia grabbed hold of his tail, and Hellboy was momentarily startled. "What are you . . ."

"I want to make sure we don't get separated," she explained. "If it makes you uncomfortable, I . . ."

"No, no," he lied. "That's okay. I don't want to lose track of you, either."

The ledge seemed to narrow slightly, and the cave to turn to the left, so that Hellboy could not see around the curve. "Slow down a minute," he instructed.

Hellboy played his flashlight over the ledge and the wall, but everything seemed sturdy enough. He stepped forward and peered around the corner.

"Looks okay," he said. "More of the same."

Back to the wall, he moved around the curve carefully, then began to walk straight ahead once again. The others followed suit.

"What is that singing?" Arun asked.

Hellboy had almost forgotten about the noise, or music, or whatever it was. It was low and insinuating and after a while it just seemed to sink into his head and disappear there. But the others still heard it and, when brought to his attention, Hellboy could hear it too.

It was deeply disturbing. Perhaps meant to turn people away. But they could not be turned away for they had nowhere else to go.

Something skittered across stone in the darkness ahead. Hellboy signaled for the others to halt as he played his flashlight further along the ledge. It was a spider. A rather large spider, at least as broad as Hellboy's left hand. It froze in the light, then began to skitter toward them once more. Hellboy hated snakes, and he hated spiders as well. But there was one sure, fast way to deal with spiders.

He lifted his right leg and brought his hoof down hard on top of the huge arachnid. Its bodily fluids spurted out from beneath Hellboy's hoof, and its legs twitched several times.

Hellboy was about to comment on his dislike of spiders, to warn the others to look out for more, when something huge shifted high up in the cavern above and ahead of them.

"What the hell is . . . ," Carruthers began, but his voice trailed off.

"Good God!" Meaney cried.

Three flashlights converged on a huge network of silver,

gleaming strands which hung across the chasm like a net. Clinging to the bottom of that web was the spider that had constructed it. It was red and black, a mammoth creature, at least six feet across its abdomen alone. Its eight spindly legs were at least a dozen feet long. And the two sets of mandibles at its gaping, pink maw were sharp indeed, more like tusks than anything else.

"Hellboy . . . ," Anastasia gasped, waiting for some kind of action.

"Well," he said, "at least now we know what Lady Catherine meant when she told us to watch out for spiders."

"Meaney! Carruthers! Kill that thing!" Anastasia barked.

The MI5 men opened fire with the SA-80's slung across their chests. The spider blossomed in a bouquet of exploding flesh and a spray of blood.

"Let's hope there aren't any more of those," Hellboy said, as the gunfire echoed off the cavern walls.

"The music stopped," Arun pointed out.

Hellboy listened intently. The professor was right.

"Well, if they didn't know we were coming before, they certainly do now," Carruthers observed.

"Good," Hellboy said. "Maybe they'll bake a cake."

"Damn!" Meaney cried and as they all turned to look, he batted something from his leg. It was another of what now appeared to be the baby spiders.

"It bit me," he snarled. "Jesus, that hurt!"

In the glare of their flashlights, the spider stared up at them defiantly. When it started to crawl toward Anastasia, Hellboy slid carefully past her on the narrow ledge and stomped a hoof down on the thing.

His hoof went right through the ledge, shattering it. Hellboy nearly lost his balance, but Anastasia grabbed hold of his arm.

"Thanks, but you shouldn't have done that," he told her. "I might have dragged you down after me."

"I go where you go," she said calmly. "Now let's move on."

They turned their attention back to the path in front of them. As Arun stepped over the hole Hellboy had punched through the ledge, a loud rumbling, cracking noise echoed through the cavern.

"Oh, jeez," Hellboy said.

Then the ledge gave way beneath their feet, and all five of them tumbled into the chasm.

CHAPTER TEN

Falling, Hellboy bellowed in alarm and frustration. End over end he tumbled, and his companions fell with him. On the way down, his only thoughts were for Anastasia. Experience told him he would likely survive, no matter how long a drop might await them. But already they had fallen too far.

The others were going to die. Anastasia was going to die, and there was nothing he could do to help her.

Cold air whipped past his face. Green light flashed in his eyes as he tumbled. Hellboy struggled to right himself, to get some perspective on the fall. If he could grab on to something . . . if there was something to grab on to . . . maybe he could reach Anastasia with his tail?

They had been falling for several seconds, a long way down, before Anastasia began to scream. Her wailing pierced his ears and his heart, for it was obvious she had held the fear at bay as long as she could. Until long after she must have realized it was too late.

Still they fell.

Arun Lahiri shrieked like a frightened monkey, chittering with terror. Hellboy tuned him out. All he cared about was Anastasia. Only seconds had passed, but a part of him was already mourning her.

Spinning, he saw something out of the corner of his eye, a silver skein across the chasm that still yawned wide and glowed green beneath them. Agents Meaney and Carruthers struck it first, grunting with the impact. The enormous, complex spider web stretched under their weight, but held.

"Oh, God!" Anastasia grunted as she hit the web.

A moment later, Arun landed on top of her, and she cried out in shock and pain. The web strained under the final insult of Hellboy's weight, then snapped taut once more.

Silently, Hellboy thanked whatever deity might be listening. With a bit of difficulty, he pulled free of the gummy web and pushed himself onto his knees. He didn't dare try to stand. His hooves would shoot through the wide holes in the network of webbing and he would have to struggle free once more. Instinctively, he checked to be certain the canvas bag in which he carried Lady Catherine's head was still tied to his belt. It was there, but she was silent as usual.

"Is everybody . . . ?"

"Get the hell off of me!" Anastasia cried, and tried to shove Arun away from her.

He wouldn't move. At least, that was how it initially appeared. Even as he cried, "I'm trying!" Hellboy realized that the professor couldn't move. None of them could.

"What the bloody hell is this, then?" Carruthers shouted, thrashing angrily and only succeeding in getting himself bound up even worse.

"Hellboy!" Anastasia called. "Come on, get him off of me!"

"I'll be right there," Hellboy promised.

Anastasia cursed and struggled to move Arun from on top of her. The professor seemed stunned, and only stared at her with a horrified expression on his face. Hellboy was tempted to find it amusing, but then he remembered how oddly Arun had been behaving toward Anastasia. His behavior had been verging on obsessive ever since they searched the lake early that morning.

Jeez, Hellboy thought. Had it only been that morning?

Hellboy crawled along the web toward Agent Carruthers, who was closest to him. He pulled at the webbing gently, but it seemed inextricably stuck to Carruthers' clothing and skin. Almost as if it had merged itself with his flesh.

"Come on, you big daft demon!" Carruthers snarled. "Get me loose!"

"What?" Hellboy asked, shocked at the insult.

"You heard me! I've lost my gun, now, and who knows what other horrors we've got to face down here? Get me loose before some of your nastier cousins come along to eat my bloody brains!" Carruthers roared.

Hellboy squinted down at Carruthers, trying to suppress his anger. The man is hysterical, he told himself. He doesn't know what he . . .

"What in God's name are you waiting for?" Carruthers shouted. "Or maybe you're thinking of sampling my choicest bits yourself, eh? Come on, then! Get me out of here!"

"Fine," Hellboy said curtly.

He grasped the skein of webbing that was stuck to and wound about Carruthers' arms and chest, and gave a single, powerful tug. Carruthers shrieked in agony as the webbing tore away, taking clothes and strips of skin with it.

"Good God!" Anastasia gasped, staring across the whimpering MI5 agent at Hellboy. "How are we going to get free?"

Hellboy stared at her, and at Arun lying silently on top of her. He winced slightly as he looked back at Carruthers' flayed skin. Desperately, he tried to figure out a way to release his companions.

"I guess, if we have some kind of a blade, I can cut you out," he said doubtfully. Then he began to search the many pouches on his belt, pushing aside the bag with Lady Catherine's head in it. He must have some kind of a blade in there, he knew. Even a Swiss Army knife would be helpful.

Someone coughed behind him. Meaney! Hellboy had almost forgotten the other MI5 agent because he'd said nothing, while Anastasia and Carruthers had been so vocal. But now Meaney began to choke, gagging loudly.

Hellboy scrambled to turn around, his stone right hand snapped through the web, and he fell on his face on the sticky strands.

"Damn!" he grumbled, and yanked his head free, yelping as the adhesive web tore a clump of hair from his goatee.

When he turned to look at Meaney, the black man was jittering with some kind of spastic fit. Green, brackish foam boiled from his mouth.

"Marvelous," Hellboy sighed. "That's all we need. The return of Linda Blair."

"Carruthers, is Agent Meaney epileptic?" Anastasia asked.

"How the Christ should I know?" Carruthers snapped, still nursing his wounds though his back and legs remained stuck to the web. "Maybe he's gone bloody rabid from that spider bite."

Hellboy shot an apologetic glance at Anastasia. He supposed that she very badly wanted to be free of the web and of Arun's sweaty presence. Arun, for his part, still said nothing. But at least he wasn't foaming at the mouth.

"It's okay," Anastasia said. "See to him first. Then let's get out of here."

Arun had panicked initially. He'd glanced quickly around and seen, in the dim green light, that the web they were on appeared to stretch from one side of the chasm to the other. That there was still no sign of a bottom to the massive crevice in the Earth they had fallen into. But there was one sign of hope.

At a far corner of the web matrix, he could see a dark patch of shadow that he believed must be another tunnel. Some kind of passage away from the chasm, away from the webs. It was on the opposite side from where they had come in, so he didn't hold out much hope for returning to the surface. But at least they could escape before more spiders, large or small, descended upon the prey trapped in their webs. Hellboy and the others hadn't mentioned the prospect, but the professor knew it must be on all of their minds.

When Hellboy had first gotten free, and Carruthers began to struggle, Arun opened his mouth to point out the tunnel he believed he saw. His eyesight had improved underground, and he wondered if it was just an adjustment to the darkness, or the weird green light.

He actually began to speak.

No sound came out.

The medallion he had found on the sandy oasis lakeshore—the one with the jackal engraved on one side and odd glyphs like those on the tablet Hellboy had found—began to grow warm in his pocket. The pleasure of it spread through his body, and he wasn't scared anymore. The medallion had exhibited these odd properties, the pleasure of which was becoming addictive, ever since Arun had found it. Even more so since they came underground.

With that warmth, that pleasure, came the overwhelming emotions he felt towards Anastasia. Lust. And homicidal mania.

Now he lay on top of her, close enough to inhale her sweet breath, and the medallion grew warmer still, nearly scalding his thigh through the fabric of his pocket. His fear melted, and he anticipated his own death, all of their deaths, with amusement. The thought of Anastasia's demise was of particular interest. She deserved to die for having spurned him for so long. Still, he was exceedingly happy to have had this chance, this last chance, to be close to her.

As he thought of their impending destruction, and Anastasia squirmed beneath him, talking to Hellboy and refusing to meet his gaze, Arun grew hard. He knew she would feel his erection and pressed it against her to be certain. To let her know. It was important that she know, at the end, what she had lost.

A grimace of disgust contorted Anastasia's face and she

looked up at him. Arun smiled down at her, a smile that told her she was finally where he had always wanted her. Where he knew she secretly longed to be.

In fact, they were so close, if he tried hard enough, strained forward without getting himself even more entangled in the webbing, he might even be able to lick the salt and grime from her face. He nearly came at the mere thought of it.

With Hellboy otherwise distracted, Arun leaned forward; his tongue snaked out. He reached, strained, but could not quite make it. Anastasia was ignoring him, perhaps not even aware of his movements. He didn't care. She would become aware momentarily.

His body felt like a furnace, the heat radiating outward from the medallion in his pocket. Arun wondered why the skein of webbing didn't simply melt away.

As he strained to lick her, Arun became distinctly, overwhelmingly aware of Anastasia's scents. As if his sense of smell had suddenly gone into overdrive, he caught the powerful aroma of her soap, her shampoo. Her sweat and body odor, and the damp visceral smell of her sex drove him wild. Arun's heart thundered in his chest.

Never mind licking her face, suddenly he was driven mad with a desire to be inside her, filling her with the erection that was quickly becoming painful in its rigidity.

He wanted to tear her throat out with his teeth. And though his tongue could not reach her cheek, he suddenly wondered if somehow, there was a way he could surge forth and sink his gnashing teeth into her soft flesh, feel arterial spray paint his face. He yearned to open his mouth and taste her gushing blood.

Arun's tongue darted out again. He surged forward, but still fell short.

"What the hell are you doing?" Anastasia asked, turning toward him.

And his tongue grew longer, just for a moment. It might have been his imagination, but suddenly, it felt as if his tongue stretched out from his mouth and licked Anastasia along her jawbone.

"Jesus!" she cried. "You disgusting pig! Get away from me! God, please, Hellboy, get him away from me!"

Hellboy looked up from the quivering, vomiting black man. Arun wanted to shout, to tell Hellboy to stay away. Anastasia was his, despite that she'd been defiled by the monstrous thing in the past. His to ravish or to eviscerate. He looked at Anastasia, mouth open in anticipation of his words, of what he might do to her given the chance.

"You're vile," she snarled, glaring at him.

Then she head-butted him with a resounding crack. The medallion's warmth dissipated. Arun blinked several times, wondering what he had done to deserve his friend's attack. He felt disoriented, and nauseous.

"I think I'm going to be sick, Stacie," he announced.

"You puke on me, you filthy little runt, I'll tear out your fucking eyeballs with a grapefruit spoon!" she shouted in his face.

"Ssssssh!" Hellboy said.

Arun and Anastasia both looked up. Arun saw the dark hole on the far side of the web and vaguely remembered wanting to tell them all about it. Too late, though. They all knew about it now. They couldn't miss it.

Or what was crawling out of it.

"Hellboy!" Agent Carruthers screamed. "Get me the fuck out of here so I can help you, dammit! I've got to get my gun!"

But Hellboy had already looked for Carruthers' gun and couldn't find it anywhere. He didn't know what to do first. Meaney needed medical attention, immediately. He was getting breath, but less and less of it as the awful green bile flowed from his throat. If he continued to choke, Hellboy could only assume that he would die quite soon.

Anastasia and Arun were thrashing against one another, helpless. Carruthers was closest to the slowly advancing arachnid, and he screamed at Hellboy, his eyes bulging from their sockets, veins pulsing in his forehead. Hellboy couldn't take it anymore.

"Would you shut up!" he snapped.

Carruthers stared at him in horror.

"Another word and I'll leave you there," Hellboy continued. "You're an arrogant, obnoxious pain in the ass. And you're damned lucky I don't hold a grudge."

He scrambled across the web, past Anastasia and Arun, past Carruthers, until he was some twenty feet from the spider. Meaney, the poor bastard, would have to wait, Hellboy thought. As quickly as he could, he surveyed the contents of his belt pouches, trying to find something, anything, that might be of use.

The spider stopped and seemed to regard him from its eight many-faceted eyes. Its eight spindly legs were matted with dark, coarse hair and its body had a kind of fur on it as well. The mandibles at its mouth twitched in silent conversation with itself, or perhaps, he thought, the spider was merely salivating at the thought of the five-course meal that awaited it.

Those prism eyes stared at him. Hellboy continued to search the pouches of his belt. When the spider did not advance any further, he began to get angry.

"What?" Hellboy shouted at it. "What are you waiting for, an invitation?"

The spider crept forward once more, slowly.

"Oh, well done, Hellboy," Carruthers snarled from behind him. "Taunt the giant spider-monster into coming a little closer. You might as well ring the bloody dinner bell!"

"Shut up!" Hellboy growled.

"Look, I don't expect you've got a big can of Raid in those mule packs you wear on your hips, but haven't you got a gun?" Carruthers sneered, his distress transforming his fear into anger.

"Yes, I have a gun," Hellboy answered. "But it's not much use against something like this!"

"Well, you can bloody well shoot it anyway, can't you?" Anastasia asked.

The spider moved forward again. Hellboy pulled out his gun and shot the spider from a range of fifteen feet, obliterating one of its eyes. It rocked back a moment, then took another eight-legged step forward. Ten feet away now.

"There, you happy now?" Hellboy asked, holstering his gun. "That didn't do a damn . . ."

The spider faltered, one leg slid into a hole in the web and it crashed onto its belly.

". . . thing."

Hellboy took a tentative step toward the spider, its remaining eyes shining in the green light, but it didn't move. Another step, and he was a little more than five feet from the huge creature. His friends were silent, all of them awaiting some kind of attack or movement.

"You think it's dead?" Hellboy asked, just as the massive arachnid lofted itself up once more. Using the five legs with which it had stable footing, the spider lurched forward, towering over Hellboy. On his knees, he was at a terrible disadvantage, but he didn't dare stand for fear of falling through.

The spider surged upward on its forelegs, and the back part of its abdomen seemed to bend under its body. A thick strand of silver shining web erupted from its rear section. It fell across Hellboy's shoulder and where it fell it burned just a little as it dried. Hellboy went to tear it off, but at first it held fast.

Then the spider ducked its head down and darted forward, trying to snap Hellboy up in its gaping maw. Anastasia screamed and Arun began to laugh hysterically. He'd gone way over the edge, Hellboy thought, and he'd been riding right on it for a long time.

At that proximity, the spider was sure to get him eventually. Unless Hellboy changed the rules, and the odds, pretty drastically. He tore the webbing from his arm, ducked down to get some momentum, and threw himself under the spider.

Flat on his back, Hellboy pulled his gun a second time and fired four rounds into the leathery underside of the beast. Green-black ichor poured from the wounds down onto his face. The stench and the taste made him turn to one side and retch uncontrollably. The spider wobbled slightly, and then began to scuttle sideways, lowering its dripping maw toward where he lay.

"This isn't working!" he shouted, though in a sense it was. He was keeping the spider away from Anastasia and the others. But if they couldn't find a way to free themselves, his efforts would be useless. As long as the spider lived!

The arachnid dipped its head for him again. Hellboy grabbed hold of its mandibles with his right hand and pulled it down, holding the spider's mouth away from his head. Its breath stank of putrescent meat, and it began to make a keening, chittering noise which might have been a scream of pain or a cry of attack.

Any second the webs would fly, and this close he didn't know what he could do. Hellboy stumbled, one hoof slipping through the webbing. He lost his grip, and the spider's mandibles closed on his left hand, slicing through his tough skin just barely. His thunderous roar of pain and frustration caused the web to tremble beneath him, but he did not fall through. The spider, unwittingly, was doing him a favor by holding him up.

But it didn't feel much like a favor.

The spider yanked his left arm and Hellboy went with it. He let the spider's strength carry him to it, lifted his massive right hand, and brought the stone fist down on top of the spider's head, among its many kaleidoscopic eyes. Again and again and again and again.

"You're. Really. Starting. To. Piss. Me. Off!" he bellowed, one word for each blow.

On the last, the spider's skull gave way beneath his assault. Its head cracked open and a sickly yellow pus began to leak out. Hellboy stopped hitting it, but when he pulled his hand away, a little of the fluid was smeared across his stone knuckles.

"Now *that's* pest control!" he said triumphantly.

Behind him, the others began to scream anew.

"Jeez!" he huffed. "What is it with you people?"

He turned, prepared to calm the others, to think of a way to free them and escape. "Look, we've got to get out of here now, before more of this guy's family shows up looking for revenge," he said. "I'm sure I've got something to cut . . ."

Hellboy stared past Carruthers. Past Anastasia and Arun, who had stopped struggling against one another and were together straining away from Agent Meaney.

Or what had been Agent Meaney.

Carruthers began to pray softly, and Hellboy suddenly felt sorry for having yelled at him earlier, no matter how much of a weenie he'd been. You couldn't blame him for his fear now, or for the way the rest of them were screaming in a hellish chorus.

Mandibles protruded from either side of Meaney's mouth, stretching and ripping his flesh. A chittering noise came from within him and he bucked and thrashed on the gluelike webs.

Increasingly, though, Meaney wasn't sticking to the web. "Come on, man, do something!" Carruthers pleaded.

Hellboy hesitated. Moments earlier, Meaney had been their comrade, perhaps the most competent and brightest of Creaghan's MI5 squad.

Then the skin and clothing at Meaney's side began to bulge. Something strained against the flesh and fabric . . . and it exploded outward. Four legs burst from either side of Agent Meaney's quaking form.

The quaking subsided, and then slowly, purposefully, Meaney turned to regard them. His eyes bulged impossibly. Then they exploded in a splash of viscous fluid and behind them, huge multifaceted spider's eyes grew. Other new eyes began to tear open in the skin of his face.

The Meaney-spider hissed, still on its back, and reached for Hellboy with its human arms. His body burst open at the pelvis, just above where the man's genitals would have been, and webbing shot from the ragged holes, whipping around Hellboy's neck and chest like bolos. Hellboy began to tear it painfully free, when another hiss came from behind him. The first spider, despite the bullets he'd put in it, lumbered unsteadily to its feet and hissed, spraying him with even more webbing.

In seconds, he was nearly fully cocooned. As hard as he

strained against his bonds, Hellboy could not snap them. He was trapped. As helpless as the others. Vulnerable.

Painfully, the huge spider began to close in. The spider-thing that had once been Agent Meaney hissed and clawed out at him with a human hand.

CHAPTER ELEVEN

Though at first he had argued, Captain Creaghan finally allowed Agent Rickman to talk him into taking a nap. He had barely slept in three days, and had begun to question his own judgment. Several hours after Dr. Bransfield's small team left to investigate the oasis cliff caves, Creaghan had given in to Rickman's suggestion and the urgings of his own body.

And slept.

When he woke, it was far darker than he expected. He had given Rickman specific instructions to wake him in two hours, but inside his tent, it seemed the day had ended. It was dusk, or past that. Perhaps five hours after he had closed his eyes.

"Damn it!" he growled.

Creaghan stood and strode angrily from his tent, prepared to shout at whomever was nearby. But as soon as he stepped outside, a hard wind and gritty sand blasted his face and eyes. He cursed loudly, and sand flew into his mouth, crackling between his teeth as he tried to spit it out.

Squinting and shielding his eyes, Creaghan looked up at the sky. The sun was still there, a dim radiance barely visible past a curtain of brown gauze that seemed to hang across the western sky.

"What the hell . . . ," Creaghan mumbled.

"Sandstorm, sir."

"What?" he asked, and turned to see that Rickman had come up behind him.

"Sandstorm," Rickman repeated. "It will be here in twenty or thirty minutes, according to the Bedouins. They recommend hiding in our tents, zipping everything up, and praying that it won't be strong enough to tear the tents off the ground with us inside."

Creaghan stared at Rickman, searching for some sign of sarcasm. He found none.

"Get the men to pack up anything vital they can in the next ten minutes," Creaghan ordered. "And send someone over to tell Colonel Shapiro that they might want to do the same."

"What?" Rickman asked. "Why?"

Creaghan stared at him.

"I'm . . . I'm sorry, sir," Rickman retreated. "I know we're not to question you. I apologize."

"Fine," Creaghan allowed. "But to save time when you pass the order along, I'll tell you why. We've established that something supernatural is at work here. Nearly twenty-five hundred years ago, fifty thousand men were erased from existence by a gale-force sandstorm.

"If that's the kind of storm whatever paranormal force is at work here has in store for us, we'll fare much better in those caves in the oasis basin than we will out here in the open desert. On the other hand, Shapiro and his men will never fit in the caves. They'll have to take what cover they can in the oasis itself. The trees and the height of the basin walls should take the brunt of the storm off them," Creaghan explained.

"But sir," Rickman paused, "how do I explain that to Colonel Shapiro?"

"Lie, Rickman! Tell the stupid American bastard that the Bedouins say it's going to be a killing storm and the only place to hide is the oasis. Now move!" he barked.

Rickman tore off across the sand and Creaghan looked up at the darkening sky, at the sun hiding away as if turning its back on their plight. Nervously, almost unconsciously, Creaghan touched a hand to the leather holster within which rested his sidearm. It was something he often did, something which gave him an odd sense of comfort.

This time, the weapon's presence failed to reassure him. What good were bullets against the desert itself?

Unbidden, tears began to well up in Anastasia's eyes. She had been this close to death several times before, and each time, Hellboy had found a way to win, to bludgeon the reaper into submission. But Hellboy couldn't help her now. Only his head was visible above the cocoon of webbing the spiders, one of which had once been human, were spinning.

Ever since they had fallen over the edge, she had felt helpless. Useless. But now there was little choice. Something had to be done. They didn't have knives, not even Carruthers, which surprised her. She would have thought MI5 agents would be armed better.

Frantically, she glanced around, squinting to see in the dim, verdant light. The tunnel entrance from which the huge spider had come was cast in deep shadows, but Anastasia didn't think there were any other spiders coming that

way. Staring into the darkness far above them in the chasm, she thought she could make out movement. Without doubt, there were further web networks up there, and probably more spiders.

"What are you doing?" Arun asked, his rank breath filling her nostrils.

"Shut up, you disgusting man," she snapped. Whatever had driven him to . . . to lick her face, she didn't want to know about it. About what perverse thoughts might lurk in his brain.

"Just let me concentrate on figuring out how to get us out of here," she snarled.

"You're mad!" he said. "We're never going to get out of here! We're going to die, and . . . oh, God, that's right. We're going to die!"

The words were hysterical, but not with fear. Arun had suddenly been overcome with an odd sort of glee. Anastasia ignored him, ignored the way he began to press his minor erection against her once more.

Carruthers had stopped shouting. Out of her peripheral vision she could see that he was still alive, still staring at the spiders. But he seemed either catatonic or simply resigned, somehow, to the death that was approaching. Once they had completed their cocooning of Hellboy, the spiders would surely attack the rest of them. He had been identified as the threat; they were merely prey.

But without a blade of some sort, how to tear free of the webbing? Anastasia's mind whirled. Above her, Arun smiled and his teeth seemed sharp and near.

"Slut," he said quietly. So quietly, she wasn't quite certain of the word. But she was sure enough.

"Piss off!" she snapped, and head-butted him again.

Arun's eyes rolled back in his head and he shuddered slightly, then was still. His unconscious weight felt heavier, and Anastasia's breathing became more labored. She longed to be out from beneath him, to shove him away.

Once upon a time he had been her friend, or at least a fond acquaintance. But something had happened. The man had obviously snapped. The signs had been limited to odd tics and other such quirks at first, but now he had gone completely overboard. He needed help, desperately needed to be returned to the surface, sent home to London for psychotherapy. But the prospects for Arun receiving help, for any of them ever leaving the chasm alive, did not appear to be promising.

"Hellboy, can you still hear me?" she called.

He tried to turn his head, but could not really manage it. Only his eyes, nose, and the stumps of his horns were visible on top. Within the web cocoon, he still struggled. Anastasia could see his arms and hands straining as he tried to reach the pouches on his belt, tried to find anything which might help them. She didn't know what he hoped to accomplish.

"Just you and me, now," a voice said softly.

Carruthers.

"Looks that way," she said. "Any ideas?"

"I haven't a one," he admitted.

Anastasia looked over at Carruthers as best she could. She couldn't really turn and look directly at him, but her peripheral vision told her enough. The man had resigned himself to death. His flesh was ragged from where Hellboy had torn the rooted webbing from his arms and face and belly. But there would be no way he could free himself.

"What I wouldn't give for a knife, a way to get us out of here, right now," she said.

"The hell with a blade," Carruthers moaned. "I'd kill my own mother for a cigarette right now."

Anastasia froze.

"Oh . . . ," she said softly. "Oh."

"Oh, what?" Carruthers asked, suddenly alarmed. "Don't tell me we've got something else to worry about? We're bloody near as well dead now, anyway."

"Maybe not," she said, and a sly smile began to spread across her face.

Anastasia squirmed and stretched. Her right arm was stuck fast to the web beneath her, only inches from her hip. Slowly, carefully, she tried to angle her body slightly so that she might reach her right-hand pocket. Arun's weight on top of her made it even more difficult. So difficult, in fact, that it might as well have been impossible. As far as she stretched her fingers, she wasn't going to be able to reach her pocket.

Which left one alternative.

Tensing her every muscle, Anastasia gritted her teeth and began to pull her forearm toward her hip with all her strength. Though she was in excellent physical condition, muscular and healthy, she wasn't an especially powerful woman. Never had been. But this was their only chance.

With a spitting sound, followed by the eerie chittering noise that had come to represent her fear of the spiders, the two huge arachnids stopped webbing Hellboy. Slowly, they inched toward him. The spider which had once been Agent Meaney still had vestigial human legs and arms, but those limbs had already begun to wither as his eight spider legs carried the burden of his transforming body. It was a revolting sight.

Death would be far preferable. But they couldn't be guaranteed of death from the creatures.

His voice muffled, still Anastasia heard defiant tones coming from within Hellboy's cocoon. He forced his head around just enough to see her out of the corner of his eye, and in that moment of eye contact, Anastasia knew she had only seconds left to act.

"No!" she cried, and with the very last reserve of energy within her, she tugged against the webs stuck to her arm, and her flesh began to tear away. Anastasia Bransfield screamed in agony. She didn't look down at her arm, but she knew the wounds were terrible. Instead, she pulled further, gnashing her jaws together like some mad dog.

Her fingertips felt denim. With a final thrust, she pushed her pelvis to one side, heard the fabric of her pants tear, and thanked God nothing was ever made as well as advertised.

Carefully, she slid her fingers into the pockets of her pants until she touched a thin, plastic tube. Slowly, she withdrew it, taking care not to drop it into the abyss waiting below. Anastasia twirled it within her fingers, turning it right-side up. She felt the metal thumbwheel, spun it, and was rewarded with a tiny jet of flame.

Thank God she had never completely given up smoking.

As quickly as possible, she burned away the webs connecting her to Arun. She was about to do the same to some of the webs holding her down, when a horrible realization dawned on her.

She would fall. She was certain of it. Even if she was careful about where she burned, the webbing would ignite and disintegrate beneath her, perhaps beneath them all. Even if that didn't happen, she might fall through, her clothes might catch on fire.

"Arun," she said, hoping to rouse him.

"Arun, wake up, dammit, I didn't hit you that hard!" she screamed.

His eyes flickered twice, then opened.

"Hmmm? What? Anastasia?" he mumbled.

"Are you you?" she cried, becoming more desperate as the spiders closed in on Hellboy. They had nearly reached him now.

"What?" he asked.

"Are you you or are you still bloody Renfield?" she roared at him. "Are you paying attention?"

"Yes, I'm bloody well paying . . . ," he began to retort, but she cut him off.

"You're free, Arun!" she told him. "You're loose! I've released you."

"Oh, God, thank you," he said, relieved, and began to roll off of her.

"No! Not that way!" she spat. "Listen to me carefully. We're only going to get one chance at this! Sit up, keep your ass on my legs, and put your feet down on the web."

He did as he was told.

"Take off your jacket!" she instructed, referring to the light tan jacket he had worn in case it was cold underground.

"What in God's name for?" he asked, shaking his head in disbelief.

"Take off your fucking jacket, you goddamned moron, or we're going to die!" Carruthers screamed from where he lay, bleeding down into the chasm and gritting his teeth in agony.

Arun whipped his jacket off. He wore a linen button-down shirt, with a white t-shirt underneath, and Anastasia wondered if they would need those as well. Something seemed to jut obscenely beneath the cloth, and she realized it was the tablet Hellboy had found in the lake.

"Now what?" he asked, quickly becoming as frantic as she.

"In my right hand is my cigarette lighter," she said. "Take it."

He did.

"Now, ball up your jacket, and set it aflame," she ordered.

"What?"

"Look at Hellboy, Arun!" she screamed. "Look at him! If we've got any hope of getting out of here alive, it means keeping him alive as well!"

Arun glanced over at Hellboy. He seemed to hesitate a moment, and a small smile began to creep over his face.

"Dying . . . ," he mumbled.

"Arun Lahiri! Earth to Arun!" Anastasia screamed.

The strange look disappeared from his face, and Arun stood, quickly, uncertain on the criss-crossed webbing. The web was tightly knit, with a gossamer sheen of lighter web connecting the strands. It was hard to walk, she saw. His feet stuck, and he had to be sure that he stepped on areas that would hold his weight, rather than on that gossamer shroud stretched within the holes.

But he did it.

"Hey!" Arun screamed. "Come on, you bloody ugly monsters, pay attention to the little guy! Meaney, turn around, you abomination! Hey!"

Half a dozen feet from where Hellboy now lay on his side, immobile within the webs, Arun stumbled and fell to his knees on the gleaming web hammock.

"Shit," he moaned. "Anastasia, I'm stuck."

The spiders turned slowly to regard him.

"Light it!" she cried.

Arun lit the ball of clothing on fire. It caught instantly, and the flames quickly spread.

The spiders began to retreat.

"You've got to be kidding," Arun said. "I didn't even get near them."

"They don't want you to," Anastasia said. "Get up, now. Go after them."

With great difficulty, Arun tore his pants away from the web and struggled to his feet once more. She saw the fear on his face as he stared at the flaming ball of cloth in his hands. One arm of his jacket hung down, fire leaping from it.

"Quickly," Anastasia said. She didn't want to tell him what she feared might happen if the web caught on fire.

He stumbled after the spiders. They retreated to the edge of the net of webbing. Arun drew even closer, and both spiders backed up right over the edge.

For a moment, Anastasia was astonished, thinking the spiders had simply allowed themselves to fall into the chasm. Then she saw the web lines. Connected to those lines, the huge spider and the deformed one that had once been Agent Meaney were descending into the abyss. Down, she assumed, to some other system of webs that they considered safer.

"Burn their lines," she instructed.

"Ow!" Arun cried. "Oh, my God, in about two seconds my hand is going to be on fire! Jesus, Stacie, it hurts!"

"Just burn the lines!" she commanded him.

Arun knelt and swept his burning hand beneath the network of webs. The lifelines the spiders hung from went up in a small puff of black smoke almost instantly. The spiders fell soundlessly away into darkness. Fire ran up the line toward the bed of webbing they were all stuck to, but stopped before it reached the main structure.

"Drop it!" Anastasia cried.

But Arun apparently didn't need her advice. He had already let go of the burning cloth, and it tumbled out of sight. He stood, cradling his right hand against his body, whimpering softly.

"It hurts," he said.

"Take the lighter over to Hellboy," she said, ignoring his pain.

"He can't even move," Arun argued.

"I don't want you to give it to him," she explained. "I want you to set him on fire. It's our only chance to get out of here."

Arun stared at her. Behind her, Carruthers began to laugh.

She knew that Hellboy could withstand the flames, that once the cocoon was weakened enough by them, he would rip himself free and snuff the fire. The web might catch. Probably would catch. How much of it would burn was another question.

But what other choice did they have? Only Hellboy might have something to cut them free.

"Just do it!" she snapped.

And prayed. Carruthers was mumbling something low to himself which might also have been a prayer. Or perhaps he had just gone away for a while, somewhere in his head. The idea was tempting.

Arun walked, stiff-legged, toward the cocoon. From where she lay, Anastasia could only see the crimson horn stumps that jutted from Hellboy's forehead, and a little bit of one of his sideburns.

Arun knelt down next to Hellboy. He recoiled suddenly, falling on his ass on the web. Stuck.

"Damn it!" Anastasia cursed. "What's wrong?"

When he turned to look at her, she thought Arun looked as if he were going to be sick.

"Something's moving around in there, down on his hip, and it isn't Hellboy," Arun said, the disgust clear in his voice. "It's her, Stacie, it's got to be. It's that damned head. And it's . . . it's muffled, but I can hear it . . . talking!"

"Well for God's sake, Arun, what's she saying?" Anastasia asked.

"I'm not completely certain, but it sounds like 'He's coming.' And then, I think, she says, 'Heaven help us all.' Then she just repeats herself," Arun explained, and Anastasia saw a shiver go through him.

She listened hard, and thought she could barely hear the muffled voice of Lady Catherine, her severed head in a canvas bag inside the thick cocoon of webbing that trapped Hellboy.

"Quick," Anastasia said. "Do it, Arun. Light him on fire."

I'm sorry, a deep, firm voice spoke in her mind. *I can't allow that.*

There was no sound for her to hear, but still Anastasia sensed the direction from which the telepathic contact had come. She strained to see the tunnel which led away from the web. In the yawning darkness that was the tunnel's mouth, two tiny red embers burned brightly.

The shadows resolved themselves into a man, the embers his eyes. He was pale and bearded, his flesh like alabaster, blue-veined and smooth. The green light from below reflected off his skin and gave it a sickening tint. Or, perhaps his skin was not perfectly white at all. Perhaps, she thought, it had that sickening tint at all times.

She knew without asking who this must be.

"Hazred," she whispered.

The sorcerer, whose linen robes hung loosely around him, smiled slightly and said something in a language so guttural she thought he might be choking. It wasn't any language she knew, or had ever heard spoken before. In truth, she believed completely that it was a language no living being outside of those caverns had ever heard spoken.

I'm flattered, his mental voice said, perhaps translating his verbal comments. *But I cannot allow your demonic friend his freedom, I'm afraid. Not as yet.*

Anastasia didn't understand. The man looked sickly. Even someone as unskilled at hand to hand combat as Arun ought to be able to hold him off. Even if Hazred could reach Arun in time.

"Arun," she said. "Do it!"

Nothing happened. She turned to see that Arun was entranced by Hazred's arrival. He stared at the man with wide eyes.

"Come on, Arun!" Carruthers screamed, another sudden outburst from a man Anastasia continued to write off as catatonic, only to have him erupt violently. "He's a murderer. He slaughtered Lady Catherine and her entire team! Set Hellboy free and we can go home! Don't you want to go home?"

"Home?" he asked. "No, I . . . I don't know."

The choice is not yours to make, Hazred's voice said in her head, and, she imagined, all of their heads.

She turned her head to see what he planned to do. The thin, pale man lifted his right hand, and green light seemed to blossom from it, sparks jumping from finger to finger. One spark seemed to grow brighter and larger and he held it in his palm. Hazred hurled the green fire at Arun. It struck his right hand, and the cigarette lighter exploded.

Arun screamed, his hand aflame, and beat his fist against his pants, trying desperately to put out the fire. Hazred waved a hand, and the flames were gone. Arun bent over, whimpering about his twice-burned hand.

"Right, then," Anastasia snarled, summoning the last of her strength and courage. "Come and get me, you decrepit old git."

I think not, Hazred said in her mind.

He barked something horrid in that choking language, waved a hand, and stepped aside.

People crowded past him, more than a dozen. But not people, really. Only a few of them looked remotely human to Anastasia. The others were even more pale than Hazred. They were stooped and short legged, barrel chested. They had large heads and huge ears.

Some of them had no eyes. Most of the others had white, bulging eyes and Anastasia assumed they were blind. The few which looked relatively human were bald and pale, and their smiles were perverse.

One of the little, twisted creatures touched her face.

Anastasia screamed.

CHAPTER TWELVE

The sandstorm was coming. No denying it now. Creaghan's men had gathered rations, weapons, bedrolls, and clothing, and tossed the provisions into two jeeps. Agent Rickman drove one of the jeeps with three other men. Captain Creaghan drove the second jeep himself, with three of his men on board. Eight of them, that was all.

They headed for the caves, leaving Colonel Shapiro and his men to hide in the oasis itself. The caves were safer, but there was no way more than a fraction of Shapiro's men would have been able to hide there. And he knew Colonel Shapiro would not have considered the caves. How could he? The man wasn't even aware of their existence. Not that it mattered. Shapiro would not even have thought to take cover in the oasis if Creaghan hadn't warned him.

Creaghan wouldn't have felt much remorse if something happened to Shapiro, but the American had a lot of good men in his command, soldiers doing their jobs. The question now was whether Shapiro and his legions would make it to the oasis at all. The man had been reluctant to respond to Creaghan's warning. Only his observance of Creaghan's own frantic actions, and those of his men, made Shapiro realize the threat was severe.

Sandstorms were common in the desert. This time of year, it would have been *un*common not to have one now and again. But this . . . this was something else entirely. The Bedouins had screamed at one another in panic as the huge brown cloud marched across the desert.

Shapiro had realized his error, but Creaghan wondered if it was too late. If the storm would arrive before Shapiro and his men could evacuate. Probably it would, at least for a lot of them. The lucky ones would make it to the oasis. The unlucky, according to the Bedouins, might have the flesh scoured from their bones by the driving sand.

Creaghan didn't plan to be unlucky.

The jeep bounced high off a slight rise in the dune, and already the grit swirled in his eyes and stung every exposed surface on his body. His men shouted curses to one another and to the wind, but the sound was lost, sucked away by the mighty storm. Beside them, the jeep that Rickman drove slewed sideways a little, then righted itself and kept rolling. Creaghan was amazed that he couldn't even hear the whine of its engine.

"There!" Agent Culpepper shouted from the passenger seat, and there must have been a lull in the gale, for Creaghan heard him, though only barely. The Captain looked up and saw the drop in the land where the oasis sat. The trees were high enough that they seemed to poke right out of the sand. Then the ground fell away and the entire oasis was spread out in front of them. But something seemed . . .

"We're off course!" Creaghan cried, then began to blare his horn to get Rickman's attention as he corrected for himself.

The jeep took air off the side of the hill and landed

with a jaw-clacking thud, then bounced and kept rolling down the path to the woods around the oasis. Agent Rickman's jeep turned in behind him and Creaghan smiled grimly, clenching his teeth to keep the sand out.

They took air again, just for a moment, and this time the wind whipping down into the oasis from the desert floor got up under them, lifted the jeep just for a second before slapping it back down again. The momentary feeling of weightlessness reminded Creaghan of air turbulence on a plane. But it wasn't something he ever wanted to feel on land again.

The wind slackened a bit. Creaghan slowed the jeep to a crawl, and Rickman did the same behind him. He scanned the hillside to his right, where he knew the caves should be. He squinted in the premature dusk brought by the storm, sand still flying at his face, though not as painfully or in such abundance.

The hillside was spotted here and there with an ugly grey scrub brush, but for the most part, it was dull and featureless sand, earth, and stone. At first, Creaghan didn't see the caves. He blinked several times, and finally, his vision began to resolve the differences between the scrub and the darker spots that were caves. The nearest was less than fifty yards away.

"Let's go!" he called, and his men responded. Further proof that the storm had lessened down in the oasis depression.

Creaghan turned his jeep from the path and it jounced over the rough terrain, every dip in the land or stone in their path a jolt to Creaghan and his men. It didn't matter. Reaching the cave was all that truly concerned him.

The jeep popped up over a small rise, then fell into a

rut. As it shot up and out, Creaghan's head bounced off the steering wheel. His nose was crushed against the wheel hard enough to make his eyes water. Momentarily, he was disoriented, but then they were at the mouth to the first cave. He pulled the jeep to a halt on the steeply angled hillside and prayed for a moment that the vehicle wouldn't simply roll over on him.

When the thought struck him, he realized how extraordinary it was that they had made it across the hillside without one of the jeeps doing precisely that. Creaghan pushed all thoughts of luck and good fortune from his mind, afraid the simple awareness of it might be enough to drive the good luck away.

He leaped from the jeep, sniffed, and ran a hand across his face. He looked down at the back of his hand and saw a deep red streak of his own blood there. His nose was bleeding.

Creaghan smiled and shook his head. He hadn't had a nosebleed since he was six years old. If he survived the chaos that he knew was coming from a number of different directions, and had nothing more severe than a nosebleed, he might actually begin to believe in miracles again. After what he'd seen the past two days, he felt capable of believing in just about anything, given a little push.

"Go! Go! Go!" he shouted.

His men hefted packs of supplies from the jeep and sprinted into the cave. As Rickman and the others from the second jeep did the same, Creaghan grabbed three large canteens from the back of his vehicle, checked to be certain there was nothing else to be had, and followed them all inside.

"Rickman!" he yelled. "Post a watch on the cave mouth

for regular updates on conditions and developments out-side."

Then he surveyed the cave they had chosen. He didn't know what the others looked like, but he felt they'd gotten lucky. It wasn't a large cave, but it would do. The entrance tunnel led perhaps twenty feet back to a small cavern large enough to have held perhaps three or four more people comfortably. As it was, with their supplies, they would have no trouble waiting out the storm inside the cave.

As long as they didn't get trapped inside by some kind of sand-slide.

"Captain!" Agent Rickman cried from the cave mouth. "You've got to see this!"

Creaghan left his men to unpack their supplies and sped back through the short tunnel to stand beside Rickman and peer out of the cave. Only when the sand and wind began to batter his face again did he register what a relief it had been to be out of it.

"What is it?" he asked, scanning.

Rickman merely pointed.

Colonel Shapiro's troops swarmed over the edge of the oasis depression. In jeeps and troop carriers, they bounced down the path toward the tree line, vehicles bearing British, Egyptian, and American flags, as well as the flag of the United Nations.

A tank appeared, its gun turret jutting out over its dark metal body, over the hill's edge, before it tipped forward and slammed down against the hill like an awkward diver doing a belly flop.

"I guess the bloody fool took me seriously after all," Creaghan said quietly.

Some of Shapiro's men were on foot. When they'd arrived, they had had enough room for all the troops aboard vehicles. But Creaghan remembered that a lot of their supplies had been airlifted in. Whatever they took in the trucks had displaced soldiers from the vehicles. The solo men, dozens of them, ran along the edges of the path, weapons at the ready, though Creaghan couldn't have said what they were ready to combat. Bullets wouldn't do a hell of a lot of good against a sandstorm.

He and Rickman watched the progress in silence. Shapiro had more than one thousand men under his command. Less than half that number had made it over, six or seven jeeps, a dozen troop carriers, two tanks.

All the while, the storm worsened. The sky darkened above, and the wind whipped even faster over the edge of the depression. Then it seemed as if there was a lull, which left Creaghan's ears ringing as he realized just how loud the storm had become. And as that thought crossed his mind, the howling gale returned, its strength vastly increased.

A jeep bounded over the edge of the depression, moving too fast. The storm got under the vehicle and shoved it, up and to one side, just enough so that the jeep went over. It tumbled, sideways, down the hill, rolling toward the rest of the convoy. The jeep struck the back of a troop carrier. Several men leaped from the back of the truck, but the jeep's passengers had been killed. The troop carrier moved on.

Another tank crested the hill and began the descent. That was it.

Several men, one after another, dove over the edge of the hill and were driven to the ground by the wind. One of them must have struck a rock, or just hit wrong, for he didn't get up when the others did.

They were the last. Creaghan judged that little more than half of Shapiro's troops had made it into the oasis. He prayed some of the rest found a way to survive the storm out in the open desert.

"Captain, do you see it?" Rickman asked, his voice hushed with awe.

Creaghan glanced back up at the lip of the depression. The storm was there, swirling, darkening with each passing second. The sand in the sky blotted out the late-afternoon sun completely. As it spread across the sky, it would be as if night had fallen. Creaghan only hoped it was over soon.

Even in the cave's mouth, Creaghan could feel the intensity of the storm increase. But there was no question the sunken quality of the oasis was cutting the power of the storm quite a bit. They'd be all right if they just stayed where they were. He wasn't as confident as to the fate of Colonel Shapiro and his men.

Then the storm began to snake tendrils of pounding sand out over the oasis. Like fingers of a giant hand, the tendrils began to whip down into the oasis and out into the air above it. The body of the storm soon followed.

"Do you see it, sir, or is it just me?" Rickman asked plaintively.

Creaghan had thought Agent Rickman just meant the massive concentrated center of the storm. But his tone said there was something else to see. Something Creaghan was missing.

Then he saw it. His testicles drew up tight against his

body and his throat con-
stricted. Up in the dark
brown center of the storm,
where he now believed his
flesh would be scoured
from his bones were he to
be unprotected up on the
surface, Captain Creaghan
saw something which in-
spired terror, bone-deep
and spreading.

In the center of the
storm, high up, were two
oblong shapes that could
only be one thing: eyes.
The storm had eyes, and
it was looking for them.

Creaghan pulled Rick-
man back into the cave
with him.

"I'll take first watch,"
he said. When Rickman appeared about to protest,
Creaghan glared at him until the other man relented.

"Yes, sir," Rickman finally said. "Try to stay out of
sight, sir."

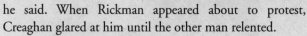 Hellboy hated being carried. It was humiliating.
The pasty-faced mutant runts were like ants run-
ning away with an apple pie in some cartoon, carting him
over their heads with prodigious strength. At least, for

their size. It still took eight or so of them to carry him. And they'd already put him down twice and passed on the burden of his weight to another set of twisted munchkins.

He was fuming.

Somewhere up ahead, the sorcerer walked with Arun, Anastasia, and Carruthers. There were pale, thin humans as

well as the squat amphibian-looking beings, and they were all armed with an assortment of weapons, from spears and clubs to axes and swords. What little he had been able to see of Hazred pretty much gelled with the man's voice: it reeked of power. But thus far, he hadn't shown more than a little magic, parlor tricks, really.

Hellboy wanted to know just what he was up against, but couldn't think of a way to find out without getting his friends killed.

Of course, friends might have been pushing it a bit. Carruthers was hardly his friend, and was not good for much more than violent ravings these days. Arun was better only in that his lunacy seemed to come and go. Lady Catherine was already dead. He could feel her spinal stump squirm against his leg from time to time, and though he had a strong stomach, it made him want to puke.

But Anastasia was another story. Hellboy vowed to himself that no matter what he had to sacrifice, including himself, she would survive this subterranean nightmare.

As their captors descended along a tunnel that corkscrewed down into the Earth, Hellboy could not hold back his curiosity. It was true that he had never put his whole heart into his studies the way his mentor, Professor Bruttenholm, would have liked. But that did not mean he felt nothing when confronted by such an extraordinary mystery.

He wanted to know the secrets of that underground world almost as much as he wanted to shatter Hazred's face with his fist. And that was saying an awful lot.

Hazred barked something at his minions in his guttural language. Hellboy knew he shouldn't be able to understand, but automatically, his mind translated. Just as it had by the lake with those Persian zombie warriors.

"Put the demon down!" he ordered. "Let the next group carry him for now."

Hellboy was jostled hastily and the dwarfish men be-

neath him were so exhausted from bearing him up that they nearly let him fall to the stone floor of the tunnel. Instead, they lowered him gently and with great effort. Throughout his cocooning by the spiders, Hellboy had continued to flex his muscles as tightly as possible. When he relaxed, there was some give to his bonds, but not enough to allow him to escape.

Now, at least fifteen minutes had passed since Hazred had captured them. The web had begun to weaken, perhaps even deteriorating slightly. And Hellboy, of course, had begun to get his strength back after taking such a beating from the spiders.

When his back touched the stone, Hellboy acted. Flexing his muscles as tightly as he was able, straining the webs to their limit, he struggled within the cocoon. It was too tight.

His bearers moved away, and the new crew moved in to pick him up. With them came spear- and sword-wielding men and gnarled halflings. They knew he was trying to escape, but couldn't realize he only wanted freedom from his bonds. And with his mouth webbed, Hellboy could not explain it to them. Not that he'd ever been all that good at explaining things in a fight situation.

Tilting his head forward, he was able to see that they had surrounded the others with weapons as well. Probably they expected Anastasia and Arun to make a break for it, given Hellboy's actions. He prayed they didn't. Now was not the time.

"Come on, you bloody freaks!" Carruthers screamed suddenly. "Come and get some if you want to die so bad! I'll be happy to go with you! Freaks!"

The mad MI5 agent launched a quick elbow at the chest of one of the tall, thin men, then drove his right hand, fingers flat and pointed, into the throat of another. Both men went down. For half a second, Hellboy stared in appreciation. MI5 trained their people better than he'd expected.

Arun and Anastasia fell to their knees, weapons pointed at them from all sides.

"Get back before I . . . ," Carruthers began to order, then shrieked as a spear passed through his right shoulder just under the clavicle.

"No!" Hellboy shouted, but it came out as more of a grunt through the webbing covering his mouth.

With a huge heave, an instinctual burst of strength as he drove both legs and arms out, and spread his back and shoulder muscles as wide as he was able, Hellboy tore himself free of the webbing.

Too late. Carruthers had doubled over in pain. A misshapen half-man buried an axe in the MI5 agent's head. He went down with a wet thud on the stone floor.

"You little son of a bitch!" Hellboy shouted. "Damn you! He was out of his mind, couldn't you tell?"

He waded through Hazred's minions before they were prepared for him, lifted the little man from the ground by the tatters he wore for clothes and slammed his stone fist into his face. At the last second, he pulled his punch. He didn't know what these guys were, or how responsible for their actions they might or might not be.

As far as he could tell, the real trouble was still standing silently a little way down the tunnel, watching it all unfold. As he turned on Hazred, whose eyes seemed to glow green in the shadows cast by the light of his followers' torches, Hellboy was surrounded once more. Spears jabbed his legs and tail, his abdomen and arms. A tall, thin swordsman stepped in and swept his blade around toward Hellboy's head. He put up his right hand and the sword shattered on his fist.

A bald, little pale halfling jabbed him in the ass with a spear. He turned and slapped the weapon away. Bent and poked his finger into the dwarf's face.

"Stop that!" he demanded. Then he turned back toward Hazred. "You're enjoying this, aren't you Hazred, you sick bastard?" he accused. "You could have prevented that."

Why should I have wanted to? he asked telepathically. Apparently, he didn't know that Hellboy could understand his spoken words. Probably a good secret to keep. *You are my prisoner. Are you going to come along, or do I have to kill your other friends as well?*

"I'll come," Hellboy agreed.

For now, he wanted to make sure Anastasia and Arun were okay. But if he saw an opening, he was going to take it. And when that happened, nothing was going to stop him from taking Hazred down as well.

You seem to know my name, demon. What is yours? Hazred asked.

"They call me Hellboy," he answered.

Oh, Hazred said, and smiled thinly. *How diminishing.*

Hellboy muttered under his breath, but said nothing more. He wanted to carry Carruthers' body with them when they set out along the tunnel again, but his guards would not allow it. Instead, he was hurried along until he walked side by side with Arun and Anastasia.

"I hope you have a plan," Anastasia said softly.

"Don't I always?" Hellboy asked.

"Oh, great!" Anastasia sighed, and rolled her eyes.

They continued in that downward spiral for about ten more minutes. After a time, the end of the tunnel began to glow with the same greenish light they had seen from far above, at the bottom of the chasm of the spiders.

"Oh my God," Anastasia said, as they exited the tunnel.

The path they were on continued down, but the tunnel opened up into an extraordinarily large cavern. Inside the cavern, a city. Well, perhaps not a city, due to its size, but

certainly a village. At least a dozen structures, two- and three-stories high, surrounded a massive citadel whose spire scraped the ceiling of the cavern. The outer buildings seemed hewn from stone and finished with iron and wood, while the citadel itself appeared to be constructed entirely of bronze.

In front of the citadel, at the center of the village, was a large pool of water which Hellboy assumed was part of an underground river system. The water rippled outward from the center of the pool, though Hellboy could not see any reason for the surface motion.

The cavern was lit with a bright, eerie, green glow. Bathed in that light, he felt queasy, and noticed Anastasia and Arun seem to react as well. His head hurt slightly, but he shook it off. The light itself emanated from the pool, from deep within the water. Somehow, he realized, all of the underground water system must be infiltrated with that light. Or a portion of it. He had seen it deep underwater when he had dived in the lake, just before battling that creature.

Which made him wonder, momentarily, what had happened to the tablet Arun had been translating. It had been among their things, but he suspected they had lost it on the web. He patted his own belt, found the pouches were apparently still full. Lady Catherine's head remained in its sack, and thankfully had stopped trying to move.

His gun was gone. He had used it against the spiders and lost it then, he realized. Of course, it wouldn't have done him a whole lot of good against so numerous an enemy, but he had grown used to carrying the weapon for backup.

The captives were marched down the stone path to the edge of the village.

"Hellboy, look," Anastasia said in a low voice. "People."

He almost asked what she meant. Clearly the tall, thin, white guys and their dwarfish kin were people, at least of some sort. Then he saw what she was referring to, and was as surprised as she seemed to be. These were, indeed, people. Paler than anyone else in Egypt, he was certain, but more definably human than any of the be-

ings they had encountered thus far. For starters, they had hair.

"Excellent," Arun said, as the people of the village approached. "Please, all of you, listen to reason. We're nothing but explorers, scientists, academics . . . we've done nothing to you. If you'll just return us to the surface you'll see that . . ."

A black-haired woman in the lead slapped Arun hard across the face, and he stared at her in astonishment. The look was almost comical, and Hellboy had to stifle a laugh at the absurdity of it all. The dwarfish creatures retreated back up the stone path to the tunnel and into other tunnels which appeared to branch out of the main village cavern.

As they passed through the village, he was amazed at how . . . well, normal it seemed. These people lived and worked down here. They were self-sufficient, at least with the help of their leader and resident magician. It was some kind of horrible society, with their twisted, tunnel-dwelling brethren surviving on the outskirts of the community. Eating their table scraps, Hellboy thought with disdain.

He saw women cradling what appeared to be infants. Some of them seemed more normal than others, and he realized that they all came from the same source, all the underground dwellers from the same race.

When Hellboy looked forward once more, Hazred had gone.

"Now where the heck did he disappear to?" he murmured aloud.

In the sack on his hip, the head of Lady Catherine Lambert began to scream.

Human guards rushed in and tried to take the canvas bag from his side, but Hellboy shoved them away, ignoring their swords and spears. He tore open the bag and pulled Lady Catherine out by her hair.

"What is it, Lady Catherine?" he asked anxiously. "What's wrong?"

Now, he wanted to add. *What's wrong now?* But he was pretty sure his point would be lost on her in her current condition.

"I remember!" she wailed. "I remember it all now! And I see through the shroud of life, I see what is to come! You must flee! All of you must flee as quickly as you can. Mar-Ti-Ku is coming, Hellboy, and you are the instrument of his resurrection."

"Me?" Hellboy asked, stunned.

CHAPTER THIRTEEN

"Flee, now, as quickly as you can!" the head of Lady Catherine Lambert cried. "Beware the jackal, and flee. Beware the jackal, and escape Mar-Ti-Ku!"

Hellboy almost told her the advice was a little late in coming, but he figured Lady Catherine had her own problems.

"What jackal?" he asked. "And what about Hazred? I thought he was the bad guy here. But he's gone."

"Hazred has gone to raise the army. He will return, a sacrifice will be made, and Mar-Ti-Ku will invade our . . . your plane of existence. Your only hope is to flee before Hazred can use you! Beware the jackal!"

The head was screaming, its ravaged face streaming blood and still managing to look terrified.

"What jackal?" Hellboy asked again, frustrated. "What army?"

"The lost army!" Lady Catherine shrieked, her voice rising until Hellboy wanted to cover his ears, but he couldn't do that without bringing the screaming head closer to him.

Then she was gone again, the head lifeless. Still, the mouth was stretched in a rictus of terror. In that moment, Hellboy realized that he hated oracles. They always gave just enough information to create fear and paranoia, but not enough to do anything constructive. With a sigh, he dumped her head back into the bag.

The sandstorm raged across the desert, its winds more powerful than any natural storm the Sahara had ever seen. In truth, the last time such a storm had carved itself across the face of Egypt had been two thousand years earlier.

Now the dunes themselves were being reshaped. All traces of the camps set up by Anastasia Bransfield, Captain Creaghan, or Colonel Shapiro were erased from the world, buried or sucked away forever into the maelstrom above.

Beneath the sand, for miles around the oasis of Ammon, something stirred. Under the very spot where Hellboy had first landed, under the camp from which Lady Catherine and her co-workers had been abducted, the lifeless forms of men who had died millennia past now drove their preserved limbs, pistoning themselves, clawing, crawling, scrabbling to the surface.

From the shroud of mystery and mythology which had buried them so long ago, fifty thousand men returned to a terrible un-life. They dragged themselves from the sand, the lost army of Cambyses.

And now they followed a new commander.

As Hellboy began to tie the bag containing Lady Catherine's head to his belt, two guards moved in and reached for it.

"You want this?" he snapped, and held out the bag to

them. "You can have it! But be careful she doesn't rip your throat out when she gets angry!"

He was pretty sure the cavern people didn't speak English, but they got at least the gist of what he said. Or maybe they were merely frightened of him. For when he went to tie the sack to his belt again, nobody tried to stop him.

"Well, that sounded bloody dismal," Anastasia said grimly. "What do you suppose it was all about?"

"I don't have any better idea than you do," he answered. "Jackals and armies and I'm the key to Mar-Ti-Ku's invasion plans. I just don't know."

They were being led past the lake now, and suddenly the procession stopped. They stood in front of a stone platform that appeared to be a stage of some kind, with a huge block of granite at the center. An altar, was Hellboy's first guess. Had to be.

No one spoke. No one approached them. In fact, the cavern people acted as if they weren't even there.

"I guess we're waiting for Hazred to come back," he said idly.

"I wish we hadn't had to leave those poor men back in the tunnels," Anastasia commented. "With the spiders and all."

"Yeah, but at least they're better off than Meaney," Hellboy noted, and saw Anastasia shiver. Throughout the exchange, Arun said nothing. He only stared at the glowing green surface of the lake with a slowly spreading grin.

"So any idea on this jackal stuff, or the army?" Hellboy asked, wondering whether he should attempt to break them all out of there before Hazred came back. Wondering if they'd have a chance of surviving.

"Well, she said the 'lost army,'" Anastasia answered, as if that explained it all. And, after a moment, Hellboy realized it did.

"Oh, jeez," he whispered. "Hey, Arun, how many soldiers did Cambyses lose in the . . ."

But Arun wasn't listening. Just as Hellboy turned to ask his question, the historian lunged past him, clawing

at Anastasia's face and breasts. He knocked off her baseball cap during his attack. Saliva poured from his mouth as if he were rabid.

"What the . . . ," Hellboy began, reaching to pull him off 'Stasia. He grabbed Arun's shoulder and spun him around. Arun growled, teeth bared like an animal and swiped at Hellboy with his fingers as if he had claws with which to tear flesh. His hand scraped harmlessly across Hellboy's chest. For a moment, Hellboy just stared at him in bewilderment.

"You've got some serious problems, Professor," he said finally.

Arun lunged for his throat, and Hellboy grabbed both his arms and held him in the air. Arun's feet dangled a foot from the ground and the professor gnashed his teeth, foam sliding down his chin. Around them, the guards retreated to a respectful distance, like children in a schoolyard making room for a fight and all jockeying for a decent view.

With Arun thrashing in his grasp, Hellboy looked up at Anastasia and frowned.

"What the hell do I do with him now?" he asked.

"Don't look at me, love," she said, straightening her clothes and then fitting her baseball cap tightly on her head. "The man needs treatment, but first we've got to get out of here."

Hellboy got his face up close to Arun's and stared at the man's red, lunatic eyes.

"Arun!" he shouted. "Arun! Listen to me! If you want to live, you've got to calm down! We can't watch out for you and figure out . . ."

Professor Lahiri lunged forward and bit Hellboy hard on the nose.

"Damn!" Hellboy yelled, and let the man go.

Arun dropped to the ground and immediately set upon Anastasia again. This time, she was ready for him. As Hellboy watched, Arun reached for her and Anastasia grabbed her friend's arm and used his own momentum to carry him over. She flipped him onto his back on the stone cavern floor, where he landed with an audible crack.

The madman groaned, but while in the past, such a blow might have snapped him back to normal, this time it only served to drive him further over the edge.

"Filthy slut!" Arun screamed as he crawled painfully to his knees. "Filthy slut, you'll die for that! I'll have you before or after, it makes no difference to me! But you've got to die after you've been defiled by that . . . that hell spawn!"

"Listen, you fruit loop," Hellboy shouted. "If your brain hadn't gone to the Bahamas, I'd pop your head off like you were a Pez dispenser. Now you'd best back off right now, before I start to get *really* aggravated."

Arun, of course, didn't listen. Not that Hellboy had expected him to. The once-mild professor roared like a savage animal and launched himself at Hellboy again. Hellboy cocked back his right arm and slapped Arun hard across the face with his stone hand, as if the man were merely hysterical rather than deranged. Well, Hellboy thought, maybe it was a little harder than that. Arun stretched back and up, as if he were standing on tiptoe, or perhaps an inch or so above the ground, then fell on his back on the cavern floor.

"Don't get up," Hellboy growled.

Arun sat up, obviously disoriented, and shook his head. Hellboy braced himself for another attack. He worried that he might have to do the man serious harm to get him to stop attacking. But if Arun came at him again, the man was going to end up unconscious. Injury be damned.

Foam bubbled from Arun's mouth, and a trickle of blood flowed through it, striping his chin. He scrambled to his feet. Hellboy prepared to knock him out.

Someone shouted in that guttural language of the cavern people, and Hellboy understood the words, "Restrain him." The village swordsmen grabbed at Arun's arms, and he tossed two of them away before four or five got a good hold of him and wrestled him to the ground where he struggled, drooling and babbling like a maniac.

"Your fault!" he sneered at Anastasia. "Your fault, you slut!"

Hellboy looked at her, to see if her eyes still reflected the hurt he'd seen in them when Arun had spoken that way earlier. They did not. Anastasia was a woman of power and confidence. Once she was over the shock of his initial attack, he knew, her anger and outrage would have turned to concern.

Well, maybe the anger was still there. She did look a little pissed. He recognized the way her nostrils flared when she was angry. Even if she'd painted a smile on her face, he always knew when she was angry.

"'Stasia," he began. "Are you all right? We've got to find a way . . ."

She narrowed her eyes and shook her head. It took him a moment to realize why she was shushing him. The guards had been commanded by a voice he had heard before. Even as he turned, he knew that the sorcerer Hazred had reappeared.

Hellboy stood a few feet from the gently rippling surface of the green-glowing pool. Slowly, he turned to face the sorcerer. Anastasia stepped to his side, and Hellboy was surprised that the guards did not move to stop her. In truth, he'd been expecting harsher treatment in general from the guards. Not that he minded, of course. But they seemed reluctant to bully their prisoners or to crowd them, other than to hold them prisoner.

Standing there, amidst homes of stone and iron, Hellboy felt even more strongly that the pool was the center of the village, rather than the cathedral, or whatever it was, that loomed just ahead of them. But the cathedral was a sight, no question about that. Its brass surface extended to the smallest detail, from window panes to the long flight of stairs

that led from the altar in front of the shimmering pool up
to the enormous double front doors of the building.

Hazred stood there, on a landing halfway up those
bronze stairs. He wore fresh robes, and even these seemed

woven from gold or per-
haps bronze, themselves.
It took Hellboy a moment
to realize that bronze and
iron might be the only
metals the strange under-
ground tribes knew how
to make. Particularly if
they had lived and bred—
crossbred really—down
there for as long as he believed.

Blue veins pulsing in
the sickly green-white
flesh of his forehead and
cheeks, Hazred stared at
his prisoners for a mo-
ment. Hellboy scowled.

The man disgusted him. Then Hazred began to smile, the
expression beginning at his wide, wild eyes and spreading
slowly across his face.

Ah, my guests, his false-friendly, slitheringly sinister
voice whispered in Hellboy's mind. From the way they
looked up, he supposed Hazred was speaking to Anastasia
and Arun as well.

"Guests?" Anastasia said in astonishment. "That's funny
as a bloody heart attack, that is. Is this how you treat all your

guests, mister wizard? 'Cause if so, I'll bet you don't get too many people visiting a second time."

Hazred's smile only grew broader.

We have never had "guests" before, so the question would appear to be moot, Hazred whispered in their heads, as he began to descend from his citadel down the forty or so steps to the cavern floor. *We've only ever had prisoners before, and no, none of them has ever returned. Primarily because none of them ever left alive.*

"So why are we your first guests?" Hellboy asked, doubtful. "I noticed your guards weren't all that pushy, so what's to stop us from just leaving?"

Hazred raised his right hand, only slightly, and the guards tightened their circle.

Perhaps guests was the wrong word, then, the sorcerer sent telepathically, and his smile grew impossibly wide. Then the smile disappeared. *I hope you'll forgive my brief absence. The preparations for Mar-Ti-Ku's return are proceeding apace, and your soldier friends have begun to take refuge from the sandstorm. In defense of our little village, I have called up our own army to combat them,* Hazred thought, still not speaking aloud, assuming neither Hellboy nor Anastasia could understand his spoken word. But Hellboy could. He hoped that was his ace in the hole.

"But it isn't really your army at all, is it, you ugly, albino son of a bitch?" Anastasia said angrily, arms crossed in defiance as Hazred continued to descend.

The sorcerer didn't pause. He merely smiled, wider than before, so that his face became a horrible rictus, almost a death grin. There was something dark in his mouth, and Hellboy didn't want to think about what it might be. But

there was also something bright that reflected the green light
from the pool.

Ah, so you know of Cambyses' folly. Excellent, the sorcerer
commended them. *Let me tell you the story then. Our story.
The tale of the people of Mar-Ti-Ku.*

*We lived around the oasis, above ground, for centuries. A
happy people, growing fruit and breeding fish, scavenging the
desert. But I was not satisfied. I left Ammon to travel the Earth,
to discover all that I had never known. Yet I found that was not
enough.*

*I wanted to know those dark and horrible things that human-
ity refused to see or believe. I sought all manner of arcane
knowledge. Thus I learned of the ancient Sumerian magician,
Mar-Ti-Ku, one of the most powerful men who ever breathed
the air of Gaea. It is said that Mar-Ti-Ku, in a jealous rage
over an unrequited love, sank Atlantis to the bottom of the sea.
Whether that sea was in our dimension or another is a subject
of much debate amongst my people.*

Mar-Ti-Ku himself will not discuss it.

*A great council of magicians banded together out of envy
and banished Mar-Ti-Ku from our plane. But he still exists,
on the other side of the veil, the oh-so-thin veil. I summoned
his voice to speak with me; his eyes burned into mine from the
wind itself, and from that moment forth, I was his servant,
dedicated to returning him to this plane, where he will rule
unto eternity.*

*Mar-Ti-Ku granted me immortality. For during his time in
exile, he has become like unto the Elder Ones themselves.*

*When I returned to the oasis, my people welcomed me
warmly. Time had not been kind to them. There was a blight
on their gardens, a sickness among them. I promised them*

blessing upon blessing if they would swear allegiance to Mar-Ti-Ku. This they did.

That was five hundred, sixty-seven years before the birth of the prophet you call Christ. Forty-two years later we received a visitor, a representative of the Persian general Cambyses, the self-styled conqueror of Egypt.

Heh. As if any one man could rule Egypt, when Mar-Ti-Ku will rule the world.

We spurned this visitor. I tore his tongue from his mouth with iron tongs and sent him back to his master. Not long after, Cambyses sent his army across the desert to punish us, to destroy all those communities which remained in opposition to him. Fifty thousand men marched toward our little oasis village. There might have been five hundred of us, all told.

But Mar-Ti-Ku knew of their coming. Among them, he suspected, there might be one who would serve as a suitable vessel for him, a body he could inhabit upon crossing between the planes. For his own physical form had been destroyed millennia earlier. "Of fifty thousand," he said to me, "surely one of them must be powerful enough to contain my essence."

When the army was but miles from the oasis, I followed Mar-Ti-Ku's instructions, and called the storm. A sandstorm as had never been seen before, nor since. Until today, of course. The day when Mar-Ti-Ku will finally return.

The army of Cambyses was utterly destroyed, save for seventeen men, who made it to the oasis and survived. These hearty souls became a part of our tribe, and their descendants are still with us today. All but the strongest among them, who was my master's intended host.

Unfortunately, when it came time for Mar-Ti-Ku to enter the host, the man did not survive the ritual. Thus, Mar-Ti-Ku

has waited. We, his acolytes, have waited. Our half-brothers of
the shadows wait in the tunnels, and we become less human
with every century that passes. But Mar-Ti-Ku shall heal us all
and lead us to grace and glory, to master the world.

Now the storm has returned. The army rises at my command.
Just as their bones have been in the unyielding clutch of the
desert sands for all these two and one-half thousand years, so
have I held their souls in my own fierce grasp. They are enslaved,
a powerful weapon, yet forever they suffer the punishment for
Cambyses' audacity.

Weeks ago, when the first humans discovered the entrance to
our underground village, where we fled at Mar-Ti-Ku's instruc-
tion after Cambyses' failed attack, we captured them, hoping
one of them might be powerful enough to contain my master's
essence. They were not. Thus, they were slaughtered as a warn-
ing, or a lure. We assumed only the truly powerful and courageous
would ignore the warning. We were correct.

The sorcerer finally reached the bottom of the stone stairs.
He paused a moment in his tale, and smiled once more,
amiably, at Hellboy and Anastasia. He did not even look at
Arun.

Hellboy stared at Hazred's mouth. Could not look away.
Though the man's robes were majestic, his beard pointed to
perfection, his flesh like the finest marble and his eyes clear
and cold, his mouth . . . Hellboy turned away. Hazred was
regal, magnificently evil, commanding in every way. Almost
beautiful. But his mouth reflected his true nature. When he
smiled, he instilled only pure revulsion. Most of his teeth
were green and crumbling with rot, save for six or seven
which had been replaced with sharply pointed bronze fangs,
embedded in his gums.

When Hazred approached, the guards parting before him as if polarized, Hellboy could not suppress a shiver. He was not afraid of Hazred, unless it was for Anastasia's safety. Rather, he was profoundly disturbed that such a man could live for so long and be so unrepentantly evil.

Mar-Ti-Ku will rejoice, Hellboy, Hazred said, and stopped before him. The man was taller even than he had first appeared, as tall as Hellboy almost. He reached out a hand and lightly stroked Hellboy's cheek with his fingers. Hellboy slapped the hand away and offered a silent snarl in return.

Hazred stopped smiling, his expression murderous. He glanced down and his eyes widened slightly. He had noticed Hellboy's stone hand, of course, perhaps for the first time.

"Can it be?" Hazred said, in that guttural tongue he could not have known that Hellboy understood. "The master will be more powerful even than he dreamed. He will unmake the world with the clenching of his fist."

Hellboy's eyes narrowed.

"What kind of crap is that?" he said. "What the hell are you babbling about?"

Hazred's eyes widened. Hellboy could almost see his mind working, considering whether he had understood the sorcerer's words, or simply objected to his lack of understanding.

We wanted to lure the best specimen we could for Mar-Ti-Ku's vessel of return, Hellboy. But I would never have hoped that one so powerful, so perfectly indestructible as you, would happen upon our home. Mar-Ti-Ku is ecstatic. As we are, in anticipation of his return. Even now, he is the storm, drives the

storm, makes war on the army on the desert sands, with the
desert sands. And I have raised the Persian dead to aid him.

"Hellboy, are you paying attention?" Anastasia asked
behind him. "He wants to . . ."

"Wait!" Hellboy said, stepping forward and glaring at
Hazred. "Let me get this straight. You want to evict me
from my body so this Marty guy can have a place to live
when he comes home?"

Indeed.

"And you talk to him pretty regularly?"

Yes.

"Then give him a message for me, will you?" Hellboy
asked. "Tell him I said, 'No vacancy!'"

Hellboy struck out at Hazred with his left hand, momentarily forgetting his circumstances, forgetting the danger to Anastasia and Arun. Not that it mattered, for his
blow never fell. Hazred lifted his hands, palms flat, and
Hellboy's fist slammed into some kind of invisible wall,
or force shield that protected the sorcerer. It returned
the force of the punch to Hellboy, and under the pressure

of his own attack, he
stumbled back three
steps, and nearly fell to
his knees.

He felt his temper
rising, felt the edges of
his resistance crum-
bling, giving way to the
rage and the frustration.
Hellboy prepared to
attack again. His tail

curled behind him in an unconscious expression of his fury.

Anastasia screamed.

Hellboy spun, his hooves clicking on the stone cavern floor, and then he froze. One of the tall, thin, mutant men held her left arm, a more normal but muscular woman held her right arm, and a third figure stood behind her with a curved, gleaming iron blade snug against her throat.

The anger drained from him instantly.

You are guests as long as you behave like guests, Hazred said in his mind, all of their minds, Hellboy figured.

For a moment, he considered going after the guards, taking the risk. But he couldn't. Hellboy relaxed and stepped back slightly.

"What about him?" Hellboy asked, and gestured toward Arun, who was still trapped beneath the weight of several guards. At second glance, the professor appeared to be sleeping.

He is beyond our control. Your companion has begun a journey he must yet complete. But I will gladly help him.

Hazred approached Arun and without being told, the guards lifted the professor into a standing position. Angry and bleary-eyed, Arun growled at the sorcerer and strained against his captors' hold.

With a sudden thrust, Hazred dug his fist into Arun's pants pocket, and withdrew some kind of medallion on a chain that Hellboy had never seen before. He glanced at Anastasia. She caught his look and shrugged, raised her eyebrows, to tell him she did not recognize it either.

Foolish man, Hazred told Arun, and they all heard his

mental communication. *The Primal Heart is a powerful charm, one of my own creation. It was left very purposefully to be found. But I credited modern man with too much sense. I expected its discoverer to wear it as such a medallion must be worn—around the neck. Already your darkest desires and emotions have surged forth, but without wearing the medallion properly, your physical form cannot comply with those desires.*

Arun seemed disoriented. Hazred dangled the medallion in front of him, then slowly slid the chain down over the professor's head. The air was charged with crackling menace, and Hellboy knew their situation was about to get worse. What was the medallion, he wondered? What did it mean?

The medallion hung against Arun's chest, harmless. Then Hazred snaked out a long, bony finger and tapped it twice, almost as if he were trying gently to wake a sleeper.

Screeching wildly and clawing at his face, Arun fell to his knees. The professor wailed in great, heaving sobs like a terrified child and began to hyperventilate. He lay on the ground, rolling back and forth over the cold stone. There was the sudden stench of urine and a stain spread across the small man's pants.

"What the hell did you do to him?" Hellboy demanded.

I have done nothing. Your friend is altering himself.

"Altering . . ."

"Hellboy?" Anastasia said. Her tone drew his immediate attention. He glanced at her, then down at Arun.

Who was changing.

CHAPTER FOURTEEN

T he tanks had bulldozed a path through the oasis forest and were quickly fortunate enough to come
upon a large clearing. The trees looked odd, but hell,
Colonel Shapiro had thought, what didn't in this godforsaken storm?

Once within that clearing, they were safely ensconced
within the trees around the oasis and down as far as they
could get from the desert floor above. The Colonel ordered all the vehicles that had survived the treacherous
journey over shattered trees to form a circle, "Like in old
John Wayne westerns," he'd explained.

Fifteen minutes later, the storm raging around them
where the soldiers clung to one another, to the ground, to
trees and to their vehicles, the Colonel called his aide to
his side.

"How many did we lose?" he asked, forced to shout to
be heard over the wind. Unable to look at the man more
than a moment or risk losing his retinas to the driving
sand.

"We won't know 'til it's over, sir," the aide said. "But I'd
guess about three hundred, maybe more."

The Colonel swore. Then he paused in contemplation.

"How many Americans?" he asked, and it was clear to

both of them that this was the real question, the only one that mattered.

"Near a hundred, sir," the aide admitted.

"Goddamn!" Colonel Shapiro roared. "How the hell can I write condolence letters to the parents of a hundred men?"

He glanced up quickly, searching for answers in the eyes of his aide, a man who'd been with him for fifteen years, loyal all the way. The aide looked back, squinting against the sand.

"Frankly, Jack," he said, "I just pray we live to write them."

Captain Creaghan had the first watch, and it was wearing on him. He could only poke his head out of the cave every couple of minutes in order to avoid the direct impact of the storm. Even then, there was very little he could see. It was hell, though; he knew that much. He could barely see the oasis itself.

Well, perhaps that was a bit of an exaggeration. He couldn't see details, but he had seen the tanks crashing through the forest. Knew that there were hundreds of men down there, trying to hide from the storm by ducking their heads and hoping it wouldn't see them.

But that wasn't going to work, Creaghan knew. It wasn't going to work because the storm *could* see. The storm had eyes. Every time he glanced out of the cave, he looked up to make sure they were still there. They'd never gone away. Like burning embers, comets at the center of the storm, the eyes stared down upon the oasis, searching for the most vulnerable spots, Creaghan imagined. Every so often, a weird and terrible thunder boomed, rolling across the sky.

It sounded like laughter. He wondered if sandstorms actually had thunder, and then realized he didn't want to know the answer. As far as he was concerned, it was thunder. He also vowed that, should he and his men survive the storm, and whatever hid within it, preying on the soldiers in the oasis, he would never come within a thousand miles of Hellboy again.

Never again. This shit followed him, and Creaghan didn't want any part of it.

When Culpepper came forward to relieve him, Creaghan couldn't have been happier. He didn't know if he would be able to sleep without seeing the sandstorm's eyes glaring down at him, but he wanted to try. Anything to escape the manic howling of the wind outside, and the horrible scream that it seemed to become as it whipped down the tunnel behind them.

"Second watch, sir!" Culpepper shouted in his ear, sand whipping into the cave entrance and piling up on the floor of the tunnel.

"About bloody time!" Creaghan replied. "I'll send Rickman up in an hour! That's about all anyone could take!"

Creaghan half-stumbled down the tunnel toward the larger cave at the end where the rest of his men were sprawled on the ground, doing their best to rest. Probably trying not to think about how they were going to survive until a search-and-rescue team showed up looking for them tomorrow. Or the next day.

"Captain!" Culpepper cried from the cave mouth.

Creaghan stopped in his tracks.

"What the hell is it now?" he called back.

"You'd better have a look at this, sir!" Culpepper shouted. "And hurry!"

Normally, Creaghan would have bristled at Culpepper, a man in his command, and a newer agent at that, telling him to hurry. But there was some indefinable quality in the man's tone, fear verging on outright panic, that brought him running. Several of the others must have had the same reaction, because Creaghan could hear them shouting and pounding up the tunnel after him.

He reached the cave mouth a second before Rickman and two others. Culpepper was wide-eyed with barely suppressed terror. Rickman had promised to warn all the men about the eyes in the storm, so Creaghan knew that wasn't what had so frightened Will Culpepper.

"Well, what is it, man?" Creaghan asked. "What do you see?"

"People, sir," he answered. "A lot of people. What are they doing here, Captain? How can they stand it out there?"

Creaghan shoved past him and poked his head from the cave. He scanned the oasis, assuming Culpepper had seen straggling soldiers come tumbling in, barely alive. He realized they would have to help those men if possible, bring them to the cave, whatever it . . .

He saw no one.

"What are you talking about, Will?" Creaghan asked. "I don't see any . . ."

"Up there, sir. On the rim."

Culpepper pointed up, toward the nearest visible edge of the oasis. But he didn't stop there. His hand swept a horizontal arc across the mouth of the cave, showing Creaghan that he meant not merely the hillside closest to them, but the entire circumference of the oasis.

Creaghan peered into the storm, squinting, trying his best to see what Culpepper was talking about. He wondered if the man had simply lost his senses, and realized he wouldn't have blamed the lad if he did.

Then he did see something. Some indefinable shape, up on the rim. Maybe some of Colonel Shapiro's men had survived, against all odds, the erosive power of the storm. If so, they would need help, and fast.

Creaghan took several steps out of the cave, peering up at the rim, trying to get a better look. There was a sudden lull, and a shape began to assert itself on the edge. Not just one shape, but several. A dozen.

More.

They stood still, straight and tall on the edge of the oasis basin. They were side by side, and it was clear, squinting through the painful, flying sand, that many of these figures carried weapons. They did not sway in the gale. They did not move at all.

More than a dozen. The lull continued, as if the storm incarnate, whatever it was that stared down at them even now from the homicidal skies, had taken a breath.

More than a dozen. Or two. More than one hundred.

Or two. More than one thousand.

Or two.

Side by side they stood, as far as the eye could see. Creaghan expected it was for the entire circumference of the oasis basin, several miles at his guess, all the way around.

Thousands upon thousands of warriors, unharmed by the sandstorm, standing as if paralyzed, weapons drawn, at the edge of the oasis. Waiting. Creaghan recalled the melee on the beach, Hellboy under attack by soldiers dead more than two thousand years. A handful of dead men fighting as if they had never died.

He looked back at the line of warriors surrounding the oasis. Then, without even being aware of it, he did something he had not done since he was six years old in a pew in the Church of England. Captain Michael Creaghan crossed himself.

Thunder rolled across the desert. Or more than thunder. A command, perhaps?

The lost army began its descent into the oasis.

"Oh my God," Anastasia gasped.

Hellboy said nothing, merely stood and stared at Arun's metamorphosis. Hazred smiled his awful, rotting grin and stepped away, the circle of guards closing behind him.

Arun changed.

His nose and mouth grew closer together, the nose shrinking, blackening. As if it had been crushed in a vise, his head fell in on itself. His forehead came down and his chin disappeared as his face thrust forward into a long, razor-toothed snout.

When his ears disappeared, only to be replaced by two pointed, brown-furred things, pink inside, which thrust up out of his hair, Anastasia screamed. It had taken several moments for her to realize that it was all real. She was terrified for Arun and for herself, disgusted and fascinated simultaneously.

Anastasia was still captive, her arms pinioned behind her back by two guards, while a third held a curved blade to her throat. She didn't want to die, but that wasn't their plan, she knew. They merely wanted to use her to control Hellboy. She wasn't going to let that happen, but first things first.

"Hellboy, can't you do something for him?" she asked.

He turned toward her, the green glow of the pool reflecting eerily off his scarlet flesh. Then he turned his head slightly to the left and gave her a small, apologetic shrug.

Arun began to howl. A terrible, mournful cry that erupted from his snapping jaws the way brown fur seemed to erupt from his body. It was that horrible cry more than his appearance which made her realize what he had become.

The jackal. Just as Lady Catherine had warned. The Egyptians called it "the howler" because of its cry. For the most part, jackals were scavengers, eating dead animals

they found. But wild? Rabid? It was a vicious beast, almost a cross between fox and hound, but sleeker. More dangerous.

The jackal-man glared at Hellboy with yellow eyes. It yapped angrily, then used its powerful hind legs to launch itself across the cavern toward him.

"No!" Anastasia cried. "Hellboy, please, you've got to find some way to stop him without killing him." But she didn't hold out much hope. The cavern people watched Arun's change and the impending conflict with amusement. This was entertainment to them.

Arun landed on top of Hellboy, slavering jaws snapping, thrusting toward his throat.

"Well, boys, what do we do? I'm leaving it up to you," Creaghan declared. "If we stay here, in the cave, we might be sitting ducks or we might just survive the whole thing. We lie down, quiet as a mouse, they might never know we're here."

He scanned the small cave quickly, meeting each man's eyes.

"Quickly now, we don't have time for much consideration," he urged. "Any minute, those dead soldiers will reach this cave. Maybe they'll come in, and maybe they won't. But it will take away our choice as to whether we help Shapiro and his men or not."

One by one, the men glanced at Agent Rickman, obviously expecting him to speak for them. After a moment, Rickman lifted his head and stared at Creaghan.

"I don't want to die, Captain," he said. "Neither do the rest of us, I suppose. But there are British soldiers down there, sir. The Americans and Egyptians deserve saving too, I guess, but if I sat back and let British soldiers die without trying to warn them, I don't think I could ever look in the mirror again."

Creaghan studied his men. They all nodded, some mumbling encouragement.

"It's unanimous then?" he asked.

"It may be suicide," a man named Baker replied, "but it's unanimous all right."

Culpepper's boots slapped the tunnel floor as he ran down toward them, toward the cave. "Sir! We have maybe a minute, probably less, and those soldiers will be upon us. If we're going, we have to go now!" he cried.

Creaghan saw the fear and desperation in Culpepper's eyes, and wondered with great interest if his men could see the fear in his own.

"Let's go, then," he said. "Let's do it."

Without any further signal, the seven MI5 agents followed their Captain out through the tunnel and onto the open hillside. The sandstorm whipped around them and Creaghan couldn't imagine what it must be like on the open desert. On the other hand, he thought, the open desert might have been preferable to their current location.

He turned and glanced up the hill. No more than one hundred yards away, the line of dead soldiers continued their descent. Flesh hung in ribbons from their bones, flayed by the sandstorm and by time, perhaps from a ghoulish resurrection that even now Creaghan began to picture in his head. He dismissed those thoughts.

"Captain!" someone cried in the storm.

Creaghan squinted, peering through the veil of flying sand.

"We got lucky!" Agent Rickman shouted to him.

He was standing by one of the jeeps. Both of the vehicles stood where they had been left. Creaghan knew they were lucky indeed. He'd thought for sure that, parked at an angle on the hillside, the jeeps would have long since been blown over and rolled down into the oasis.

"Let's not waste our good fortune!" he called.

As quickly as they could, Creaghan and his men climbed into the jeeps. As he pointed his jeep's nose down toward the oasis, Creaghan worried momentarily that they might get lost in the storm and drive into an open cave mouth. But there was nothing to be done for it.

Behind them, the army quickened its pace. The dead were on the march.

The jackal-man that had once been Arun Lahiri, professor of history, drove its snout again and again at Hellboy's throat. He held the beast back, but only barely. While Arun had been a small man, of little strength, the jackal was phenomenally strong. It had knocked Hellboy down without any problem, put him on the defensive in an instant.

But it was time to turn the tables. Hellboy solidified his grip on the jackal-man's throat, pushed it back, and slammed his stone fist into its face. There was a crack, a noise Hellboy recognized from experience as the sound of bone breaking. Though he was fighting a creature that had been a friend not long ago, though Anastasia had pleaded with him not to harm Arun, he could not help but feel a sense of satisfaction at that sound.

The jackal whimpered and staggered back on its deformed hind legs. It was not a man, not a jackal. It was nothing nature had ever intended to exist. A tiny, niggling thought wormed its way into Hellboy's brain, a thought which threatened to compare him to the jackal-man. He denied it. The jackal-man was savage. Hellboy was, if nothing else, civilized.

When the jackal came at him again, Hellboy was ready. His own tail bobbed as he dodged to one side and brought his left hand down on the yapping creature's head again. The broken bones in the jackal's face must have grated together painfully, for it cried out in agony and despair.

"Hellboy, please!" Anastasia cried.

There was so much distress in her voice, that he turned to face her.

"I'm trying," he said. "But it's not like this fight was my idea!"

Even as he turned, he discovered that the jackal had recovered more rapidly than he expected. Its teeth clamped onto his left arm, tearing flesh but not sinking too deeply. Times like this, he thought, almost made up for having leathery red hide for skin.

With his stone hand, he gripped the jackal around its neck. He couldn't pry its jaws apart just with one hand, but he could choke it until it had to let go. His fingers tightened, and the strength of its bite lessened.

"Back off, Fido!" he roared.

The jackal let go, and Hellboy tossed it toward a group of cavern people gathered around to watch the spectacle as if it were their own Roman forum. In a way, he supposed it was. But he'd be damned if he was going to be put on display like some sideshow attraction. He wasn't about to perform for Hazred's subterranean freak show.

The cavern people scattered as the jackal got to its feet once more.

"Down, boy!" Hellboy snapped, then sighed. "There's never a rolled-up newspaper around when you need one."

He crouched low, his hooves wide apart, preparing for the jackal's latest attack. The only hope he could see that he might stop Arun without killing him was to cut off the jackal-man's air supply just enough to knock him unconscious.

But the jackal was faster than it looked. Hellboy heard Hazred laughing both in his head, and in the cavern. The mocking sounds echoed in the vast underground complex. Then the jackal slammed into his legs and lower torso, and Hellboy felt himself going over once more.

"Damn!" he cursed as he fell backwards, the jackal on top of him, snapping and yapping once more.

He braced himself to hit the stone floor. But did not. Hellboy fell past the level of the cavern floor. The green light flared around him and he knew, then, what had happened.

A fraction of a second before they hit the water, Hellboy inhaled.

The green-tinted pool slapped his back hard, and water shot up on either side of them as they splashed down. Hellboy hadn't gotten much of a breath, but he held out the small hope that the jackal might have gotten even less.

The tablet Hellboy had found in the oasis lake tumbled from inside the linen shirt the jackal-man still wore. Nine inches high and four wide, it was heavier than it looked, but it fell slowly through the water, end over end, until it came to rest at the bottom of the pool. Hellboy saw it, but could not have gone after it even if he had wanted to.

As they struggled, Hellboy could see a warren of tunnels under water, leading away from the pool. One even seemed to go up, and that was where the green light actually emanated from. It was nearly blinding in its brightness when he stared directly at it.

He blinked.

The jackal tore into his shoulder.

Furious, he heaved his fist at the jackal's body and shoulders again and again. He pummeled the creature with every ounce of the rage he'd been holding in to preserve Anastasia's life.

Put simply, for those few moments, Hellboy lost his temper. It was a common enough occurrence, given the right circumstances. And after seeing what Hazred did to Lady Catherine and her people, and knowing what he planned . . . it was too much.

Then he stopped. It was Arun, after all. Somewhere under that fur, and those fangs, was a human being. Annoying, perhaps, but not deserving of what had happened to him. Hellboy was glad they were in the water. It had slowed his punches, hindered him enough that he did not think he had done lethal damage to the creature.

Running out of air, he shoved the jackal-man away with his hooves and whipped his tail behind him. With broad strokes, he began to haul himself to the surface. He had not realized they were so deep.

Clawed hands grabbed his tail, pulled him back. His breath began to run out, his chest tightening. He had to reach the surface, or he would drown. Though it was rarely useful, Hellboy found a use for his tail now that it was causing him such pain. With incredible power, he whipped it back and forth in the water, the jackal hanging on with its jaws clamped on Hellboy's flesh.

After a few moments, the jackal's jaws slackened and shook loose.

Hellboy surged upward, breached the surface of the pool and sucked in vast lungfuls of air.

He turned to deal with the jackal's latest attack. But none was forthcoming. The hirsute body of the beast-man floated idly beneath the surface, slowly rising through the green-lit water.

"Oh, damn it," he whispered. "Oh, no."

Hellboy looked up and saw the stricken look on Anastasia's face.

"'Stasia, I'm sorry," he said. "I tried not to . . ."

She nodded, but wouldn't look at him. She understood. She knew him too well not to. But that didn't make it any easier for her.

Hazred stepped forward from the gathered spectators and motioned to the guards.

"Take them, now," the sorcerer said. "It is almost time."

"So much for your hospitality, buddy," Hellboy sneered. "The Plaza this ain't."

CHAPTER FIFTEEN

The clearing was standing room only. Colonel Shapiro was from Cincinnati, and remembered all too well what had happened to eleven unfortunate concertgoers trying to get into a Who concert. The poor bastards were trampled. Too many people crammed in too tightly, trying to get through the same door.

This wasn't at all the same thing, but that was the analogy that came into his head. That one and the old saying, "stacked up like cordwood." All around the clearing, the men in his command jostled against one another, some cursing, some joking and laughing. Even those who crowded into the back of the troop carriers, taking turns getting out of the driving wind and sand, were unruly. He was tempted to call them on their behavior, but now was no time to try to force order upon them. Chaos was the rule, that day.

A day that was quickly waning. With the sandstorm effectively blotting out the sun but for errant rays that strained to reach the ground, it was already quite dark. But even that meager light seemed to be dimming. Afternoon faded into evening.

Shapiro sat on the turret of a tank, surveying the clearing as best he could while shielding his eyes from the sand.

It was much easier to see down among the trees, he'd found, and was bitterly grateful for the advice of that arrogant MI5 man, Creaghan. If not for him, they might not have taken cover. Shapiro didn't want to think of it, nor of the men who had not made it to cover.

There would be time enough for recriminations later.

After the gore they'd found strewn among the trees on one side of the clearing—thankfully the wind was driving the stink of death in the opposite direction, for the most part—Shapiro wanted badly to talk to Creaghan, find out what MI5 were really doing there. But there might never be another chance for that conversation. They hadn't seen Creaghan down in the oasis, and the Colonel wasn't at all sure they would ever see him, or his men, again.

The wind battered his eardrums until everything became white noise, yet out of that cacophony, one sound rose and crystallized. A man, shouting his name. The Colonel turned, and saw two men scrambling across the top of a troop carrier, down into a jeep, and then onto the top of the tank where he was perched. The vehicles were linked in a classic wagon circle, keeping the elements out.

When the men reached him, they still had to shout to be heard.

"Colonel!" the lead man barked. His name was Major Dawson, one of the higher-ranking Brits in Shapiro's command. "We've got company!"

"What's that?" Shapiro asked, squinting and shouting back. "What did you say?"

"We've got company!" the man repeated. This time Shapiro understood him just fine. "An advancing army. Thousands of them!"

Colonel Shapiro narrowed his eyes and looked at Bryan Dawson as if he were out of his mind. He didn't want to look at the Major that way, particularly since the young man had taken command of the British troops now that Colonel Williams had been lost in the storm. He didn't want to, but he couldn't help himself.

"What the hell are you talking about?" he cried.

Dawson repeated himself. Shapiro stared at him. Finally, he summoned the energy to shout one word. "Thousands?"

Dawson nodded. Shapiro's mind was racing with thoughts he didn't want to be thinking. Far too many to be stragglers from his own troops. Thousands. His troops, American, British, and Egyptian, had not even made it over the edge of the oasis in time to be shielded from the storm. Out in the open desert, they had probably all died. Suffocated by the wind, torn at by the driving sand . . . eroded.

How could a man, never mind thousands of men, an entire army, have come through that storm?

"Libyans?" he yelled.

Dawson shrugged, wincing under the onslaught of sand. It didn't make any sense to him either.

"Sir!" the man with Dawson cried, and pointed out of the clearing, along the path the tanks had bulldozed through the trees.

A jeep—two jeeps—were lurching over shattered tree limbs and navigating the stumps, coming straight for them. Dawson drew his weapon immediately. The other man wore an SA-80 across his back, and he swung it forward in one smooth movement, which Shapiro envied. He wished his own men were that fast.

The jeeps had gotten a lot of other attention now. Perhaps two dozen weapons were pointed in the direction of the advancing vehicles. Nobody fired. Most of them looked up to Shapiro, waiting for his signal to fire. Others merely waited. Thus far, none of them knew about the advancing army.

Shapiro glanced at Dawson, eyebrows raised.

"They were all on foot, sir, as far as I could tell!" Dawson cried. "And much farther away. I don't know who . . ."

The rest of the Major's words were taken by the wind, but Colonel Shapiro had already turned back to look at the advancing jeeps. He could make out the passengers now. Four per vehicle, it looked like.

"Creaghan," he muttered to himself, voice colored with just a little bit of wonder. Not quite astonishment, but in the neighborhood. Colonel Shapiro scrambled forward on the tank turret and slid over the edge. He dropped down directly in the path of the pair of jeeps. Seconds later, the lead vehicle, with Creaghan at the wheel, rumbled to a halt several yards from where he stood.

The MI5 man jumped out and ran to greet the Colonel. Shapiro was smiling, actually glad to see the man had lived despite their previous animosity. But when he saw the look of panic on Creaghan's face, he recalled Dawson's report. An advancing army. What the hell was going on around here, he wanted to know. And whose remains had been hanging in the trees when they arrived, now nearly gone, torn away and buried somewhere by the storm?

"Creaghan, we've got a . . . ," he began, but Creaghan wasn't waiting. Creaghan wasn't even looking at the Colonel.

He was looking past him, at the tank, and the circle of vehicles in the clearing.

"Jesus!" Creaghan shouted. "This is bloody suicide! But there's no time for . . . all right, listen!"

He rounded on Shapiro, the two officers eye to eye. Shapiro thought the Captain had lost his mind, but with an unknown enemy on the march, there wasn't time to investigate.

"Captain, I'd advise you and your men to take cover!" Shapiro shouted over the howling gale.

"Are there any openings in your circle?" Captain Creaghan demanded. "Any holes in the blockade?"

Shapiro pointed to his left, past the tank and a troop carrier, to indicate that in that direction, there was a gap in their defensive circle. Creaghan turned and motioned to the rear jeep to follow along outside the line of vehicles. The jeep bumped over two thin, downed trees and tore open a tire on a stump. The tire fell flat instantly, but the jeep rolled on. Colonel Shapiro saw the same desperate expressions on Creaghan's men that the Captain himself wore.

"Captain, I . . . ," he began, but once more Creaghan cut him off.

The MI5 officer stepped closer to the American Colonel, close enough to inhale his breath, if it weren't for the storm. He shouted, and at that proximity, Shapiro heard every word.

"Listen quickly, and maybe a miracle will happen!" he roared. "You know Hellboy's reputation. You know what he does! Accept it now, or we're dead."

That last was almost a question, and Shapiro shrugged

in response to indicate that he was noncommittal, but that Creaghan should continue.

"You Americans always talk about the Alamo," Creaghan yelled. "Here's your own personal Alamo, Colonel. Get all your men on and behind those vehicles with their weapons ready. Turn the tank turrets out. We've got a killing circle, quickly closing in. Nearly fifty thousand men if I'm correct."

Shapiro blanched. "Fifty thousand? We don't have a chance! What are they, Libyans?"

Creaghan's eyes narrowed. "No, Persians!"

"What? There aren't any more Persians, you lunatic!" Shapiro shouted.

"Look here, we have one chance!" Creaghan told him. "They don't have any projectile weapons! No guns! Just swords, axes, and the like. If we can hold out, hold the circle, we might survive. But you can't take any prisoners, Colonel, and they won't surrender. You've got to destroy them all!"

"What are you . . . ," Shapiro began, bewildered.

"They're dead, Colonel! They're already dead! They have to be obliterated!" Creaghan screamed. "Now prepare your men! We have a few minutes, no more than that!"

Hellboy couldn't move. While one of Hazred's goons held a knife to Anastasia's throat, the sorcerer had ordered his followers to secure Hellboy to the stone altar at the foot of the steps to the citadel. With Anastasia screaming for him to fight, not to worry about her—yeah, right—Hellboy had allowed them to chain him down with heavy iron fetters. All the while, he had assumed he could break them easily if necessary.

The moment Hazred turned his attention away, Hellboy had tested the chains. Not intending to escape, he merely wanted to get a feel for their strength. But he couldn't move at all. No mere chains could hold him, but Hazred had obviously added a little something, a sorcerous recipe of his own.

"Damn," Hellboy grumbled, and lifted his head slightly, scanning the cavern, trying to figure how he was going to get them out of this one.

The altar stood on a stone platform between the glowing pool and the citadel. Around the pool and the altar, and massed around the steps up to the citadel itself, which he guessed was some kind of religious cathedral, as well as Hazred's twisted little hacienda, the sorcerer's followers gathered. There were hundreds of what Hellboy could only think of as normal humans. Not because they were normal, really. Not hardly. They were odd looking, pale as Atlanteans, and brutally strong.

Quiet, too. But then, they were all quiet. As if they didn't dare speak, at least not in the presence of their great leader.

"Pay no attention to that man behind the curtain," Hellboy whispered to himself. But there was no man behind the curtain, no charlatan in wizard robes. Hazred was the real deal, and the magician he worshipped, Mar-Ti-Ku, obviously far more so. A god, a demon, whatever he was, Mar-Ti-Ku wasn't human anymore. Hadn't been for thousands of years.

Hazred wanted to bring the ancient, evil bastard back

to Earth. Hellboy had an idea it might be better for everyone if he could keep that from happening. But with Anastasia at knifepoint and himself trapped with enchanted bonds, it didn't look very promising.

A group of gangly mutant under-dwellers stood beyond the humans gathered around the altar and pool. Seven feet or taller, awkwardly thin, ugly with white, almost blind-looking eyes, there were perhaps a hundred of these. No more. They didn't seem to be much of a threat, so he paid them little attention.

Not like the others. The dwarves, or whatever they were, protecting their "King under the Mountain." The little troll-like men and women were descended from humans, Hazred had made that clear. But they were the product of centuries of inbreeding, and Hellboy had to wonder how bright they actually were. He expected their brains to be as stunted as their bodies, but thus far, had no proof of anything except that they were vicious.

"My people!" Hazred cried, and if Hellboy thought those gathered around the altar had been silent before, the new hush proved him wrong. Hazred was speaking in that guttural language, and as far as Hellboy knew, the sorcerer was still unaware that he could understand those words.

"We have arrived at a momentous occasion! The time has come to join our spirits and to summon, as one, our great leader and father from the wasteland where he has been exiled all these long millennia. In a few moments, the spell will begin.

"Mar-Ti-Ku will come to inhabit the extraordinary body of the mighty demon before you. He will lead us to a new age of dominance over the Earthly plane. Coupling

with the women of our tribe, Mar-Ti-Ku will father a new
generation of immortal warriors who will enslave the
world! And he will begin with this one!" Hazred shouted,
and pointed at Anastasia.

Though she could not understand his words, Anastasia
shrieked, her face contorted with horror, and struggled
with her captors. Hellboy realized she must have assumed
that the order had just been given to kill her. It occurred
to him that such an order would have upset her far less
than Hazred's actual words. He had to get them out. But
he still couldn't see a way to do so without getting 'Stasia
killed.

The sorcerer dipped his hands into a large bucket by
Hellboy's head on the altar, and then began to smear it
across his chest. The concoction was obviously blood, but
there was something more to it. Something Hellboy recognized but could not put a name to. It smelled disgusting,
whatever it was.

He wished fervently that he could wash it off.

The stuff dripped across his chains and the deep crimson of his chest. The dark stubble on his chest bent with
the spread of the liquid, and it felt sticky. Hazred picked
up a canvas bag that Hellboy recognized immediately.

"I was wondering what you'd done with her," he commented dryly.

The sorcerer reached into the bag and removed Lady
Catherine's severed head. He stared at her in silence, at her
eyes. He held the head by the hair on top, and the stub of
spine on the bottom, and shook it, trying to elicit some response.

"You must really be lonely," Hellboy said, and smiled.

In the silence, his words sounded hollow, reaching out to bounce off the distant cavern walls and ceiling but not quite loud enough to make it, to echo in return.

Hazred ignored him. Instead, he concentrated on Lady Catherine's head.

"Foolish woman," he said, again in that ancient, ugly tongue. "Rather than avenge yourself you have only succeeded in supplying me with precisely what we needed to resurrect our God."

Lady Catherine didn't respond.

"Hey, pal," Hellboy observed in a conspiratorial tone. "I don't want to upset you or anything, but has it occurred to you that's a head? The lady's dead, in case you weren't sure."

She is still here, demon. Be certain of it.

Hazred placed Lady Catherine's head just next to Hellboy's, and smiled down at him. His idea of a joke, maybe, Hellboy thought. It wasn't funny. Lady Catherine had done her best to warn them to leave the area. She tried to tell them about the spiders, and about Arun's succumbing to the jackal medallion.

But she'd done a damned half-assed job as far as Hellboy was concerned. Not that it was really her fault. The dead were confused, as a rule. Death did that. The lure of the afterlife and the need to complete unfinished business was pretty stressful, from all accounts. So as an oracle, Lady Catherine had been less than perfect.

"I tried," she whispered in his ear, startling Hellboy.

He waited a moment to see if his small grunt of surprise would draw Hazred's attention. When it didn't he turned as far as he could to get a look at Lady Catherine.

Her eyes were open, but bleary and unfocused. It was the look of someone who'd had far too much to drink and was near to passing out.

"You did great," Hellboy replied. For all her vagueness, Lady Catherine tried hard. That had to count for something.

"How do I get out of these chains?" he whispered.

"The soldiers need your help, Hellboy," she mumbled in a dazed, distant monotone, like a radio with the batteries nearly worn out. "Your friend Creaghan needs your help, at the oasis."

Hellboy knew immediately what had happened. They'd been told, hadn't they? Hazred had raised the lost army.

"That's all well and good," he said, a little too harsh on a woman who'd lost everything, her life first and foremost. "But I'm a prisoner right now myself. I can't even break these

 bonds. How the hell can I help those guys if I'm trapped here? And I'm not going anywhere without Anastasia."

Lady Catherine's eyes closed and she exhaled noisily through her nose. Her eyes fluttered open, as if she were falling asleep, or in the throes of passion. But it was best not to think that way of a supernaturally animated severed head.

"Hazred is powerful but not omnipotent," she said.

"Calling his master will require great focus. Remember, you will need the tablet."

"What?" Hellboy asked anxiously. "But it's in the water. It fell when . . ."

The ravaged features of Lady Catherine Lambert's face went slack. Her eyes remained open this time, but they were vacant, staring. Dead. Just as Hellboy began to get the idea that she might be gone for good this time, the head began to decay rapidly. It hadn't occurred to Hellboy that, beyond the injuries she had received previous to her death, Lady Catherine's features had not changed. But now, her face went through rapid color transitions and the flesh began to sag as if rotting.

It smelled, too.

Hellboy held his breath, and tried to figure out how he was going to get his hands on that tablet. And what he needed it for. Or even if Lady Catherine's words made any sense at all.

"My people!" Hazred shouted suddenly in that guttural tongue, startling Hellboy. "It is time."

"Utukk Xul!" he shouted. "The accounts of the generations of the ancient ones here rendered, here remembered. Cold and rain that erode all things, they are the evil spirits in the creation of Anu spawned.

"Plague Gods. Pazuzu and the beloved offspring of Eng, the offspring of Ninnkigal, rending in pieces on high. Bringing destruction below. They are the Children of the Underworld, as are we. Loudly roaring on high, gibbering loathsomely below, they are the bitter venom of the Gods, the great storms directed from heaven."

Hazred reached within his robes and produced a long,

gleaming dagger whose blade curved back and forth like a still, unmoving snake. Wordlessly, he sliced the blade across the palm of his left hand and then held the hand above Hellboy's face.

"Hey!" Hellboy cried. "Cut the crap, will ya!"

But he couldn't avoid the blood dripping onto his forehead, onto the stumps of his horns.

There was an electric crackle off to his right, between the altar and the cathedral, yet still on the platform. He glanced over and saw a hole in the world. In reality. A dimensional tear whose outer edges swirled like heat mirage sweltering above pavement in August. The center was pure darkness, but not flat. It had depth, and a fetid breeze seemed to flow from that opening.

The limbo realm where Mar-Ti-Ku had been imprisoned for millennia had been breached. And Hellboy was to be his host on Earth.

"I don't think so!" Hellboy said, and tugged against his chains.

Nothing happened. They didn't slit Anastasia's throat, and the chains didn't give. He guessed they were all entranced by Hazred's sorcery. He tried the chains again and maybe, just maybe, they gave a little bit.

"The highest walls, the thickest walls, the strongest walls," Hazred intoned, slicing his other palm. "Like a flood they pass from house to house, they ravage. No door can shut them out. No bolt can turn them back. Through the door like snakes they slide. Through the bolts like winds they blow.

"Pulling the wife from the embrace of her husband. Snatching the child from the loins of man. Banishing the

man from his home, his land. They are the burning pain
that presses itself upon the back of man.

"They are the ghouls. The spirit of the harlot that died
in the streets. The spirit of the woman that died in child-
birth. The spirit of the woman that died, weeping, with a
babe at the breast. The spirit of an evil man. One that
haunts the streets. One that haunts the bed. One that
haunts the desert.

"Mar-Ti-Ku!" Hazred screamed.

All of his silent followers finally opened their mouths,
and chanted that name. "Mar-Ti-Ku!" Then silence descended again. Or ought to have. For in that absence of
voice, Hellboy heard another sound. A buzzing, or chittering noise, like locusts or crickets or ten million ball bearings shaken together, tossed against one another.

He stared at the dimensional rift as it began to grow
wider.

Hellboy blinked in surprise when the first scarab beetle flew from that hole. It fluttered straight for him and landed on the stump of one horn. Then another followed, flying out into the cavern. Several more. Several dozen. Several hundred.

Thousands of them. And the noise was deafening.

"There!" Agent Rickman shouted.

Creaghan and Shapiro were together, several feet away, and they heard him at the same time. Creaghan knew what to expect, but Shapiro obviously still didn't believe what they were up against. He knew there was something terribly odd, had no real answers to the questions whirling in his mind, but dead men?

He knew what Hellboy did, sure. Just like Creaghan had said. But to accept it as reality was another story entirely. Now he didn't have any choice.

The first dead soldiers, Persian warriors dead twenty-five hundred years according to Creaghan, began to shuffle through the trees toward them. They were immediately visible, as Shapiro had expected, along the path the vehicles had used to get into the clearing. And now they were here. Flesh hanging in strips indistinguishable from their linen rags, they advanced upon the living, breathing soldiers under his command.

He scanned the woods, squinting against the driving sand. Which, gratefully, did seem to be lessening somewhat. There were so many of them. Fifty thousand was hard to believe, but thousands nevertheless, just as Major Dawson had said.

There was no denying what they were once he had seen them. Instead of thinking about it, trying to deal with something so irrational in a rational manner, Colonel Shapiro did the only thing left for him to do.

He screamed, "Fire!" as loud as he could.

The men lay across the roofs and hoods of vehicles, sat inside jeeps and troop carriers with their weapons pointing outward, lay along the tops of tanks. Hundreds of them, crowded in together in an incredible defensive effort. When they discharged their  weapons, all in such a small space, the noise was deafening. Louder, even, than the storm.

The tanks fired almost simultaneously, and on the other side of the clearing from Colonel Shapiro, a tree went down.

The first wave of dead warriors fell to the ground, limbs and weapons tumbling to the sand and grass. Obliterated. Harmless.

But there were oh-so-many more where that came from.

CHAPTER SIXTEEN

T he bodies piled up fast. Some were little more than skeletons. Dead Persian soldiers, on their feet and trudging through the oasis forest, climbing on the backs of their broken, unmoving fellows in a mindless quest, bent on stealing life almost as if they believed they could claim it once again for themselves.

Creaghan's ears rang with weapons fire, and every time one of the tanks fired, its blast seemed to echo around the inside of his chest. But still the dead kept on coming. There seemed to be an endless supply of them.

Shapiro had accepted the truth faster than Creaghan had expected. There was nothing more convincing than physical evidence. They had tens of thousands of savage dead men wielding razor-sharp weapons, trying to take their lives, to prove that the impossible was possible. The dead could walk.

Could kill.

Fortunately, they hadn't been doing much killing thus far. Quite the other way around actually. Though it was still growing darker as the evening began to encroach upon the clearing, though the storm still raged about them, their wagon-train circle defense, while coincidental, almost seemed providential as well.

Or at least, that was how it had seemed to Creaghan early on. His feelings were changing rapidly, for several reasons. For starters, night really was coming on. As he watched, some of the dead men slipped from behind one tree to another, their stealth in direct contradiction to the actions of the rest. Perhaps that was the plan, for some to sacrifice their un-life, lull the living into a false sense of protection, of superiority, and then attack.

The other thing that disturbed Creaghan was the sheer number of Cambyses' dead soldiers. When the first round had been eliminated, and the rest began to move in, Creaghan had been ebullient. But when the second wave of soldiers died on top of their comrades they effectively created a buffer, a bunker of bone and sand and cloth for the others to take cover behind.

The dead Persians climbed over their fellow soldiers and made it several additional yards before they, themselves, were obliterated. Skulls and chests exploded in showers of bone and metal shrapnel. But they had come that much closer and created a second tier of bunkers for the others that came behind.

Night inched ever closer, the dead fell under the torrent of gunfire. But there was a limit to their ammunition supply. Certainly they wouldn't have enough to kill fifty thousand men, even if the tanks did a good portion of the work. Morale slipped. Light drained from the sky

And a third tier of defensive shielding was built from the bodies of the undead.

Fifty thousand.

"It's not going to work," Creaghan whispered to himself.

Beside him, Shapiro didn't seem to even be aware Creaghan had spoken. The man was maniacal, spittle flying from his mouth as he barked orders that were immediately stolen by the gale force winds and carried away. Still, the weapons fire went on. Shelling from the tanks brought down trees and blasted holes in the corpse barriers the enemy were using as shields.

None of it mattered. Through the madness, the certainty had descended upon Creaghan mercilessly. They couldn't win. He felt the eyes of the storm above him, though he couldn't see them. Whatever was up there in the savage winds controlled the army. At least partially. He was certain of that. And they were as unstoppable as the storm itself.

"Captain!" Agent Rickman cried, off to his right.

Creaghan looked up to see that a new corpse mound had formed half a dozen yards from the circle of vehicles.

"Fuck," he whispered.

The military men watched as knobby-knuckled hands, bone jutting through withered flesh, grabbed hold of the top of the pile of corpses. One of the dead men launched himself, with surprising strength, over the hill and into the trench between cadavers and vehicles. His nose was gone and his jaw hung loosely by a few strands of dried muscle.

Silently, the dead man drew his sword. He raised it above his head as he charged the front of the tank. Creaghan aimed his sidearm and shot the Persian zombie in the forehead. Its skull exploded in a spray of bone and sand and it fell three feet from the tank. It didn't move again, but the image of its exploding cranium, sand flying, stuck in Creaghan's mind.

The dead soldiers on the lakeshore, the ones Hellboy

fought, had pretty much disintegrated into a pile of sand before their eyes. Why wasn't that happening now, he wondered?

They're stronger now, more powerful, driven by a force that is also more powerful. And they needed the corpses for cover. The answers were quick in coming to him. He wasn't certain they were correct, couldn't possibly have known for sure either way. But they felt right. The idea that whatever malevolent force drove the dead men was powerful enough to prevent their decomposure disturbed him profoundly. But he was confident that was the truth.

Captain Michael Creaghan fought harder than ever before to keep faith in himself and his men. They were righteous and just, and they would prevail. He so wanted to believe that.

Dozens of dead men came over the pile of bodies and launched themselves toward the human soldiers. They howled in open-mouthed silence, brandishing gleaming weapons.

Soldiers cranked up their vehicles' engines and turned spotlights on the oncoming dead. The night had come, and so had the true struggle. A hopeless struggle, Creaghan told himself, and then fought against that pessimism.

Shapiro's men slaughtered the Persian zombies, but there were simply too many. They began to pull themselves up onto military vehicles, grappling with British, American, and Egyptian soldiers.

Someone screamed to Creaghan's right, and he knew before he turned that it was Rickman. A beautifully inscribed crescent-shaped battleaxe with a six-foot handle

was buried in Agent Rickman's chest. The man lay dead
on the tank, and the walking corpse that had killed him
had one foot on Rickman's chest, trying to pull its weapon
out of the man's ribcage.

Creaghan bounded over to the dead Persian warrior
and blew its head off at point-blank range. He knelt,
swept up Rickman's SA-80, and took two long strides before leaping to the top of the tank's swinging turret.

Then the real slaughter began.

Scarab beetles poured through the dimensional rift
in swarms of thousands. A terrible dark cloud, a
plague of Biblical proportions, a vast wave of insects
whose chittering grew louder and louder within the cavern. The beetles descended upon the denizens of Hazred's
underground world, upon Hazred himself.

The sorcerer began to scream. His followers wailed in
terror and agony. The wave of beetles moved out, away
from the altar where Hellboy was chained. Eating. Mar-
Ti-Ku's harbingers were gnawing the flesh from the bones
of his worshippers, including Hazred, their high priest. As
those further away began to realize what was happening,
they turned and fled in terror.

Screams battled with the clicking of the beetles in a
chaotic war of nightmare sounds.

Dozens of the beetles had landed on Hellboy, but he
did not receive a single bite. He was to be Mar-Ti-Ku's living host, after all. It wouldn't do to damage him.

"Some guys have all the luck," he grumbled.

Hazred screamed again, and batted the beetles away

from his face. Bright orange light the color of ripe pump-
kins erupted from his hands, enveloped him, burned the
beetles from his body. He was bleeding from tiny wounds
all over, eyes wild, drool trailing on his chin. But he was
safe, for the moment. His magic made him safe.

But Hazred wasn't Hellboy's concern. His only thought
was for Anastasia. He scanned the spot where she had
been standing, held fast by Hazred's sycophants. There
were only beetles there now, flying and crawling over the
writhing, screaming bodies on the ground.

"No!" Hellboy screamed.

He sat up. Simple as that. Hazred was occupied trying
to keep himself alive. His magicks were no longer focused on
keeping Hellboy bound.
When Hellboy surged
forward, horror and fury
and worry for Anastasia
driving him, the iron
chains snapped easily.

"Damn   you!"   he
shouted at Hazred, who
didn't even glance at him.

Then he screamed her
name. "Anastasia!"

And   she   answered.
Across the cavern, just
ahead of the tidal wave of beetles devouring the flesh of
Hazred's followers, of Mar-Ti-Ku's worshippers, Anastasia
stood and cried out to him.

"Hellboy! Over here! We've got to get out of here!" she
screamed, standing directly opposite him, across the pool

of water which still glowed green. The verdant light pulsed now, as if its energy was being leeched by Mar-Ti-Ku's impending arrival.

And what of that? Where was the all-powerful Sumerian sorcerer-turned-elder-god, anyway? It occurred to Hellboy that Hazred might not have finished the spell. That Mar-Ti-Ku might have jumped the gun by sending in his hungry little scarab beetle buddies. Hazred was too terrified to speak, never mind finish any spell.

Hazred. Hellboy knew Anastasia needed him, that they had to go, but part of him resisted. Hazred deserved more than just a slap on the wrist and an attack by carnivorous beetles. He had slaughtered so many, and caused the deaths of numerous others. Carruthers and Burke, Meaney and Professor Lahiri. They'd all died because of Hazred. And they were only the most recent.

Hellboy took a step toward Hazred, who still didn't look at him. The sorcerer gibbered incoherently, spittle spraying from his mouth, limned by that bright orange light.

"Hellboy!" Anastasia called again.

Then she shrieked. He spun, saw that several beetles had landed on her. Anastasia swiped at the air to keep others away. That decided it. She was much more important than kicking Hazred's ass.

"'Stasia!" he roared. "Get in the water!"

She looked at the pool doubtfully for a moment. Then a beetle landed on her face and she screamed as it bit into her flesh. Anastasia arced a perfect dive into the pool. Hellboy did a cannonball from the stone platform into the water.

Where the water splashed up on the cavern floor, the beetles flew away, leaving gleaming bones behind, stripped clean of meat. Hellboy took notice, even as he swam to meet Anastasia in the center of the pool.

"There's something in the water they don't like," Hellboy informed her.

"How did you know that?" she asked, obviously surprised and pleased.

"I didn't," he confessed. "But there are tunnels underwater here. They're the only way out without having to go through the swarm again."

She stared at him. Anastasia had lost her baseball cap as she dove into the water, and her hair was slicked back behind her now, dripping wet. There was a welt on her face, and a trickle of blood from several places where the beetles had bitten her. Otherwise, she was unscathed.

Anastasia opened her mouth as if she were about to speak, then closed it again. She gnawed her lower lip, raised her eyebrows, and said, "Maybe we should go now?"

Hellboy grabbed her and pulled her into his arms. He held her to him tightly, and a tiny burning ember in his gut began to die out. His fear for her safety had been almost overwhelming near the end. It wasn't over yet, but just being free, knowing he could protect her, made him feel so much better.

"Good idea," he replied, and kissed her on the forehead. No romance in the kiss—well, perhaps a trace—but the love of a vital friendship.

She glanced down, into the water, even as some of the more courageous beetles swooped low over the pool, hoping for something else to nibble on.

"How long a swim do you think it is?" she asked him.

Hellboy swatted at an errant scarab beetle, then froze as he considered the question. How long, indeed? They were a great distance underground, but he had suspected the moment he saw the green glowing pool that it connected somehow to the lake tunnels. Their exit, he had presumed, and still believed.

But how far?

He could hold his breath for a long time. But what of Anastasia? How long could she go without taking a breath? How far could she swim? And did they have any other choice?

"That may be a problem," he said finally, and focused on her fine features once more. But Anastasia wasn't looking at him. She was staring over his shoulder, mouth agape and eyes wide with horror. Hellboy whirled in the water.

Atop the stone platform, Hazred had lain down on the huge granite block which served as an altar. He lay, bathed in orange light, on the shattered chains which Hellboy had snapped only moments earlier. The sorcerer's body bucked and spasmed. Even from that distance, Hellboy could see that Hazred was bleeding from his eyes. His mouth opened, and three scarab beetles crawled out in quick procession, like ants at a picnic.

The voice which issued from Hazred's mouth was not the sorcerer's own. It was a horrible, rotting voice, seething with hatred and evil. The voice of Mar-Ti-Ku, most certainly.

"They dwell within the caverns of the Earth," the voice cried, "amid the desolate places of the Earth they live. Amid the places between the places unknown in Heaven and Earth. They are arrayed in terror and they have no name. They ride over the mountain of Sunset, and on the mountain of Dawn they cry."

Every word like the shattering of glass combined with the sound of dull, jagged blades tearing through human flesh. The voice of evil. Hellboy understood more than merely the words. He understood their intention.

"Give me a friggin' break!" he roared, finally giving in to his temper. Mar-Ti-Ku had commandeered Hazred's body the best he could and was using it to complete the spell which would throw wide the passage between dimensions.

"Stay here!" he instructed Anastasia.

"Wait!" she said. "What are you . . . ?"

"I've got a few frustrations and hostilities to work out," Hellboy snarled as he pulled himself from the pool. He ran across the cavern floor, tail high. Beetles blinded him, beetles crunched beneath the heavy tread of his hooves, beetles tried to get into his mouth. Several landed on him, tried to bite, but couldn't tear through his thick skin.

"God damn it!" Hellboy yelled, and brushed the bugs away from his eyes.

The platform was right in front of him. Hellboy hauled himself up, expecting to trounce Hazred, prepared to do whatever it took to keep Mar-Ti-Ku from returning to the Earthly plane. He had no idea what the Sumerian really was . . . or even if the story Mar-Ti-Ku had fed Hazred all those years ago was even true. It might never have been human at all. There was no way to tell, no way to know what to expect.

He sure didn't expect to get kicked in the face while he brought his hooves under him and tried to stand. But Hazred was up, and looming over him. The sorcerer caught Hellboy under the chin with his bony foot. A blow that should have done little more than turn Hellboy's head, but instead sent him reeling backwards off the platform.

Hazred jumped off after him, stalked toward him as Hellboy scrambled to his feet. The sorcerer, magically powered by Mar-Ti-Ku, clamped an iron grip on Hellboy's throat and actually lifted him off the ground. An impossible feat for anyone remotely human.

"Through the caverns of the Earth they creep!" Hazred announced in Mar-Ti-Ku's death-cry of a voice. "Their place is outside our place, and between the angles of the Earth. They lie in wait, crouching for the sacrifice."

Hazred brought his face within inches of Hellboy's. He could smell the sorcerer's rancid breath, the stink of his rotting teeth.

"They are the children of the underworld!" Hazred screamed. "Falling like rain from the sky! Issuing like mist from the Earth! They . . ."

With all his strength, Hellboy grabbed Hazred's shoulders and slammed his own head forward. His skull knocked against the sorcerer's with an echoing crack. Hazred let him go and stumbled backward.

"Shut up," Hellboy ordered. "Shut up, shut up, shut up, shut up!"

"Uruku they are, giant larvae, feeding on the blood . . . ," Hazred cried.

"That's it! That's enough!" Hellboy shouted, and then he was gone, lost in his temper, over the edge. "Now you've really pissed me off!"

He launched himself at Hazred. The sorcerer reached for his throat again, but Hellboy knocked his hand away.

Beetles chittered nearby, but most of them were underhoof now, bloated with human flesh, weighted down. Hellboy grabbed Hazred by the shoulder and pummeled the sorcerer's face with his stone fist. Hazred's head snapped back, cracked against the granite platform, bounced. He looked up as Hellboy came at him again, and grinned.

Hazred began to float, to levitate off the ground. He drifted, rapidly rising above the platform. Hellboy scrambled up after him, barking his shin on the platform's edge. Hazred continued to rise. Hellboy stood on the platform. In front of him, the dimensional doorway yawned wide, and tendrils of some horrid-smelling yellow gas snaked through it, feeling the air like fingers, searching.

Invading.

Hazred floated above the cavern floor, midway between the platform and the stairs to the brass cathedral; floated, in fact, just above the dimensional doorway which looked like nothing so much as a cigarette burn on the cloth of reality.

"No door can stop them!" Hazred cried. "No bolt can . . ."

Fury driving him, Hellboy leaped on top of the stone altar, kicking his chains aside. He swung his arms low for momentum, gathered his strength, and jumped.

Hazred looked surprised when Hellboy's hands clamped around his ankles, crushing the bones with a sound like crumbling plaster. His weight dragged them both down on top of the stairs. Hazred tried to speak again, but Hellboy crushed his windpipe with a quick jerk of his right hand. He hauled back his stone fist, righteous anger overwhelming him, and let it fall.

The sorcerer's face exploded in a spray of sand and bone under the force of the blow, and Hellboy's fist shattered the bronze stairs beneath them. There was a terrible rumbling, a profound shifting of the Earth, and a massive crack opened along the center of the stairwell. The stairs ripped apart as if an earthquake had struck, but the rift did not end at the top of the steps. The crack continued up the side of the cathedral, the bronze tearing itself apart.

Hellboy scrambled backward, falling down the last few steps to avoid the growing rift. He stood for a moment in front of the dwindling dimensional gate and looked up at the crumbling cathedral. Its pinnacle, which he had thought reached nearly to the top of the cavern, split just as the rest of the building had.

The tip snapped half a dozen feet from the top, and that six feet just hung there from the roof of the cavern. The realization was fast. The cathedral had not only been the center of the cavern, but its central support. The pinnacle had actually reached the ceiling, actually held up the weight of the desert above.

But now it was shattered.

The rumbling grew worse. To it was added an additional, terrible sound, a grating noise that did not bode well. A long crack suddenly appeared in the cavern's roof, and massive chunks of rock began to fall all around the stone and iron village. Hellboy saw several people who had survived the beetles running for cover once more. He tried to feel bad for them, but couldn't. Not after all they had done.

Which reminded him of Hazred. The sorcerer had crumbled to dust just like the dead Persian soldiers Hellboy had fought. He knew then that the man had been dead, not immortal. Somehow his magic had allowed him to retain himself, to stay animated and in control. But he fell apart just like any ancient corpse.

A hunk of stone hit Hellboy on the head, clacking against the stump of a horn.

"What the bloody hell are you waiting for?" Anastasia screamed.

Hellboy turned, saw her head poking out of the pool, which still pulsed a weird green, and whatever trance he'd been in broke instantly.

"Good question!" he called, and ran for the water, scarab shells crunching under his hooves. Absurdly, the sound reminded him of plastic bubble wrap.

He dove in the water and swam to Anastasia.

"How long can you hold your breath?" he asked.

"It'll have to be long enough," she replied.

He was afraid for her again, but they didn't have much choice. They went under and swam for the largest tunnel, the one from which the green glow emanated.

Time to find out what the source of the glow really was.

CHAPTER SEVENTEEN

Creaghan stood twenty feet away from the tank he'd been laying on only minutes before. Colonel Shapiro stood by him, shoulder to shoulder. They were among the fifty or so humans still moving, still alive, still shooting in the clearing. The corpses, both long-dead Persians and newly slaughtered soldiers, were piled up on all sides like some grotesque atoll island of carrion and gore.

"Die!" Colonel Shapiro screamed, letting loose a string of invectives with a hail of bullets from an SA-80 he had snatched from a dead man's hands.

Creaghan didn't even recognize the weapon he was using. Egyptian issue he thought. Not that it mattered. They had another few minutes to live, certainly no more. The odds were overwhelming. The Persian dead swarmed over their barricade, climbed over the mountain of corpses and moved relentlessly forward, intent upon the total destruction of any breathing human being in sight.

The sandstorm had thinned, the winds died down. Soon it would be over. The eyes were gone from the sky, and Creaghan assumed that whatever had powered the storm was otherwise engaged. Initially, he'd hoped that

would mean the zombie soldiers would slow down as well, or even fall dead in their tracks. But it wasn't to be. They were as powerful and as vicious as ever. The ground was muddy with blood underfoot, and when Creaghan pulled his boot up to take a step back, there was a nauseating, sucking sound.

Deep within Captain Creaghan was a white-hot core of rage which held the chill of despair at bay. Surrender would have been so simple, but he had never been anything like simple, no matter what anyone else said.

He fought on against the horror of the inevitable.

There was a falsetto scream to his left, and he glanced over to see a Persian soldier impale a man on its sword. The corpse warrior used both hands to pull up on the pommel of its blade, tearing the human's belly open and spilling his steaming viscera on the ground.

"Damn you!" Creaghan screamed.

In the space between heartbeats, Creaghan saw in his

mind's eye what he would do next. Surge forward, driven by rage and desperation, press the barrel of his weapon against the back of the zombie soldier's head and fire. Not just once, though once would have been sufficient. But three, four times, as many times as he was able before jeopardy forced him to face other enemies.

But none of that happened.

In the eyeblink before he moved, Creaghan was brought to a halt by pure astonishment. The Persian cadaver withdrew its sword from its victim, and glanced up, seeking the next. It faced away from Creaghan, and so did not see him. But as the Captain watched, something came between himself and the walking, murderous corpse. A snow-white mist, shapeless, featureless. Quickly it shifted, coalescing into the shape of a woman, but translucent, floating weightless yet in control of its movements.

Quite in control. This wraith, for Creaghan was certain that was precisely what it was, extended one arm, fingers like long tendrils wrap-ped around the Persian warrior's neck. The ghost's other hand clamped itself on the dead soldier's head, and ripped it off.

"Good Christ!" Creaghan shouted, awestruck.

The wraith turned then, its attention drawn by his exclamation. For just a moment, he worried that it might do the same to him. But the ghostly woman smiled at him, and he recognized her at once: Lady Catherine Lambert.

Creaghan remembered her words then, when she spoke to them all from a ravaged mouth, her head severed from her body. Her people were all bound to haunt that clearing until the power that held them, the power that had slaughtered them, was destroyed. But obviously there was more to it than that. Somehow, Lady Catherine had a powerful enough will and sense of self that she was able to make contact with the physical world.

And now that she had done it, the other members of her expedition who had died there were also invading the clearing. Creaghan spun in a circle, astounded and exhilirated to see that the cavalry had arrived in the form of at least twenty powerful wraiths, ghosts who had a score to settle with the Persian dead, and the force which controlled them.

"Creaghan!" Colonel Shapiro shrieked just behind him, letting loose a stream of fire from his SA-80 that cut three dead Persians in half. "What the hell are they?"

Creaghan smiled thinly. "They're on our side," he

replied. "That's all you need to know."

The Captain blew apart a zombie's head, and bent to pick up the SA-80 of a fallen human soldier. He didn't even have time to look to see if it was one of his men, or a stranger. He was too busy just staying alive. After all, the cavalry may have come, but it remained to be seen if they would be able to turn the tide.

Anastasia swam for the tunnel, and Hellboy stayed close behind her. Just before he entered the underwater passage which pulsed with green light, Hellboy glanced down and saw the stone tablet that had fallen from Arun's clothing during their skirmish. He almost left it behind, but remembered Lady Catherine's warning that he would need the thing. He turned, kicked his hooves off the stone wall of the pool, and dove for the tablet.

Then he followed Anastasia into the tunnel.

The water churned with the trembling of the Earth, and he had a sense that the chain reaction he had started above was not anywere near over yet. Who knew what delicate balance had been destabilized. The flow of water had already increased. Water apparently flowed into the pool from a tunnel behind them, and out through the tunnel they approached. Eventually, he was certain, it dumped into the lake.

But the current had strengthened dramatically, and continued to grow with each new tremor. For the first time, Hellboy dared hope that he might get Anastasia out alive. He hadn't wanted to admit it to himself before, but there was no way she could hold her breath long enough to swim out on her own, and with his hooves, he wasn't the best swimmer in the world himself. He didn't even know how far they had to go.

The tunnel seemed relatively straight and level, and Hellboy wondered how deep the oasis lake was. He tried to calculate how far above the level of the lake they had been when they entered the cave on the hillside above the water, as well as how far they had descended to get to Hazred's underworld.

Then he pushed the calculation away—math had never been his forté—and put all his energy into stronger, broader strokes. He watched Anastasia carefully as she swam ahead of him. There was some temptation to be distracted by the beauty of merely watching her move through the water. But not much. Not when he knew she must already be panicking. Hellboy could hold his breath at least twice as long as she, and already he could sense the end of his air supply. It was a ways off yet, three or four minutes at least, but it was there.

Sixty seconds left for her, Hellboy thought. Give or take.

The light ahead had grown so bright they couldn't see any further into the tunnel. It took Hellboy by surprise when the right side of the tunnel opened up to a deep cave into which the underground river swirled and eddied. The cave was the source of the green glow, so bright now that they could barely look at it.

Hellboy had to grab hold of Anastasia's hand to keep her

from being pulled in by the whirling current. Luckily the flow of the river itself was strong, and pushed them from behind. He looked at her face, and was disturbed by the fear in her darting eyes. Not quite panic. Not yet. But on the verge of surrendering to it, certainly. No time to lose, he thought, and kept swimming.

A tentacle whipped out from the green, glowing cave and just missed snagging Anastasia. Hellboy put himself between her and the cave, though they were almost past it.

His eyes had adjusted somewhat to the glare, and suddenly, he could see what was inside that cave. The tentacle had only given part of it away. For the lake monster, the creature he had battled many hours earlier—battled and blinded—lay within. It searched with its tentacles, but could not see them.

It wasn't alone in the cave. It was protecting something, a cluster of bulbous green spheres which shone like tiny suns where they stuck together in a corner of the cave. They were the source of the light, and if Hellboy guessed correctly, they were the lake monster's offspring. Its eggs.

At once he felt both horror—at the thought that there would be more of the monsters—and sympathy for its parental defensive instincts. Then it snaked out another tentacle, reaching for him, and this time it seemed to have sensed his position correctly. He could fight it, but in the time that would take, Anastasia would have drowned. But what . . .?

Of course!

Hellboy held the stone tablet in his left hand. He lifted it up in front of him, holding it away from his body, separating himself from the lake monster. Lady Catherine had told him he would need it, and need it he certainly did. The tentacle waved uncertainly in the water, then began to retract. Concerned that it might still launch an attack on Anastasia, he tucked the tablet under his arm again and began to swim as fast as he could to catch up with her.

He didn't have far to go. Just past the cave where the lake monster tended its unborn children, Anastasia thrashed in the water.

She was drowning.

Colonel Shapiro was raving. Part of him knew it, and the rest of him didn't care one bit. The dead—both recent and ancient—were stacked around them in mountains, and zombies crawled over them like an army of ants. They stood atop piles of bodies and leaped down on the few of his troops who had survived thus far. Swords whickered through the air, axes entered flesh and bone with a horrid sound nothing at all like chopping wood.

Like carrion birds, the vengeful spirits of Lady Catherine's slaughtered expedition fluttered across the battlefield. They fell upon the walking corpses of the Persian soldiers, cracking their bones as if to savor the marrow. Still the tide of dead warriors rolled in.

Twenty men, maybe fewer, still lived within that clearing. Shapiro himself, Creaghan, a handful of Egyptians and Brits, and an American named Felix to whom Shapiro had never spoken, despite the fact that the man was in his command.

He regretted that fact profoundly as he watched Felix die.

The ghosts were fast, swooping and dipping in the air, dodging among the trees, ripping the dead Persians apart so that sand and bone and linen flew into the clearing and onto the vehicles with almost celebratory abandon.

Shapiro was raving. Of course he was.

The SA-80 in his hands, perhaps the fourth one he'd fired, jammed suddenly. Two dead Persians rushed him. One seemed to be madly grinning, although he realized it might be that the damned thing just didn't have any lips. Shapiro returned the grin, long since having begun the slide down into insanity. He rushed forward rather than wait for them, and the one on the right missed him with a long sword stroke even as the other lifted a long-handled crescent axe.

The Colonel kicked the axe-wielder in the chest and rammed the butt of his SA-80 into the skull of the swordsman, crushing it. The thing dropped at Shapiro's feet in a spray of sand. He turned to face the other, but he was too late. Before he could even begin to block, the dead Persian warrior's axe split Shapiro's chest, embedding itself irretrievably in his ribcage. Blood fountained up from the wound onto the face of his attacker. The last thing Shapiro saw was a withered tongue snaking out of a dead, lipless mouth and licking that wound clean.

"No!" Creaghan shouted as he watched Shapiro fall. "Damn you, no!" He held his finger on the SA-80's trigger and scythed a cutting spray of bullets across a half-dozen dead Persians. Nearby, a pair of restless ghosts lifted another zombie warrior off the ground and literally tore it apart.

It wasn't enough. The wraiths had not turned the tide, only prolonged the inevitable. They were all going to die. Of that, Creaghan was now quite certain.

In the crumbling underworld village where Hazred once ruled, seven people still lived. There might have been a handful of halflings in the tunnels somewhere, and it was possible they would survive. But the seven in the cavern they had once called home knew that their lives were over.

Hazred was dead, destroyed, nothing but dust.

The ground shook, fissures appeared in the walls, floor,

and roof high above. Massive hunks of stone shook loose from above and crashed to the cavern floor, crushing people and destroying homes. And the tremors were getting worse.

At the center of the cavern, eight feet from the heaving, shattered stone floor, was a hole in the world. A hole in the fabric of universal reality, edges burning, crinkling . . . diminishing. The hole was closing. Little by little, without any anchor to perpetuate the power of Mar-Ti-Ku in the world, reality was repairing itself.

In moments, it had dwindled to no more than a pinprick through which a terrible orange light radiated. The roof of the cavern finally gave way, thousands of tons of rock and earth sliding, pouring down to fill the massive natural chamber. The floor of the cavern bucked and

quaked, and surged up to meet the falling roof.

It is said that nature abhors a vacuum.

That horrid orange light winked out, the hole ceased to be. The space where it had been was filled as the earth collided and contracted, eradicating any trace of the existence of Hazred or his people.

The shockwave might have resulted from the convulsions

of the earth, or the repulsion of Mar-Ti-Ku. There would never be any way to tell.

Anastasia was drowning, sucking water into her lungs in greedy gulps as if she had never wanted anything but to die in that underground river. Hellboy was frantic, swimming away from the light and the lake monster, and toward what he hoped would be the exit. He held the tablet in one hand, and dragged Anastasia with the other, praying he could keep the monster away and get Anastasia to the surface in time.

Then the shockwave hit, the water pressure pounded on his eardrums, and suddenly swimming was redundant. The river surged up behind them, almost seemed to vomit them up through a much wider tunnel which the lake monster had left behind when it first went after Hellboy. The water pressure forced them up into the open lake. They broke the surface and shot several feet above it before splashing back down. Hellboy inhaled vast lungfuls of air as he dragged Anastasia to the shore.

She wasn't helping. In fact, she wasn't moving at all.

There was a thunderous sound, as if a bomb had gone off somewhere close by. Night had fallen and Creaghan was prepared to feel the slice of a blade at any second. He stood in a rough circle with five other men, the only survivors of that nightmarish massacre, desperately fighting off the onslaught of dead men. Ghosts flitted about their heads. One of the human survivors screamed, and Creaghan knew that he and four others were all that remained to defend themselves.

Then he heard the explosion, if that's what it was. He risked a quick glance up above the treeline, and saw the hillside where he and his men had hidden abruptly collapse on itself, bringing acres of desert and tons of sand down after it.

"Oh, God!" someone shouted behind him, and Creaghan spun to defend himself, holding up his useless weapon to ward off a sword stroke. But there was no sword. No sword, no dead Persian soldier attacking. In the instant of the explosion, the rest of them, all that remained of the lost army of Cambyses, imploded in a shower of sand and began to merge with the desert which had preserved them for so long. The spirits which had aided Creaghan and his comrades retreated into the stretch of trees which were still draped with their tattered entrails.

It was over. Hundreds of men had died that day, without explanation. Night had fallen. But it was finally over.

Creaghan let his weapon fall to the ground. Without a word, he had resigned his commission as Captain with MI5.

Hellboy pumped Anastasia's chest half a dozen times. He exhaled air into her lungs. He pumped her chest again.

When water trickled out of her nose, hope ignited within him. A second later, she began to choke, then rolled onto her side and threw up about a gallon of water.

She groaned, her eyes fluttered open.

 Anastasia looked up at Hellboy, her stomach still lurching, her breath still coming in ragged gasps. Her throat hurt and she felt too weak to move anything. Even in the gathering dark, with his crimson features melding with the night, she couldn't miss the broad grin on Hellboy's face.

It gave her the strength to smile back.

"You alive?" he asked. Her eyes began to adjust and she could see the outline of his horn stumps against the night sky.

"Barely," she replied, her voice harsh and low. "What happened?"

"I guess I started some kind of chain reaction," he explained, rather sheepishly.

"Bloody well right you did," she teased. "Of course you know you obliterated the archaeological discovery of the century."

He brushed damp strands of hair away from her face and Anastasia wanted to hug him but didn't have the power to sit up.

"Hey," he said, shrugging his shoulders, "somebody had to do it."

EPILOGUE

"You know, you really should get rid of that goatee," Anastasia said archly. "It's so fifties."

"What do you want?" Hellboy asked. "I'm an old-fashioned kind of guy."

Anastasia's smile was painful to him, because he knew it would be a long time before he would see her again. Their lives led them down vastly different paths, and from time to time pushed them together as well. For that, he was very grateful. He was also happy that she smiled at all, after everything they'd been through the previous few days. They had seen a lot of death; Anastasia had lost a lot of friends.

The noonday sun beat down on them, its heat shimmering over the desert which had swallowed Hazred and his people and absorbed the remains of the lost army, but left the corpses of hundreds of soldiers to be bagged and tagged by horrified United Nations workers.

Of the U.N. soldiers who had not made it to the oasis with Colonel Shapiro, no trace had been found. As it had been with the Persians two thousand years before, Hellboy suspected that no trace ever would be found. The sandstorm had taken care of that. It had changed the topography of the desert completely. Their campsite had vanished as well.

They had spent the morning in the oasis, but far from the carnage—Hellboy, Anastasia, Creaghan, and four other men, two British and two Egyptian—until they heard the familiar pounding rhythm of military helicopters cutting the air. Creaghan and the others had already gone, anxious to be on the first helicopter departing the area. Anastasia had amazed Hellboy by offering to stay behind and help with the cleanup and investigation.

There wasn't another woman like her on Earth, he'd often said. And that day, he was painfully aware of the truth of those words.

Hellboy scratched the stubble on his head and shifted his hooves uncomfortably where they sank into the sand. He wasn't any good at saying good-bye. Never had been.

"Thanks again," Anastasia said.

"Hellboy, come on! Let's go!" Liz Sherman shouted from the BPRD chopper. They had arrived several hours after the other helicopters, having finished their mission in Scotland just in time to airlift him home. Professor Bruttenholm fussed over him like any anxious parent. Hellboy had felt a familiar relief when Abe and Liz followed his mentor out of the chopper. His family had arrived. He was going home. The prospect was decidedly bittersweet.

Liz beckoned him from inside the chopper. Abe lifted his hand in a wave of greeting. Professor Bruttenholm said nothing, made no beckoning gesture, but he smiled warmly.

They were waiting for him.

"Hey," Anastasia said, and he turned his attention back to her. Looked at her tan face, her fine, proud features. The smile that reached her eyes.

"I'm going to miss you," he confessed. "Even more than before, I think."

"Me too," she said. "But I'm sure we'll see each other again soon."

Hellboy smiled. "Okay. But next time, I'd settle for dinner and a movie."

Anastasia grinned, reached up, and pulled his head down toward her. She kissed him firmly on the mouth, let her lips linger over his, a memory for both of them.

"I love you, big guy," she said. "Always will. In all the ways that matter, you're my best friend."

"And you're mine," he told her. "Why else would I keep saving your life?"

She punched him in the shoulder, and he squeezed her hand once, then turned and walked toward the helicopter. His tail swung in the air behind him, and as his hooves slid in the sand he realized how happy he was going to be to get away from the desert. To get home.

"What's that?" Professor Bruttenholm asked as Hellboy approached the chopper. The old man was pointing at Hellboy's right hand. He glanced down and saw that he was still clutching the tablet he had pulled out of the tunnel under the lake. He'd completely forgotten.

"Sorry," he said. "Give me one more second."

Hellboy trudged several steps away from the chopper, and waved the tablet above his head to get the attention of the U.N. investigative team. One of the investigators trotted over to him.

"What is it?" the man shouted to be heard over the helicopter's rotors.

"Found it in the lake," he replied. "It might be the only

artifact not destroyed by the cave-in. Other than the weapons and stuff."

The man looked at it, squinting as he stared at the glyphs inscribed on the stone.

"What's it say?" he asked.

Hellboy smiled. "No swimming," he replied.

He turned and climbed into the helicopter. When it lifted off, carrying him away from the oasis, his smile was bittersweet.